The Day After Never

Rubicon

Russell Blake

Published by

Reprobatio Limited

Chapter 1

West of Dallas, Texas

A short column of riders trotted along a forlorn ribbon of highway toward the gates of a compound that jutted from a morning blanket of fog. A pair of gunmen sat in the bed of a rusting pickup truck beneath a tree inside the barbwire fence and watched the newcomers approach. When the riders had drawn near enough for the guards to make out their features, they visibly relaxed and lowered their rifles.

The lead rider waved from atop his horse. "*Hola,*" he said in Spanish.

"You're up early," one of the gunmen replied in kind.

"Got a lot of ground to cover today. We need to see the *jefe.*"

The guard motioned for his partner to open the gate. "Everyone's up and starting the day. You know the way."

The score of riders followed their leader down a hard-packed dirt road that led to the main building a quarter mile in the distance. A windmill spun lazily atop a steel tower, and nearby dozens of men were bathing by the stone lip of a well. A tall bearded man with swarthy, sunbaked skin pulled on a threadbare flannel shirt as the riders drew closer, and called to several of the farmhands, who quickly moved to retrieve their rifles from the side of the well.

The horses drew to a stop, and the lead rider swung down from the saddle and approached the bearded man.

"Morning, Cruz," the rider said in Spanish.

Cruz wiped water from his forehead with the back of his sleeve. "Morning, Gera. What brings you out here?"

Gera gazed at the farm, which had been a sprawling cattle ranch before it was taken over by the Mexican ranch hands, who'd slowly added to their ranks with migrant families interested in forming a community on the land.

"How many do you have here now?"

Cruz faced the cartel lieutenant. "Probably almost a hundred, give or take. Why?"

"It's tax time, Cruz. We need to draft as many able-bodied fighting men as you can spare."

Cruz's expression didn't change. "For what?"

"We're raising an army."

"You've got thousands in Houston. What do you need my people for? We've got our hands full trying to work the land. There aren't a lot who aren't needed."

Gera's expression hardened. "It's not a request. We've been ordered to bring men to Dallas, and that's what we're going to do."

Cruz glanced over his shoulder at his men, who'd been following the exchange. Several more had donned their shirts and stood with their weapons at the ready.

"I can ask, but you should know these people don't belong to me. They're here of their own free will. If they want to join up, they can, but I can't force anyone. That's not how we're set up."

"Then you'd better be persuasive. We're not leaving empty-handed."

Cruz drew a tense breath and lowered his voice. "This isn't right, Gera. We've never bucked you, and we've pitched in when we could. We've always given you your share of what we produce. You can't just ride in here and leave with our men. That's not how it works."

Several of the riders cocked the bolts on their rifles. The ranch hands responded by raising their weapons, and more of them moved to their guns.

Gera fixed Cruz with a cold stare. "The cartel needs some of your men, Cruz – this isn't a negotiation." He paused. "Look, you have women and children here. Don't make this a standoff or it'll get ugly. We want at least fifteen of your best. The rest can stay. And consider yourself lucky we don't take thirty."

Cruz's lips tightened into a thin line. "You want men, take it up with the group. I don't own them."

"They listen to you."

"Because I've never asked them to do anything I wouldn't do myself. But I can't order them to leave their families to help you out. I don't have that power."

Gera frowned at the men. "Convince them. Or this'll end badly."

More ranch hands emerged from the buildings, some carrying rifles, others with picks and scythes. All were bronzed the color of saddle leather from long hours under an unforgiving sun, and their faces were gaunt and determined, their eyes dark beneath their hats. Women's faces peered from the doorways, and a few children's heads peeked from beside them as the men slowly moved toward the riders.

When at least fifty armed figures surrounded the horsemen, Cruz called out to his men, "Some of you know Gera here. He's one of the top dogs in the Dallas cartel. He's here to talk to us." Cruz turned to him. "Go ahead. You've got their attention."

Gera's scowl deepened as he surveyed the armed mob.

"I'm here to recruit men for an army to defend Dallas. We need as many able-bodied men as we can get. You'll be fed and armed, and when the threat's over, you're free to return to the ranch."

"Defend Dallas from what?" one of the men asked.

"An enemy army's headed our way. Marauders. Our orders from Houston are to stop them."

"We're already free and doing well here," the man said. "Don't think you're going to find many takers."

Gera glowered at him. "I'm not asking. We're leaving with at least fifteen of you, one way or another."

A murmur drifted from the crowd. "We're not townies you can push around," one of the gunmen closest to Cruz snapped. "We can defend ourselves. If nobody wants to join, that's our decision to make. Threats won't work. We've all had our share of fights, and we're still standing."

"Which is why we need you."

Cruz took a step forward. "Doesn't sound like they're interested, Gera. I'd look elsewhere."

"You don't defy the cartel. You know that."

"I'm not. I told you, this place is a cooperative. Nobody's here by force. We all share an equal cut of what we produce, and nobody slacks. So it isn't like the men work for me. They're all free agents."

Gera shook his head. "If nobody steps up voluntarily, we'll do this the hard way." He paused to allow his words to sink in. "That what you boys want? To have the cartel come down on you?"

Cruz squinted at Gera. "You're a long way from Dallas, Gera. Seems like if there's marauders headed your way, you'd do better to look for those who'll go willingly. We aren't picking a fight with you."

"That's how it's shaping up."

"Then I'm sorry. We're just working our plot and keeping our heads down. We don't ask for anything from your cartel, and we pay your tax like we agreed. But that's as far as it goes."

Gera's expression soured further, and he shook his head in disgust. "You're making the biggest mistake of your life."

"Not me. Everyone heard what you have to say. If there's no takers, that's just how it is."

"You're not leaving me any choice," Gera snapped.

"Probably best you ride on," one of the hands by the well called out. "We got work to do."

Gera sized up the men and returned to his horse. He mounted up and then stared death at Cruz.

"You were warned."

"We're not looking to butt heads. Maybe some of the men will change their minds once they think on it some."

"That's not how this works."

Cruz shrugged. "It is today."

Gera snapped his reins and his stallion turned. The riders followed him back to the gate, where they rode back onto the highway without a word to the guards.

Cruz walked to the gate carrying his rifle, accompanied by four gunmen. "We're going to beef up security today," he announced, and gave the guards a brief rundown on what had happened. By the time he finished, the color had leached from their faces.

"If they come back, they'll be out to make an example of us," one said.

Cruz shrugged. "Maybe. Maybe not. Sounds like they've got bigger fish to fry, and they might not want word to spread that they got nowhere with us. This isn't Houston, and we're well armed and fortified. There's no reason to go to war with us over something like this. Not like we weren't polite."

The guard looked uncertain. "I don't know…"

Cruz nodded. "I do. Keep your eyes peeled. My money says they won't be back."

"Hope you're right."

Cruz gazed at the heat waves distorting the horizon and nodded again. "Me too. But if they do, let's make sure we aren't caught by surprise."

The day crawled by, and apart from the occasional tumbleweed blown by an arid wind, nothing stirred on the highway. As the sky darkened and a pair of new guards approached the gate to relieve the day shift, their demeanors were more relaxed, the threat apparently abated.

"Time to feed your fat asses and catch some shut-eye," one of the newcomers said, holding out a canteen.

"While you sleep the night away, as usua–"

A series of explosions from the farmhouse blew debris and siding into the air. Screams echoed across the field as orange flame blossomed skyward. More blasts destroyed the main structure. The guards watched in horror as the whistle of incoming mortar rounds screeched overhead and the grounds were obliterated.

"Carlos, the highway!" the first guard said, pointing at the road. They wheeled around to where ten riders were galloping straight at them in the gloom. The guards opened fire, as did the riders, and three of the horsemen fell from the saddle before a withering assault from the mounted men silenced the guards' defense.

Twenty minutes later, the farm was ablaze. The cartel gunmen overwhelmed the surviving ranch hands and rounded up the fittest. Gera walked over to the group and waited as his second-in-command reported.

"Thirty-one that aren't wounded. Another six that are lightly wounded but can walk. The rest are either dead or in bad shape. And there are a few dozen women and kids."

Gera studied the survivors for a few seconds before he spoke. "This is what happens to those who defy us. It could have been prevented. You'll now be prisoners instead of volunteers, and if you step out of line or in any way disobey, you'll be killed." He looked to his subordinate. "Shoot the wounded. Leave the women and children for the wolves. Prepare to march in ten minutes. Anyone who can't keep up gets a bullet." He looked around. "Anyone find Cruz?"

"Negative. He must have been hit by the mortars."

"Serves him right. He should have known better. A shame. He was a good man." Gera paused. "Now go finish off the injured, and let's get clear of this rathole."

The lieutenant hurried off, pistol in hand. Gera didn't flinch at the duty – he was a veteran of the most brutal cartel Mexico had ever spawned, and he had no pity for those who tested him. There was only one way to rule, and that was with overwhelming force; a lesson that none of the survivors would forget. If he'd allowed the ranch to defy him, he would have been weakened in front of his men, and he couldn't afford them to think him spineless. By refusing to join his ranks, the ranch hands had doomed themselves. It was nothing personal, and they'd been fools not to expect it.

He gazed at the blazing skeleton of the farmhouse for a few moments and then turned to where the horses stood waiting, and slowly strode toward them as the crack of pistol shots echoed from the dark.

Chapter 2

South of Oklahoma City, Oklahoma

Daybreak painted the eastern sky salmon before the sunlight diffused into a kaleidoscope of neon crimson and gold. A rifle with a sniper scope appeared from behind the edge of a ruined building and slowly swept the dusty freeway, now little more than a wash of beige with an odd rusting vehicle carcass mired in the topsoil like metallic driftwood.

Conejo exhaled heavily and lowered the rifle. It had been a grueling two days since the disastrous incident in which the cartel's ambush force had been wiped out, leaving him the lone survivor, as far as he knew. His side hurt where he'd been grazed by a stray round, and his leather vest had an entry and exit hole from the bullet, with the interior crusted with dried blood. He was running on fumes, his food stock gone and only a few mouthfuls of water left.

Conejo had managed to elude the army's attack by retreating at the first salvo of unexpected gunfire, his loyalty to the cartel as transitory as his courage. His allegiance had been a huge benefit while he'd been in charge of a Dallas neighborhood that he'd rolled in before the collapse, but had turned into a liability when it had become obvious that the cartel had been sideswiped by the attackers and wasn't going to be able to hold the hill. Ever the pragmatist, he'd dog-crawled from his position by a machine-gun nest and slunk into the night as his companions were cut down, and he'd been on the run ever since.

The army had marched past him late the prior day, and he'd watched from the second story of a partially collapsed building as thousands of heavily armed men paraded by, a seemingly unending procession that it now seemed like lunacy to have attempted to ambush. There was no question that the fighters would be able to take Dallas, and Conejo had decided that the fastest way to increase his value to the cartel was to make it there ahead of the army and warn them that what was on its way was an organized, well-armed force that had destroyed Dallas's best in a matter of minutes – a far cry from the ragtag mob Roman had assumed he'd be bushwhacking. Conejo figured the remaining cartel fighters would abandon the city and hightail it to Houston, with him in tow, now a valued survivor who'd saved their bacon in spite of the great personal risk in attempting to do so.

Unlike many of the others who'd died, Conejo wasn't a hardened killer. Rather, he'd climbed the ranks when his gang had been absorbed by the cartel, and he'd worked tirelessly to make himself indispensable to them, even when it had meant turning on his former gangmates and sacrificing them so he could advance. But he'd never been a fighter and had always relied on his wits rather than brutality, which had served him well – until now. When he'd been selected by Roman to be part of the ambush party, it hadn't seemed a prudent time to reveal that he wasn't as seasoned as he'd pretended, and he'd figured he'd be able to keep his head down while the cartel battled the army. Nothing he'd experienced, even after the collapse, had prepared him for the ensuing carnage, and now he was on his own, with nobody to rely on but himself, the rifle he carried of little comfort given his lack of familiarity with it in a gunfight.

He swatted at an errant fly and took another look at the highway. Nothing was moving. Much as he disliked traveling during the day, he saw no other alternative if he was going to warn Dallas in time. With Roman dead along with most of his command, Conejo would be a senior cartel lieutenant upon his return, and he didn't plan on allowing that opportunity to escape him if he could help it. He sighed and stepped from the building's shade and then jogged to the next structures that lined what had been a major artery before the plague but was now a desolate stretch slowly being reclaimed by the elements.

Conejo was exhausted from having skirted Oklahoma City the night before, and every bone in his body ached from fatigue. But he told himself that it had been worth it, because he'd managed to flank the army and get ahead of it for his trouble, which gave him the advantage he needed to make it to Texas in time to warn the cartel. There was no sign of an army having trekked along the highway, which told him that it had made camp near or in the town while he'd been moving stealthily south. Now he simply needed to maintain his lead and he would be in Dallas well before the army – assuming no unforeseen problems.

Once he was clear of the city, he would need to steal a horse to put some distance between himself and the army. He couldn't risk it in town, because horse thieves were pursued relentlessly – it was considered a more serious offense than murder, since a horse often meant the difference between survival and death, and Conejo didn't need half of Oklahoma hunting him down.

He spotted the hulking outline of a truck stop a mile south and pushed himself toward it. The route between Dallas and Oklahoma City was well known for marauders and scavengers who preyed on the unwitting; he didn't want to wind up roadkill. He picked his way along the pavement, keeping low and pausing periodically to scan the surroundings. He was panting hard by the time he made it to the sprawling truck stop, and his shirt was soaked through with sweat from exertion. He darted through the shattered doors of the fuel station and made his way into the ransacked space.

After a brief exploration of the building, he lowered himself into a dark corner where he could see the entrance, and laid his rifle across his lap. His eyes fluttered shut, and within moments he was dead to the world, snoring softly after almost fifty hours with no rest.

Conejo jolted awake at a metallic snick from the entrance and found himself staring down the muzzles of a trio of M16 rifles. He belatedly groped for his gun, but a gravelly voice stopped him cold.

"Move another inch and you're dead."

He blinked at the daylight streaming through the doorway, where the gunmen were silhouetted as they stepped into the room. One of the men, a large figure with curly hair cropped tight, studied Conejo as he approached, his weapon trained on his head.

"Toss the gun aside. Slow," he said.

Conejo did as instructed, and the weapon clattered against the concrete floor. "I don't have anything to take."

"Nice gun," the man replied, and pointed to Conejo's wound. "Looks like you're winged."

"A scratch."

"How'd it happen?" one of the others asked.

Conejo didn't answer.

"You alone, or got some buddies with you?"

Conejo just stared at him.

The first gunman motioned with his rifle. "Get up."

"Why?"

"You're coming with us."

Conejo's expression hardened. "You don't want to mess with me. You have no idea what you're biting off."

"Yeah? What's that?"

"I'm cartel. Dallas. You don't want to make an enemy out of us."

The men exchanged a glance and the first one grinned. "Nice of you to confirm it. Now get up."

Conejo tried not to let the confusion show on his face, but the man's tone sent a chill up his spine. Even in Oklahoma, mention of the cartel should have commanded respect, but the man's response was anything but awed.

"Did you hear me?" Conejo demanded. "You're best off moving along."

"We gonna have to hog-tie you, or you going to stand? Either way, you're coming with us."

"I…"

"Last chance. Move, or you'll have some broken ribs to keep your wound company."

Conejo struggled to his feet. The men looked like Crew. Which should have meant they'd be cooperative, or at least more careful with him.

"Where are you taking me?" he asked.

"Got someone who'll want to meet you, I expect."

Conejo's eyes darted from face to face before settling on the leader. "Who's that?"

"You'll find out soon enough." The man looked to one of the others. "Cuff him, and let's get going."

The smallest of the trio slid his rifle sling over his shoulder and moved to Conejo to frisk him. He confiscated a nickel-plated revolver and a folding buck knife, and then cinched Conejo's hands behind him with a plastic tie wrap. The leader scooped up Conejo's rifle and looked him over a final time, his gaze lingering on the bloody hole in his vest.

"Looks like you got lucky on that one."

Conejo shrugged. "You're making a mistake."

"Wouldn't be the first time."

The men laughed, and the short one prodded Conejo in the back with his rifle, causing him to grimace from the lance of pain that shot through his side. The leader turned and retraced his steps through the entrance, and the remaining two gunmen escorted Conejo into the sunlight, where he blinked like a startled cave dweller as visions of his triumphant return to Dallas faded like morning mist.

Chapter 3

The army was bivouacked on the outer reaches of the city, where the new volunteers were being equipped and fed along with the animals. Over three hundred men had joined the force from Oklahoma City's ranks, most of whom were relatively healthy by post-collapse standards. Years of scarcity and deprivation had eliminated the doughy layer of fat that had been a perennial byproduct of a diet filled with corn syrup and carbohydrates, and in the new reality the survivors were whippet thin, the chronic obesity of the past a seemingly impossible memory of a society gorged from endless prosperity.

A file of men shuffled forward toward the mess tent, where they were handed plastic trays containing bowls of stew. Once fed, they each received an M16 or M4 with two hundred rounds of 5.56mm fully jacketed military spec that had been recovered from the ambush site. Any shortfall was made up from the army's stores, still heavy from the defeat of the Colorado force.

Lucas sat in the shade by the command tent, Elliot and Duke by his side, watching the recruits without expression.

"What do you think?" Duke asked.

"They'll do," Lucas said.

"Anything for a meal and a bath," Elliot agreed.

"Not entirely," Duke said. "Most of them have had their fill of the gangs. Trying their luck with us at least offers the promise that if they survive, they'll be able to live without looking over their shoulder every morning."

"Let's hope they're willing to fight for their freedom," Elliot responded.

"We get deeper into Crew territory, they won't have much choice," Lucas observed. "Is Tyler all set to run Oklahoma City until it's self-sufficient?"

"Absolutely. He's going to stay put with fifty men for a couple of months, until they've organized a working government."

Lucas and Elliot had selected Tyler, one of the brighter lieutenants, to oversee the city so it didn't fall into chaos as warring factions sought to dominate the locals. They'd agreed that they couldn't just pass through major hubs without establishing a presence, or the country would return to anarchy within weeks of their departure.

"You thought about how we're going to proceed? Once we're on the move again?" Elliot asked.

"If Wink's right about Dallas, it shouldn't pose a big problem. Houston will be the real battle."

"What do you make of him?" Duke asked.

"He's out for whatever he can get, like most," Lucas said. "Long as his interests are the same as ours, he'll watch our back. Second they aren't, he'll try to snakebite us."

"When do you want to move out?" Elliot asked.

Lucas drew a long breath. "We need to talk about that. I've been thinking on how to minimize our casualties and keep the men supplied. Not much to forage between here and Dallas, if Wink's telling the truth. Which means we're going to have a hell of a time feeding five thousand hungry mouths."

"We can carry enough food to go eight, tops," Duke reminded him. "Dallas is two hundred twenty miles as the crow flies. That won't get us there. We're talking ten to twelve if we don't run into any problems."

"I know," Lucas said. "Which is why I'm going to leave the army under Elliot's command and ride ahead with a handful of men."

Duke blinked in disbelief. "Why in God's name–"

Lucas held up a hand. "There's an Indian nation about halfway to Dallas. Choctaw Nation. I might have some pull with their chief. Worth a try."

Elliot shook his head. "Generals can't be riding off every few days and leaving their army behind, Lucas."

"Didn't know there was an instruction book."

"Send someone else."

Duke raised a hand. "I can go."

Lucas exhaled heavily. "Nope. Has to be me. There's a personal connection there…assuming nothing's changed."

"Changed? Personal?" Duke asked.

"That's right," Lucas said, and described what he had in mind. When he was done, Elliot shrugged.

"I'll do what you wish, but with reservations."

Lucas looked over Elliot's shoulder and his brow knit. Duke's head swiveled around to see what had drawn his attention, and he pushed to his feet. "We can take this up later. We gonna spend another night here, or hit the trail?"

A glance at Lucas convinced Elliot to rise as well. "Perhaps we can regroup in a half hour?"

Lucas nodded. "That'll work. As of right now I'd say let's stay put tonight, but I'm not married to the idea."

The men left just as Sierra arrived, her face tight with a frown. "Do you have any time for me?" she demanded, hands on her hips.

"Sorry, Sierra. It got away from me."

She sat across from him. "I've been thinking."

Lucas's expression didn't change. "About?"

"Why risk crossing Texas and losing men to take Houston? Why not go directly to Washington and bypass it completely? Just return once you've beaten the Illuminati?"

"We need the fuel and vehicles, Sierra." He paused. "As I explained before."

"Why? I mean, on horseback you might be able to sneak up on

them. But with a bunch of tanks and trucks, they'll spot you from halfway across the world."

"We can move far faster with vehicles, even clearing the roads all the way."

"If the cartel was able to take over Houston, they're nothing to mess with, Lucas. And there's no way they won't be expecting you after this. They probably have spies in Oklahoma who've already radioed your position."

"Maybe. Maybe not."

She gave him a disbelieving look. "They knew you were coming and tried to ambush you, Lucas. They'll do it again."

"How did that work out for them?"

She shivered involuntarily. "You can't rely on being lucky all the time."

"Point taken. But we're still going to Houston. Without fuel and trucks, we don't stand a chance. Just trying to keep everyone fed while crossing the country on horseback would be damn near impossible. So we don't have much choice."

"I don't like it."

He held out a conciliatory hand, which he withdrew when she didn't respond in kind. "Noted. But that's what we're going to do."

She glared at him and said nothing.

He shifted in his camp chair. "I'm going to be gone a couple of days, Sierra."

Her eyes widened. "What? Where are you going?"

"South. I've got to talk to some people. But I'll meet back up with you soon enough."

She crossed her arms across her chest. "I don't understand."

Lucas explained what he intended to do. Sierra listened in silence. When he was done, her face was clouded. "We barely see each other anymore, Lucas."

"That's not true. But I'm trying to lead an army, Sierra. I told you it wasn't going to be a picnic. You still wanted to come. This is what it's like."

"You didn't tell me that you'd be gallivanting off every couple of days."

His brows rose. "Gallivanting? I have to do this, Sierra. Nobody else can."

She stood. "Isn't that always the story – you always have to leave? What about me? The kids? Send someone else."

"There is no one else. I'm sorry."

She pressed her lips into a thin line. "When are you planning on leaving?"

"In a few hours."

"And when were you going to tell me?"

"As soon as our meeting broke up."

Sierra turned and started walking away. Lucas called after her, "Sierra…"

She slowed, and then continued walking. "Go do what you have to do, Lucas. As usual."

He watched her disappear into the sea of tents and shook his head, and then returned to his seat, preoccupied with the preparations he would need to make before he left.

Chapter 4

Houston, Texas

A hot wind blew from Galveston, carrying with it the scent of the sea, of rotting vegetation along a barren coastline. Treetops baked in the late afternoon sun, bowing in the breeze like courtesans, their leaves rustling gently. The boulevards were empty of life, with nothing visible but the hulks of rusting cars and a sandbagged guard outpost that blocked two of the lanes of one of the largest streets in front of a government building that the Zeta Cartel had commandeered.

Inside, Julio was lounging in a second-story office, the stone walls cool in spite of the heat, studying a handwritten ledger with two of his subordinates. He'd been questioning some of the numbers in the long columns, periodically scowling at the explanations they offered.

"Why is our take from the southeast lower this month? What changed?" he snarled.

"Less people around, so less traffic in the bars."

"This is, what, down twenty percent from last month? That doesn't add up." He sat back. "I want you to take some men there tonight and do a head count. Then do the same tomorrow night. If anyone's skimming, I want them to know we're looking over their shoulders. You see anything suspicious, make an example out of them."

"Those are mostly our men now. We cleaned out the last of the Crew."

"I don't care. If any of ours think I'm asleep, they'll find out the hard way I'm not."

A knock at the door interrupted them, and Julio looked up from the ledger.

"What is it?"

One of his guards poked his head through the doorway. "A messenger. He says he'll only talk to you."

Julio frowned. "Messenger from where?"

"All he said was back east. A gringo, but he speaks Spanish with a Colombian accent."

Julio grunted at the information. "Colombian? Did he say what he wants?"

"Just that he needs to see you as soon as possible." The man swallowed hard. "His weapons are expensive. So's his saddle. And his horse is in excellent shape."

"Where are you holding him?"

"Downstairs in one of the back rooms. We took his guns and his knife. He's unarmed."

Julio eyed his two lieutenants. "Wait for me. This shouldn't take long."

He pushed back from the table and made his way downstairs, nodding to the fighters who stood every twenty feet, rifles in hand. The guard led him to a mahogany door, where a pair of dark-skinned men with long black hair were sitting on metal chairs, AK-47s at the ready. The guard stepped back, and Julio twisted the knob and entered the room, which was heavily paneled in dark wood, and found himself facing a man in his late thirties, his hair neatly trimmed, his gray eyes dead as a shark's.

"This'd better be good, or you've seen your last sunset," Julio growled.

The man indicated a pair of upholstered chairs beside a small circular marble table. "I trust you'll find it worth your time," he said, and moved to sit as though he owned the place.

Julio stiffened almost imperceptibly, but he took the offered seat and stared holes through the gringo. "Well?"

"My name's Lorne. I represent the group that reached out to you on the radio and tipped you off about the army approaching Oklahoma City. We spoke on that occasion."

Julio's expression remained impassive. "That was you?"

Lorne dipped his head. "Yes. I bring you more news. Not good, I'm afraid."

"Spit it out. I don't have all day."

"The ambush your Dallas group attempted failed. It was a complete rout. The army is on the move and wasn't even slowed by your men."

Julio grunted. "First I've heard of it."

"They're on the march towards Dallas. They'll be there within two weeks, on the outside."

Julio waved the news away. "I'm not worried. Houston is well fortified, and there's little in Dallas I care about. It's a trading hub now, nothing more."

"You have another opportunity to stop them there."

"I'm not going to split my forces and commit any to Dallas. I'll order my people there to do as much damage as possible and then retreat. We'll weaken them, and then when the army reaches Houston, we'll rain death down on their heads. We're far too strong to defeat here."

Lorne nodded, but his face betrayed his doubt. "Weaker is good, but dead is better." He steepled his fingers. "It would be wise to stop them before they reach Houston. If the refinery were to be damaged, that would be a major blow."

Julio sat forward. "I said I'm not worried. Now, why are you here?"

"We can help you in Dallas. Arrange for a little present they won't be expecting. While we agree that there's little strategic value for them there, it could well turn out to be their undoing if things play out well for you."

"I don't like riddles. What are you proposing?"

"There's a chemical weapons storage facility in Fort Worth that I can get you the blueprints for, along with detailed instructions on what to secure and how to deploy it. I trust you have personnel in Dallas who are ex-military?"

"Of course. You think we're amateurs?"

"No disrespect, but based on how the ambush went, I wouldn't overestimate your Dallas contingent's skills."

Julio shook his head in disgust. "I still can't believe it."

"If you have anyone in Oklahoma City, you can confirm. Although from what I understand, there were few, if any, survivors."

Julio's eyes narrowed. "How do you know this?"

"We have ears everywhere." He looked around the room. "Even here. That's how I knew where to find you."

The threat implicit in the statement was clear.

"And if I decline your…help?"

Lorne's lips tugged into a tight grin. "With an army bearing down on you, that would be most imprudent. You need our assistance as much as we need your manpower. It's a good marriage in that regard. And as I said on the radio, we're going to be consolidating our hold on Texas and the surrounding states over the next year, and we'll want a strong, disciplined hand to manage it. We feel your group has all the necessary attributes."

Julio's eye twitched. "Your Spanish. Where did you learn to speak it?"

"Medellín."

"You're a long way from home. It would be wise to remember that."

"As are we both. I'm not here to threaten you. I've come with a legitimate offer that will benefit us both. If you don't accept, that's fine. I'll relay your answer, and we'll step aside and allow events to play out as they will."

Julio considered him for a long beat. "Explain precisely how you would propose that we pull this off."

Lorne's smile was as cold as a crypt. "You'll first need to know how to blow the main doors of the storage facility, which are reinforced steel. Once in, identifying the target material will be simple, as will deploying it."

He spoke for fifteen minutes, and when he was finished, Julio peppered him with questions. When Lorne had answered them all, Julio stood.

"I'll be back with some of my men. You'll take us through this again, and they'll take notes."

His demeanor relaxed, Lorne nodded as though he'd been expecting the response. "I'd be delighted."

Chapter 5

East of Ardmore, Oklahoma

Dawn was breaking across the plain as Lucas led Sam, Logan, and a party of four others on horseback along a strip of cracking asphalt. Tango's head was hanging after another long night's ride, and Lucas sat low in the saddle with his M4 across his lap. His riding jacket was coated with a film of beige dust, as was the stubble on his chin and his dry, chapped lips. Everyone was on guard after having passed through Kingston just before sunup, the place now a ghost town, the only sound the muffled clatter of their horseshoes and the moan of the wind through abandoned, partially burned homes.

The group had been riding at night and resting during the day in order to avoid drawing attention to itself, even though according to Wink, the area between Oklahoma City and Texas was a desiccated wasteland devoid of anything but coyotes, rattlers, and the odd collection of human predators that preyed on travelers. They'd stayed off the main highway and worked their way south along secondary roads. They snatched a few hours of sleep in abandoned buildings, and pushed their horses as hard as they dared, covering thirty or more miles per day under cover of darkness.

Sam spurred his steed forward until he drew abreast of Lucas.

"How much farther?" he asked in a hoarse whisper.

Lucas squinted at the horizon. "Lake's up ahead. Other side of it's Durant. That's the seat of the Choctaw Nation. Maybe a dozen miles off the water."

"Remind me again what the plan is once we get there."

Lucas sighed. "Back when I was a ranger, I got the son of one of the tribal leaders out of a jam in Texas. He told me that he owed me a solid for doing that. I'm going to call in the marker."

"What are the odds he's still alive?"

Lucas shrugged. "You never know. It's not like Durant's a high-traffic area, and the Indians tended to keep mostly to themselves. But even if he isn't, if anyone who knew him is alive, they might be kindly disposed toward us." Lucas patted a leather satchel hanging from his shoulder. "And there's the gold. That should convince them to help."

"They could just take it at gunpoint."

"True. Wouldn't be the first time. But that's never as easy as it sounds."

Sam's expression soured. "Still sounds like a long shot."

"Not saying it isn't. But it's the only one we have. Army won't make it to Dallas in fighting shape with what we can carry. You've seen how barren it is. We don't have any choice but to see if the Choctaws will help."

"That assumes they have the means to help, if they want to."

"They're an enterprising bunch. Been living off the land here for longer than anyone."

"What about the lakes? Worst case, couldn't we camp at one and fish until our stores are refilled?"

"That's an option, but it will take a week or more, assuming there are enough fish to catch. That's one more week for Dallas to get word and prepare a welcoming committee. I'd rather not press our luck if we don't have to."

"May turn out that way anyway."

Lucas shrugged. "No guarantees in life."

They continued along the road until they reached the bank of Lake Texoma. A bridge stretched two miles across the greenish water, and trees shimmered in the morning sun on the far shore. Lucas raised his binoculars and studied the span, and then lowered them and turned to Sam and Logan.

"We'll make camp back at the airstrip we passed until late afternoon. Water the animals and get some shut-eye. Three-hour watches. We've got nine hours till we saddle up again. Make them count."

They led their horses to the lake and let them drink their fill, and then retraced their steps to a gutted filling station by the roadside and settled in. Two men watched the road while the horses sheltered beneath the branches of a grove of tall trees. The sun blazed its arc across the sky as they slumbered, and when Lucas emerged from the building an hour before twilight, he was rested, the trail dust brushed from his coat.

"Mount up, gentlemen," he said. "Let's get across while we can still see. Don't want to get caught out in the open."

The men retrieved the horses, and Lucas swung up into the saddle while Tango stood obligingly, his coat shining in the late afternoon light. Lucas goaded him forward, and the others followed him to the bridge. He paused and studied it for a long moment through his spyglasses.

He lowered them and turned to the men. "At a trot. No point crawling now."

Lucas guided Tango forward with Logan and Sam by his side, and the big stallion eagerly answered his master's coaxing and sped up. Lucas bounced in the saddle and adjusted his hat, the air redolent with the aroma of stagnant water. The horses' hooves clomped on the pavement like the beating of drums. Nothing moved along the far shore except a flock of black birds that flapped into the sky at the unexpected clatter of the approaching party.

They skirted several rusting vehicles that had run out of fuel on the span, and Lucas slowed as they passed the halfway point, eyes fixed on the way ahead. He peered into the deepening gloom and then held up a hand, signaling for everyone to stop.

"What is it?" Logan asked.

"Up ahead. Something funny about it," Lucas said, pointing.

Logan strained to make out what Lucas was indicating. "Yeah. That doesn't look right."

Lucas urged Tango forward a dozen yards, and he and Logan dismounted. Lucas took cautious steps, M4 gripped tightly in his right hand, and then stopped so abruptly that Logan nearly ran into him.

"See it?" Lucas hissed in a low voice.

"Yeah."

Lucas probed the dusty surface with the toe of his boot, and it shifted. Sam met his gaze with a worried look and scowled. "A tarp? Why?"

"Don't know. But whatever it is, it can't be good."

Logan shook his head. "It's a trap."

"Which we almost tripped." Lucas glanced around and then looked back at the men. "We'll find another way. There's another bridge farther south we can tackle tomorrow."

Tango whinnied, and Lucas moved to calm the big horse. Bats darted above his head, pursuing mosquitoes in the waning light, and he was stroking Tango's neck when movement at the section of bridge they'd just traversed caught his eye. He raised his M4, but not before dozens of rifles materialized along both sides of the bridge railing, all pointed at his group.

"We've got company," he growled, and dove for cover as the rest of the men did the same.

A voice rang out from down the bridge.

"Drop your weapons or we'll cut you down. This is your only warning."

Chapter 6

Woodsmoke drifted in aromatic clouds across the field where the army had made camp for the evening. Thousands of tents were pitched on either side of the highway to Dallas, where barricades had been hastily thrown together and manned by scores of troops, alert for any hint of threat. Fires dotted the gloaming like neon ulcers. Groups of fighters huddled around them, speaking in low voices while they ate their rations or cleaned their weapons with determined concentration.

Wink was sitting near the flames at the edge of the camp, where he and his group had settled. They had reunited with the army when it had begun its procession south several days earlier, but were still outcasts, remaining apart from the main body in a continuation of their uneasy truce.

One of his men approached out of the gloom and sat across from him.

"That guy we captured keeps demanding to talk to you."

Wink made a face. "He's a pain in the ass. Has he told you anything useful?"

The man shook his head. "Nope. He spent the better part of a week denying everything and stonewalling, and must have changed his story a half dozen times. He's a real character."

"He had to be part of the ambush party."

26

"No question, but he hasn't fessed up. Until now. He's now claiming that he can help us."

"Help us how?"

"He won't say. He'll only talk to you."

Wink frowned. "Sounds like another stalling tactic."

"Maybe. But it might be worth listening."

"Why waste my energy? We have bigger fish to fry."

The gunman looked around, and his gaze settled on the army's sprawl. "True. But if he knows something and is ready to come clean, it might be valuable – and it's never a bad thing to have something to trade, even if it's only information."

Wink sighed and poked at the fire with a branch. "I suppose it couldn't hurt to listen. Where is he?"

"With the horses. Got him hog-tied, with two of our men watching him."

"Waste of food and water, if you ask me," Wink grumbled. "Fine. Bring him on over."

Five minutes later the lieutenant reappeared with Conejo, who stumbled alongside him with his arms bound behind his back and a length of rope hobbling him so he could only take short steps. They stopped beside the fire, and Wink considered the prisoner.

"My man here says you have something to say?"

Conejo sized up Wink for several beats before speaking. "You the head honcho?"

Wink nodded. "That's right. So say your piece."

"You ex-Crew?"

"I thought you had information for me."

Conejo's eyes darted to the fire, then back to Wink. "I heard you're headed to Dallas. I can help."

Wink snorted. "Help how? Not like it's hard to find."

Conejo looked to the lieutenant. "In private."

Wink glared at Conejo. "You waste my time, I'll carve you up like a Christmas ham."

"You'll want to hear what I have to say."

Wink glanced at his lieutenant. "Take a walk."

When they were alone, Wink leaned forward. "So talk."

Conejo cleared his throat. "First of all, you were right. I was part of the group sent to bushwhack the army."

"Which you've been denying. What changed?"

"I'm not really part of the cartel. I mean, I am, but I'm not from Mexico. More like a local recruit."

Wink gave him an annoyed look. "Why do I care about any of this?"

"I was born and raised in Dallas. I know it like the back of my hand."

"So?"

"I also know everything there is to know about the cartel's strength, where they're holed up, the works."

Wink's expression grew more interested. "Which you would share with us…for a price?"

Conejo nodded. "I like to bet on winners. There's no way they can defend the city against this big a force."

"Tell me something I don't already know."

"There's more. A lot more."

"Such as? So far all you've done is repeat the obvious. The cartel's presence in Dallas is common knowledge. Unless Houston sends reinforcements, they'll be overrun. Just a matter of time and casualties."

"I can tell you how to minimize the damage to your army. In detail." Conejo spoke for five minutes. When he was done, Wink regarded him thoughtfully and then stood.

"If you're lying again, I'll personally drag you all the way to Dallas behind my horse. Naked. You read me?"

"I'm not lying."

Wink called out to his lieutenant, who materialized from the darkness. Wink indicated the rope tied around Conejo's ankles. "Lose that."

Once Conejo could walk, the trio set off toward the command tent at the far end of the camp. They were stopped by guards as they neared, and had to wait ten minutes while news of their arrival was carried to the tent. Elliot emerged with Duke and his commanders, who dispersed, leaving Elliot alone by the entry.

After being relieved of his sidearm, one of the sentries escorted Wink and Conejo forward. Elliot met them a few steps from the tent and looked Conejo over before addressing Wink.

"Who is this, and what's so important? We have a lot of logistics to work out if we're going to keep moving with full bellies. I don't need interruptions."

"This is the prisoner we captured after the ambush. He was wounded, but nothing serious. Up till now, he's been claiming he wasn't part of the attack. Now he's changed his tune."

"And?"

"He says he can help you with Dallas."

Elliot turned to Conejo. "That true?"

Conejo leaned forward. "I know everything there is to know about the cartel there. Stuff nobody else would know. Including how to beat them without losing a ton of men."

Elliot considered him skeptically. "Why would I believe anything you say?"

"I don't have any loyalty to them. As far as I'm concerned, they're just another gang. I was willing to work with them when there was no choice, but now, far as I see it, I've got more options with you."

Elliot considered Conejo for several seconds. "Which options are those?"

Conejo managed a trace of a smile. "That's what I want to talk about."

Elliot nodded and motioned to the tent. "You have as long as it takes me to eat; no more." He looked to Wink. "Bring him in and let's hear what he has to say."

Wink pushed Conejo forward, and Elliot followed them in, pulling the tent flap closed so he could listen to the prisoner's story without being disrupted. Wink's lieutenant remained outside with his rifle at the ready, wary as he studied the surroundings, his eyes never ceasing to scan the area for any hint of danger.

Chapter 7

Oklahoma City, Oklahoma

A tangerine moon hung low in the night sky, the stars glittering like blue diamonds, the only illumination torchlight seeping from some of the downtown building windows and a scattering of fires ringed by bedraggled travelers.

A yell rang out from the doorway of a dilapidated bar, followed by a roar of drunken male laughter. A hand-painted sign depicting a bare-chested biker atop a chopper with a nearly nude cartoonishly breasted woman behind him hanging on for dear life hung crookedly over the twin saloon doors.

A rider stopped his horse in front of the bar and eyed the sign, and then swung slowly down from the saddle and tied the animal to a makeshift hitching post before limping toward the doorway.

A bouncer with a ten-day beard and eyes like a ferret stared at the newcomer for a long moment before he nodded and stepped aside.

Snake didn't return the gesture and looked over the crowd as he stepped inside. Most of the drinkers were trail bums, judging by their looks, with a few hardcase scavengers or raiders keeping to themselves in one of the corners, huddled around a table with a bottle of rotgut in the center. Snake's eyes didn't linger on anyone for very long, and he was glad for the hat and the camouflage jacket he'd liberated from the trading post. Nobody would recognize him as the ex-leader of the Crew in his dusty trail getup, and he welcomed the anonymity now that he was back on what had once been Crew turf.

The antibiotics and painkillers he'd stolen had done their job; his wound was healed, although it still hurt like hell after a day in the saddle – of which he'd had many since being instructed by the voice on the radio to follow the army south to Oklahoma City, where he would be able to restock on gold. This bar was operated by an ex-Crew thug named Red, who had in his possession a coded map that was the key to locating a Crew stash of gold. Apparently Red had no idea how to decode it, and was unaware of its contents beyond that it was valuable in some way. How the Illuminati knew this had gone unsaid, and Snake hadn't asked. He was familiar enough with the organization's resources to be unsurprised by anything, although for whatever reason they'd refused to provide direct assistance to him in Denver.

The radio operator had given him the information necessary to locate the place and recognize Red, but Snake's cursory glance around the room hadn't picked out any red-bearded Viking types. He made his way to the long, polished wood bar and climbed on one of the stools, wincing at the twinge of discomfort from his side. The Vicodin he'd been popping like candy had run out a week before, and the withdrawals and return of the pain from the gunshot wound were vivid reminders that he was lucky to be alive. If not for the antibiotics and a healthy dose of luck, he would have been dead within forty-eight hours of raiding the trading post. Every day he awoke above ground was borrowed time, as far as he was concerned.

A scrawny man with lank hair and a thin beard the color of wet hay approached and looked Snake over. "What'll it be?"

Snake eyed the bottles that lined the shelf behind the man and indicated one. "Is that rum?"

The man shook his head. "Nope. Tequila. From Mexico. Been seeing a lot of it lately, what with the way things are going in Texas."

"The real thing?"

"Sure. Kicks like a mule, too."

"How much for a shot?"

"Three rounds."

Snake reached into his pocket and withdrew six 9mm cartridges and slapped them on the table. "Make sure they're generous pours. I'm parched."

"You bet. Anything with it? Water? Some salt?"

"Don't suppose you have any limes."

The bartender laughed, revealing several missing teeth and a few more not long for this world. "Shipment's supposed to be here any day now, along with the French champagne and caviar."

Snake barely resisted the urge to shoot the bartender. "Then just the tequila."

The man fished a tall shot glass from beneath the bar, blew in it, and set it down in front of Snake. He turned and snagged a bottle of blanco tequila with no label, withdrew the cork with his teeth, and poured the glass to the top. "Just holler when you want the other."

Snake raised the glass to his lips and downed the shot in a single swallow. He blinked once and held up his finger. "Ready."

The man grinned and poured the glass full again, and then set the bottle on the bar. "Not bad, is it?"

Snake drank half the shot and exhaled slowly. "For diesel fuel. Where does Red keep the good stuff?"

The bartender's eyes darted to the left before returning to Snake. "Got no idea. Way before my time."

"You should. He owns the place."

The man shook his head. "Not anymore. I been here two months and never seen him."

Snake could see the man was lying, and could smell the distinctive scent of fear on him. Why he would be afraid to admit to knowing of, if not knowing directly, Red was unknown, but Snake intended to find out.

Rather than alarm him further, Snake dunked the last of the second shot and slid three more rounds onto the bar. "Shame. Buddy of mine knew him back in the day. Said he was good people."

The man shrugged and refilled the glass. "Maybe so. But like I said, it's before my time."

"Whatever. Just keep the tequila flowing, brother. Damn right about it having a bite."

The man visibly relaxed. "Told you."

Snake drank half the bottle over the course of the evening and then made a show of staggering out to his horse and riding down the street. When he circled back on foot a few minutes later, his steps were sure and none of the drunkenness he'd displayed earlier was evident. He entered a building across from the bar and sat inside the darkened doorway and waited for the inevitable, rifle in his lap, his breathing steady.

Two hours later, the bartender exited the watering hole, looked both ways down the empty street, and pulled a steel cover down over the door. He locked it in place with two padlocks, and then hoisted a backpack over one shoulder, an AR-15 in hand, and strode quickly down the sidewalk, glancing around furtively.

Snake followed at a safe distance, keeping to the shadows and darting from doorway to doorway. That there was nobody else on the street was fortuitous, but made avoiding detection that much harder. When the bartender finally stopped in front of a three-story building that had once housed what looked like a sporting goods store on the ground floor and apartments above, Snake hung back and watched as he knocked on a metal barrier that protected the apartment entry, and waited for someone to open it.

A pair of men appeared and had a hushed discussion before the bartender handed over the backpack. Snake squinted to better make them out and was rewarded by the taller of the pair turning toward him briefly, his face and lush red beard illuminated by the moonlight. The three slipped through the opening in the barricade and bolted it shut, leaving Snake alone to consider how to get to Red now that he'd located him.

Chapter 8

Flickering torchlight warmed the exterior of a former medical center near Lewisville Lake, in the Dallas area, where several small cooking fires blazed on the grounds of the cartel's headquarters. Four gunmen guarded the hospital entrance from behind a sandbagged outpost while roaming patrols orbited the grounds, the expansive paved perimeter making it easy for them to spot anyone approaching. The night air was cool and the wind from the east mild except for an occasional frigid gust, the only sound the mating chirp of amorous cicadas from the trees at the edges of the complex and an occasional gunshot from across the lake as a drunken brawl resolved decisively.

Inside the building, a lean man with an olive complexion and gleaming black hair pulled into a tight ponytail sat at a table with two others in what had been the administrative offices. Half-empty shot glasses rested in front of them, and his pockmarked face creased when he finished the liquor in his and slammed the glass down against the hard plastic. He twisted to look over his shoulder and called out to a barefoot teenage youth standing in the corner.

"Miguel, another round!"

The youth hurried to the table with a bottle and poured each man's glass full with careful precision.

"Bernard! I don't know if I'll be able to walk if we keep this up!" one of the men said to their ponytailed host.

"Then we'll carry you to your bed," Bernard said, his eyes lingering on the youth as he wordlessly padded back to his corner.

A voice rang out from the doorway. "*Jefe!* We just heard from Oklahoma City!"

Bernard tore his gaze from Miguel and sat forward. "Enter," he ordered.

A gunman crossed the room, his expression tense, and stood before the table. "It isn't good. One of our partners up there said that the ambush failed, and that nobody survived."

The color drained from Bernard's face. "What? And Roman...?"

"Your brother didn't make it. I'm sorry."

"How could this have happened? What went wrong? And why are we just now hearing about it?"

"He said that the army was in the city until two days ago, and he wanted to get as much intelligence as he could before he radioed us. He couldn't call from town – they left a small force there to organize the locals. So he pretended to join the army and then deserted when they passed a trading post a few days south of the city, which is where he contacted us from."

One of the drinkers threw back his shot and exhaled forcefully. "That means you're in charge now, Bernard. You're the boss now that your brother...isn't."

"Are we sure this informant's news is accurate?" Bernard growled at the messenger.

"He's never contacted us with anything that wasn't."

Bernard glared at his two drinking partners and then returned his attention to the newcomer. "What else did he say?"

"That he wasn't the only volunteer, and the army is huge. Many thousands, all well equipped...and headed our way."

Bernard couldn't keep the worry from his face. "We only have three hundred and fifty core fighters left, along with the deadwood we drafted from the outlying compounds. We wouldn't last an hour against an army that size. How far away are they?"

"At their rate of travel, maybe eight days, maybe less."

"Damn." Bernard licked his lips and took a deep breath. "Are we sure my brother couldn't have somehow survived and be on his way back to us?"

The messenger looked reluctant to answer. "Anything's possible, but our contact said nobody lived except one man, who they've kept apart from the rest."

"Who? Couldn't it be Roman?"

"Not from what he said. He described him. Too young, and not one of us. Not from Mexico. Probably one of the gangbangers we got when we took over Dallas."

Bernard tapped his glass absently and then waved his hand at the messenger. "All right. Let me think some. Don't tell the men anything. This is top secret till I say it isn't."

The messenger nodded and left, seeming to take the air from the room with him.

Bernard drained his glass again and signaled for a refill. Miguel poured another round while Bernard brooded, his interest in the teenager no longer as intense as earlier.

"We'll have to evacuate," he said, once the youth was out of earshot.

"Julio would draw and quarter us," one of the men observed.

"There's no way we can stand up to an army that made mincemeat out of Roman's men. Those were the best we had. And it sounds like we'd need twenty times that number to have any chance at all." Bernard paused. "What are the odds Houston is willing to send an army to help us?"

His two drinking partners exchanged a glance. "Not likely."

"Then we need to plan to pull out." Bernard sipped his drink. "There's no other choice. I'll have to radio Julio and explain the situation."

"That's signing all our death warrants."

"So's staying here and making a stand against a tsunami."

"Then what do we do?"

Bernard guzzled the remainder of his shot. "Shut up and let me think."

A knock on the doorjamb was loud as pistol shots in the room.

The messenger poked his head in, and Bernard threw him a murderous glare.

"I told you to leave us be," he snarled.

The messenger held up a folded piece of paper. "I have a message for you."

"Then give it to me and get out of here."

The man hastily handed Bernard the note and scurried away lest he be the target of his master's frustration. Bernard unfolded the paper, read it, and then reread it carefully before putting it on the table and staring at the wall.

"Who's it from?" the man closest to Bernard asked.

"Headquarters. They know about the ambush."

"And?"

"They want us to remain in Dallas and arrange a surprise for the army."

"A surprise?"

"Yes."

"They know we only have a few hundred men?"

Bernard glanced at the paper. "That shouldn't be a problem. We're to draft anyone who can hold a rifle."

"How's that going to help? They'll just turn tail and run at the first shot."

"There's more to it. But that's the first step."

The man's eyebrows rose. "More? Sounds like suicide to me."

Bernard nodded slowly and then pointed to his glass. "Miguel! Another bottle. And be quick about it, you lazy boy, or I'll have to punish you."

Miguel approached the table, a hint of a smile tugging at his mouth, and stood close to Bernard as he poured his glass to the brim. "Let me know if you want anything more," he said, his voice lilting, and after refilling the others' glasses, ambled unhurriedly back to his position in the shadows, the bottle swinging loosely in his hand.

Chapter 9

Lake Texoma, Oklahoma

The tense standoff on the bridge exploded into gunfire when Logan began firing at the nearest gunmen. The horses bolted back the way they'd come, and Lucas cursed under his breath. His M4 rattled in his hands as he sprayed the attackers with rounds, and his men opened up with everything they had, peppering the sides of the bridge with slugs, their muzzle flashes bright flares in the encroaching darkness.

"Hold them off and move to the sides, where the lip will give some cover," Lucas yelled, as he unleashed measured three-round bursts, rolling toward the edge of the pavement between every few volleys. Rounds tore chunks of asphalt around him, but he kept calm and continued his careful aim and was rewarded by screams of agony from down the bridge as his bullets found home.

Logan groaned when a shot tore through his shoulder, but he continued to return fire, lying flat and pounding at the enemy positions until his magazine was empty. He crawled toward Lucas while he ejected the spent mag and slapped a new one into position, and Lucas laid down covering fire as he inched closer. He was only a few feet from Lucas when another round blew the top of his skull off and showered Lucas with crimson. Logan shuddered and lay still as the light went out of his eyes.

Lucas redoubled his onslaught as he screamed instructions to Sam, and was met with another hail of bullets as he pressed himself against the concrete lip of the bridge. Ricochets whined and whistled off the pavement where he'd just been, and he grimaced as a shard of road sliced his cheekbone, nearly blinding him. Blood welled in the gash and then streamed down his face, but he continued shooting, ignoring the burning pain as he picked off another shooter twenty yards away.

He did a quick count of his men. With Logan dead and one of the others now lying motionless, they were down to four against at least triple that number of enemy shooters. The deepening darkness was working in their favor, but not quickly enough; at the rate they were going, they'd be dead in another few minutes.

Lucas freed a grenade from a pouch in his flak vest and lobbed it at a cluster of attackers firing from behind one of the concrete buttresses. When it detonated, he forced himself to his feet and climbed over the railing while the enemy was momentarily stunned. He screamed to his men to try to make it to the water, but his voice sounded distorted in his ears from the blast, and he had little hope they could hear him. Gunfire barked from down the bridge again, and he lowered himself down the outside of the structure and winced as rounds pocked the metal where his hands gripped the lip.

He dropped toward the dark surface of the lake and hit feet first with a loud splash. The weight of his flak vest, weapons, and the satchel filled with gold pulled him down in spite of powerful kicks, and he struggled to hold his breath as gravity's inexorable drag sucked him deeper. After several fruitless attempts to make it to the surface, Lucas drew his survival knife as he fought to rise, and he cut through the satchel's strap and let the gold sink to the bottom.

Twenty pounds of metal no longer weighing on him was the break he needed, and ten seconds later his head exploded through the surface beside a tall concrete piling – one of two legs of an inverted U-shaped structure that supported the bridge. The sound of gunfire above continued in fits and starts. He shook his head to clear it as he swam to the square piling and grabbed onto one of the corners with cold fingers. Able to regain his breath, he noted that he was only two pilings from where the iron superstructure rose above the road, and scanned the surface of the lake. He saw his hat floating nearby, dog-paddled over to retrieve it, and then returned to his handhold and eyed the bridge above. He could barely make out some of the men who'd attacked his group, standing on scaffolding that ran along the exterior of the bridge a good thirty yards back. He debated trying to take them out from the water, but then a cloud darkened the sky and obscured his view.

Lucas adjusted his M4 so the strap wasn't choking him and the weapon was cinched across his back, and then pushed from the piling and swam with steady strokes toward the next in the line of supports, taking care to be as quiet as possible. When he reached it, he rested and regarded the attackers again; they were climbing over the steel railing and onto the bridge. The night was silent now, the gunfire abated.

The chance to mount a surprise counterattack lost, Lucas concentrated on making it to shore. He swam from piling to piling, taking his time. The wound on his cheek throbbed with every stroke. When he reached the bank, he lay panting for several minutes and then pushed himself to his feet, dripping oily water, and moved away from the scene of the ambush, the fate of his men unknown, the imperative now to survive without freezing to death as the temperature dropped with the onset of night.

Chapter 10

The moon and stars were nowhere in evidence on what Snake had decided would be his final night of staking out Red's hideaway. He'd spent most of the week watching for the elusive thug, but had only been rewarded with infrequent glimpses, and he was out of patience and time. He needed the map so he could replenish his gold stock, without which he was just another drifter, and with the army having passed through the city only a few days earlier, the clock wasn't his friend.

Snake had tracked the comings and goings of the bartender each night, as well as those of visiting scumbags, and had found no rhyme or rhythm to the visitors' arrivals other than the barkeep's, who was regular as a metronome. His initial instinct on his second night's vigil had been to follow the bartender into the building and shoot the men who opened the gate for him, but he'd dismissed the idea. Snake had no doubt the bartender had told Red about his visit, so the ex-Crew enforcer would be doubly on guard until enough time had passed for him to go on to something else. Snake had resigned himself to patience and used the delay to study Red's lair so that when he did make his move, the chances of his getting in without being killed were as good as they were going to ever be.

Snake checked his weapons a final time and peered at the building. Given the two guards that were there at least part of the night, a frontal approach would be disastrous, so he would have to make it in from the adjacent building, which was the same height and uninhabited – he'd reconnoitered it the prior day in the early morning hours, long after the bartender's departure. Tonight he'd brought a coil of rope from his saddlebag, which he fingered nervously as he descended the stairs and crept to the exit of the building he'd chosen as his perch.

The street was ghostly still in the wee hours. Even the scavenging dogs and cats had long since retired, leaving the sidewalk to Snake. He stood in the shadows of the doorway and waited five minutes, senses on alert for any sign of life, and when he didn't hear or see anything, he made his move.

Snake darted along the pavement until he reached the corner, the night so dark he could barely make it out, which had been one of the deciding factors for him in choosing to make his play now. If he couldn't see three yards in front of him, neither would the guards – assuming they were even still awake, which he was betting they wouldn't be. By his reckoning it was around five in the morning, and the bartender had come and gone four hours earlier, so the odds were in Snake's favor that everyone was sleeping.

The door to the building he'd targeted yawned open like a black mouth, but Snake felt no trepidation about ducking inside after having spent several hours in it the prior night. Unlike before the virus, there were no junkies or vagrants to squat in a vacant tenement – the collapse had turned everyone into a predator if they were to survive, and the weak and addled had long since expired, leaving only the fittest to battle for whatever resources remained.

Snake blinked in the darkness as his eyes adjusted to the gloom, and when he could discern the concrete stairs to the second floor, he took cautious steps toward them, wary of kicking a bottle or can that might alert his prey next door. When he reached the stairway, he ascended slowly; a misstep could result in a tumble he might not recover from, and he wasn't about to end his journey with a skull cracked open from a stupid mistake.

The flat roof's tar and pebble coating crackled under his feet as he worked his way to the edge, where several pipes jutted from the surface. The same architect must have designed both buildings, because Red's also had the same fittings extruding from its roof across the fifteen-foot alley gap – a piece of trivia that Snake intended to put to good use.

He tied a loose slipknot loop and tossed it at Red's. The loop hit the rim near the pipes but bounced off the lip, and Snake quickly retrieved it and tried again. The next pitch was closer, but still failed, and he swore under his breath, frustration bubbling in his throat. Finally, on the fifth try, the loop settled around one of the pipes, and Snake pulled it tight and leaned back with his full weight to cinch the knot so it was secure. When he was satisfied there was no give, he wound the free end around the pipes beside him and tied it as snugly as he could.

Snake peered down at the alley below while he tightened his rifle strap across his chest so the weapon was hard against his back, and then checked his pistol holster to ensure it was snapped shut. He lowered himself to his knees and gripped the rope, and worked himself along it to where he was supporting his upper torso with the line while his legs and hips remained on the roof. He held the position for a moment, his arms shaking the rope slightly, and then pushed himself farther out over the alley, gasping when he swung upside down with his legs and hands gripping the rope, the cord the only thing between him and certain death three stories below.

He inched towards Red's roof, and when he was slightly more than halfway there, the knot on the far side gave a few inches with a heart-wrenching lurch. Snake's breath hissed through clenched teeth when he froze, and he hung suspended over the alley, waiting for any further surprises before he attempted to finish his trip. When the rope held, he edged the rest of the way and felt for the roof rim with one hand while the other clutched the lifeline.

Moments later he'd pulled himself up and over the edge and lay shaking on the tarpaper, his breath coming in rasps. After a full minute he rolled and studied the knot he'd tied, and saw that there were only three inches of free line remaining – the rest had slipped as he'd made his way across. Snake frowned at how close he'd come to plunging to the alley below, and then shrugged to himself. The gambit had worked, which was all that counted, and he'd be walking out of the building under his own power or carried out in a body bag; there would be no need for rope on the return trip.

He pushed himself to his feet and moved stealthily to the hatch that accessed the building, taking his time, careful to minimize the crunch of his boots on the roof. When he reached it, he eased the slab upward, wincing at the creak from rusting hinges, and paused with his rifle in one hand and the handle in the other. He listened for sounds of life below and, when nothing greeted him, lowered himself down the rungs of a steel ladder bolted to a wall and froze once on the landing.

The interior was black as pitch, and he waited for his eyes to adjust to the dim light seeping through a window at the end of a long hall. Once he could make out the stairs that led down to the ground level, he crept along the corridor and stopped at the first of four doors, which he believed from his vigil to be one of the empty rooms – he'd never seen a light on at night and so had concluded that it wasn't being used.

Snake twisted the knob and eased the door open, and a quick scan of the empty room revealed his assumption had been right. He proceeded to the next room and confirmed that it was also uninhabited. Once he'd established the upper floor was clear, he made his way to the stairs, his Kalashnikov at the ready. Another pause, and then he was taking cautious steps to the second level, where the faint glow of a lantern illuminated the surroundings.

He stopped at the landing and cocked his head. Snores reverberated along the corridor, which he could see led to a living area. Snake listened intently for several seconds and, when he had placed the source of the snoring, inched toward one of the doorways on his right as he slid the rifle sling over his shoulder and unsheathed his buck knife.

A slumbering form lay on a mattress, and Snake squinted in the darkness. After a pause, he could just make out a man's bald head, so it wasn't Red – it was one of the muscular goons that he'd seen greet the bartender at the barrier. Snake approached the sleeping man and, when he was beside the bed, crouched and lowered the blade to the guard's throat.

The man's eyes snapped open at the cool touch of the metal.

"Not a peep," Snake whispered, and pressed the knife edge into the man's skin until it drew blood.

He sniffed in fear, and he nodded almost imperceptibly.

Snake knelt closer. "Where does Red sleep?"

The goon's arm shot up in an effort to knock the knife away, and caught Snake in the esophagus. He retched and slashed the man's throat with all his might, and a spray of crimson painted the headboard and sheet as Snake rolled away, gasping for breath. The knife clattered to the floor, and a rasping burble from the dying man ended in a wet groan before he shivered and lay still, his blood soaking the filthy sheet while Snake fought for air, his hands at his throat.

Footsteps pounded from the hall, and Snake whipped his pistol from its holster just as a gruff voice called out, "Carl? What the hell's going on?"

Snake shifted and forced himself to steady his shaking hand so the pistol wouldn't wobble like a falling bowling pin, and waited for the man to show himself. His throat was a pressure point of pain, but he managed a swallow and sucked air through clenched teeth while he blinked away involuntary tears.

"Carl?"

A dark silhouette filled the doorway, and Snake cocked the hammer on his gun. "That's far enough," he managed, his voice tight from the aftereffect of the blow.

"Who–" the figure growled, and then disappeared as he threw himself away from the doorway and hit the hall floor hard.

Snake grimaced and held his fire – he didn't want to use his guns if he didn't have to. The building was on a deserted block, but he didn't need prying eyes for his escape, and gunshots would be unmistakable in the still of the night.

Running footsteps thumped back down the hall, and Snake swore under his breath and forced himself to his feet. He was sure that the only occupants were Red and his two men, but in an unfamiliar layout with his throat on fire, he didn't relish a gunfight with two against one, his element of surprise now gone.

Snake stopped just inside the door and peered around the edge. The hallway was empty, which left him with several choices, all of them bad. There was only one way to get to the main room, and he'd be fully exposed in the corridor no matter what he did.

He looked over his shoulder for anything he could use as cover, but there was nothing suitable – just a rolling chair, a filing cabinet, and a cheap chest of drawers. The distinctive click of a round being chambered in a pistol from the main room reached him, confirming his worst expectations, and he swore silently. There was no way to do this without getting shot.

His eyes roamed over the room a final time before settling on the dead man. Snake's lips curled in an ugly grin, and he hurried back to the bed, the coppery stench of fresh blood strong in the confined space, and heaved the corpse up and dragged it to the corner.

Ten seconds later he was back at the door with the body slumped in the rolling chair. He took a deep breath and then pushed the dead man down the hall, staying low as he shoved the chair ahead of him. The corpse's feet skidded along the floor, leaving a pair of ragged red streaks.

Gunfire exploded from the main room, but the dead man's body absorbed the slugs. Snake reached the living area, and the chair collided with the shooter, knocking him backward. He landed with a thud on the hardwood floor, and Snake was instantly on him, his pistol crushing the man's wrist, forcing him to release his hold on his gun.

The man's face twisted in pain at the blow, and Snake knocked his handgun out of reach and sat back. Snake studied the shooter, raised his pistol, and trained it on his face.

"Where's Red?" he demanded.

"Ain't here," the man sputtered.

Snake's brow furrowed. "What do you mean, he's not here?"

"He took off earlier. To see his squeeze."

Snake snorted. "How? He never left. I've been watching the building."

"Back way. Through the cellar."

Snake's frown deepened. "Shit."

The man studied his face for a long moment. "You look…familiar."

"That so?"

"Yeah. You Crew?"

Snake's expression remained unreadable. "Could be. Why?"

"Me too. Out of Dallas. Old school – OG straight up. Always loyal. Up to the end. Same with Red."

"Then what are you doing here?"

"I got out with my skin when the beaners took over Houston. I was down there on a run when it happened. Headed north and kept going, after hooking up with Red. Pretty obvious it was just a matter of time till Dallas fell." He paused. "You…you're Snake, right? Took over after Magnus passed?"

Snake sighed. "I was."

"What's your business with Red? What did he do to cross you?"

"When will he be back?" Snake snapped, ignoring the question.

"Never know with Red. Sometimes a day, sometimes a week." The man winced and licked blood from the corner of his mouth, where he'd bitten his cheek when he'd fallen. "Name's Pete. They call me Petey." He glanced at the pistol in Snake's hand. "You won't need that now I know who you are. But it might help if you told me what you want with Red."

Snake eyed Petey and slowly lowered his weapon. "You try anything and you're dead."

"Hell, I know that. You got nothing to worry about." He sat up. "So what's the deal with Red?"

"He's got something of mine. I need it back."

Petey cocked an eyebrow. "What's that?"

Snake stood. "A map. Coded. You seen anything like that?"

"Of course. We spent hours trying to figure out what to make of it. All Red would tell me was it was some kinda treasure map or something. I figured he was pulling my leg, you know?"

"Where is it?"

"He keeps it in the safe," Petey said. "I'm gonna get to my feet, all right?"

"Well, hurry up. I don't got all night."

Petey rose, one hand pressed against his ribs, and glanced at the corpse that had spilled onto the floor when it had hit him. "He wasn't a bad sort. But he wasn't Crew."

"Didn't see as I had a lot of choices," Snake said. "I figured Red wouldn't be too excited to see me." He looked around the room. "Where's the safe? And do you know the combo?"

Petey nodded. "Of course. I'm in charge of making deposits half the time."

"Then let's have a look." Snake paused. "One wrong move…"

"Yeah, yeah, I got it. This way."

Petey walked into a smaller room off the main one and switched on an LED lantern. A large black metal box hulked in one of the shadowy corners. Petey led Snake to it and knelt in front.

Snake raised his pistol and pointed it at Petey's head. "Open the door and then step away. Wouldn't surprise me if there was a gun in there. Just in case."

"There is. But it ain't for you."

"If you say so."

Petey spun the dial back and forth and then twisted the steel lever that protruded from the door and cracked it open a few inches before standing and moving away. Snake motioned with the gun. "Over there where I can keep an eye on you."

Petey complied, and Snake moved to the safe and opened it the rest of the way. Inside were ziplocked bags of ammo, a few gold coins, three handguns, and a rolled-up document. Snake removed the document and shut the door before spinning the dial and straightening. "I'm no robber," he said, holstering his gun and unfurling the paper.

It was a map of Texas, with handwritten characters scrawled across the bottom. Snake peered at it in the dim light, and then looked up at Petey.

"How tight are you with Red?"

"We get along okay, I guess. Ain't like there's anything better than what he's got going."

"What if there was?"

Petey scowled. "Like what?"

Snake rerolled the map tightly and tapped his leg. "This will lead me to a fortune in gold and weapons. Enough to do anything – one of the stashes we set up, just in case. You want to be a part of what I do once I find it, say the word. If not, you can stay here and rot, waiting for the cartel to make it to Oklahoma. Your call."

Petey considered the proposal, looked at the dead man, and shrugged. "Not like anyone's getting rich here except Red."

"I've got no beef with him. He's on his own, far as I'm concerned."

Petey grunted. "When do we leave?"

"Grab your gear. No point in waiting to see if anyone's curious about the shots, is there?"

"Shots won't draw anyone. Not around here." Petey fixed Snake with a hard stare. "Thing is, I don't want to have to worry about getting back-shot all the time. Nothing personal."

Snake extended his hand. "If we do this, you're part of my deal."

Petey took Snake's hand and shook. "Well, all right then. Let's get to it. Give me a couple of minutes." He paused. "Where we headed?"

"You'll know when we get there. You got a horse?"

"Sure. Got a bunch. I keep them a few blocks from here."

"Good. I could use a fresh one."

"You want me to leave a note or something for Red?"

Snake shook his head. "Nope. Just make tracks and let him figure it out."

Petey nodded and sighed. "All right, boss. Whatever you say."

Snake watched Petey walk into the other room and smirked. "That's the spirit."

Chapter 11

Lucas shrugged out of his soaking clothes and wrung them out, shivering so hard as the temperature dropped that his teeth sounded like castanets in his head. He worked on his trail coat first, and then his jeans and shirt, but damp they would be of little use, and he knew he'd be hard pressed to survive the night without protection from the elements. When he'd squeezed as much of the water from the garments as possible in the dark, he donned them again, and the cold moisture caused another racking shiver fit as his body struggled to maintain its temperature.

He glanced back over his shoulder and, after verifying that nobody had followed him, willed his legs into motion and walked unsteadily through the trees until he reached a clearing. He stopped and scanned the small open area and felt with numb fingers in his flak vest for the disposable lighter he kept in one of the front pockets. He withdrew it clumsily and cursed when he dropped it into the grass. Agonizing moments ticked by as he knelt and groped for it, and after retrieving it, he flicked it several times to confirm it still worked.

Lucas groaned as he stripped off his coat and shirt and moved bare-chested to the nearest trees, survival knife in hand. Once he'd cut enough branches for kindling, he returned to the center of the clearing and the black lump of his discarded clothes. He kicked gravel

51

and small rocks into a rough circle and then arranged the branches into a rough pyramid. He studied his handiwork and then made for the tree line again, knife at the ready.

The pine branches caught with a crackle, and soon the small pyre was a modest blaze. He luxuriated in the warmth of the dancing orange flames until he'd stopped shaking, and brought his coat and shirt over to hang on one of the thicker branches he'd staked into the ground at the fire's edge. Lucas squatted by the flames in a trance and held the coat steady, and only pulled it back a few inches when steam bubbled and hissed from it.

The fire consumed its fuel with surprising speed, and Lucas shrugged into the coat and returned to the pines to gather more. He made three trips over the next half hour, by which time his jeans were nearly dry, and his coat and shirt were stiff as bark and reeking of woodsmoke – a concession he figured he'd gladly make to stave off pneumonia.

He pulled the clothes on and adjusted his flak jacket and was picking up his M4 when a shot rang out and a spray of dirt fountained by his left leg. Lucas threw himself to the ground with his rifle clutched to his chest. Two more shots snapped past his head, missing him by inches. He rolled to his right, away from the fire, and squeezed off two three-round bursts at the trees before vaulting to his feet and sprinting for cover at the far edge of the clearing, driving himself as hard as he could, staying low and zigzagging through the darkness to avoid making an easy target.

The fire had been a risk, though a necessary one – for which he was now going to have to pay the price. His damp boots squished with each thumping footfall, and he'd just reached the trees when more shooting barked from behind him. Divots of wood flew from a nearby trunk no more than a yard away. He considered turning and returning fire as he entered the woods, but discarded the idea when more shots echoed from the clearing, their different tones confirming his worst fear – there were at least four shooters. Chilled to the bone, with his night vision scope waterlogged and out of operation for the time being, the odds of prevailing in a firefight were suicidal.

Lucas had no choice but to run, which rankled after having had to abandon his men on the bridge. He continued deeper into the trees, moving in a crouch, ignoring the branches that tore at his face as he raced through the brush. The absence of any more shooting meant that his pursuers would hear him crashing through the bushes, the sound of branches snapping beneath his boots as loud as firecrackers to his ears, which would lead them directly to him.

He forced himself to slow, straining to make anything out in the darkness, and moved through the trees until he came across a game trail that led away from the lake. He followed it, pausing periodically to listen for sounds of pursuit, and kept moving until he'd put a half hour between himself and the clearing. When he stopped, heart thudding in his chest, he took cover behind a large tree and crouched with his rifle trained on the path, liking his chances better now with a good position to take out whoever was hunting him – assuming they hadn't given up, which was his hope.

Minutes crawled by with the only sound the treetops shivering in the breeze, and he fiddled with his NV scope to try to coax it to life. It didn't cooperate, and he gave up and concentrated on the trail. His feet were freezing in his wet boots, but the coat and flak vest provided enough insulation that his core temperature remained stable.

When nobody appeared after an hour of lying in wait, he crawled farther from the trail and leaned back against a tree trunk, his M4 in his lap, the moonlight seeping through the branches barely sufficient to make out the way he'd come. He cocked his head and listened intently, but no sound greeted him, and as the adrenaline seeped from his veins, his eyelids grew heavy. Lucas blinked away sleep for as long as he could, but eventually he drifted off, coat wrapped tightly around him, gun in hand.

He jolted awake when the cold steel of a rifle barrel pressed against his cheek, and a voice growled at him from three feet away.

"Set the rifle aside. No fast moves."

Lucas inhaled sharply and willed his eyes to focus, but the darkness was impenetrable. He raised his left hand and shifted the

M4 with his right until it was lying by his outstretched leg.

"Now the pop gun," the voice instructed. "Two fingers."

Lucas drew his Kimber from its holster using his index finger and thumb and tossed it by his feet.

"That all of 'em?" the voice demanded.

"All I've got," Lucas replied, his words clipped.

"Shoot him," someone else said from Lucas's left.

A pause that seemed to last a minute stretched in silence, and Lucas waited with gritted teeth for his life to end. A wooden rifle stock slammed into his temple, and his vision exploded in a kaleidoscope of stars, and then the myriad lights pinwheeled dizzily with a sound like a monster wave breaking against a rocky shore, and everything faded to nothingness.

Chapter 12

South of Oklahoma City, Oklahoma

The command tent was large enough to hold ten men, and Wink, Conejo, and Elliot easily sat at a camp table set up in the center, Elliot's meal resting half eaten in front of him as he listened to the enemy's account. Wink's expression was unreadable in the half-light of the lanterns, and Elliot's could have been carved from alabaster, his eyes locked on Conejo seated across from him.

"I know everything about the Dallas defenses. Everything. How many men they have, where their armory is, where they keep their horses…the works. It'll save hundreds of your men if we can work a deal between us."

"You asked me to listen. I'm listening," Elliot replied. "There's no deal; just you talking about how valuable your information could be. Which for all we know is lies."

Conejo shook his head. "It isn't. I swear. I've been with them since they booted the Crew out. I know all about them."

Elliot pursed his lips. "You're a member of the Zeta Cartel, but you're willing to turn traitor and help us? Forgive me if I'm skeptical."

"It's not like I went to Houston and signed up. I was working with the Crew before, but they always treated me like an errand boy. When they got their asses handed to them by the Zetas, it wasn't like it broke my heart. Because I'm Latino, I caught a break with them.

But I'm not Mexican. I'm second generation. Born and raised in Dallas. Never even been south of the border."

"Why did they accept you, then?"

"I speak the language because of my folks. And I…because I was working with the Crew, they assumed I was hardcore, you know? But I've never popped a cap in anyone. Before the virus, I was part of a local gang that sold weed and meth in a two-block area. That's it. It was a nothing operation in a lousy area nobody else wanted, you know? So we never had to defend it except from other homeboys, and they weren't gonna die for a corner. Worst we ever did was bust each other up with pipes, and even then that was only once."

"So far I'm unimpressed," Elliot said.

"When the cartel showed up, I kept out of the fight until they ran the Crew off. Then I sort of made my pitch. I told them I was Dallas OG and ran my gang before the Crew took over. My homies were all dead, so there was nobody to say I wasn't." Conejo smirked. "Sure, I exaggerated some. I mean, to them I was a stone killer and homegrown, you know? I made up stories, and they believed them. And since the virus, I've had to off a couple of guys, but in self-defense. That's it. But I told them that I'd run half of Dallas before the Crew showed up, and there wasn't anyone left to say I was full of it. Plus I made myself useful, showing them where everything was and telling them who was who with the locals." Conejo sighed. "One thing led to another, and pretty soon I was one of them."

"Enough to have been one of the men they sent to ambush us."

"That's part of what you need to know. They're really thin in Dallas. Nobody hard wanted to be there – Mexico or Houston's where all the action is. I mean, yeah, it was a good gig for me, because I got my own area to run, but that don't make me one of them. More like I was in business for myself, and they were the new city government, you know? I paid my dues every week and made sure nobody stepped out of line, and that's about it." He eyed Elliot's food. "You gonna eat that?"

Elliot pushed at the mushy stew with his fork. "When I'm ready. Cut to the chase. I'm running short on patience."

"There's only maybe a couple of hundred cartel left in Dallas. They sent everyone else north to get you. But of the two, two fifty, only forty or fifty are from Mexico. The rest are like me – recruits from Dallas, most of us Crew-affiliated. The cartel guys are the ones you need to worry about. The rest won't die for the Zetas, but their men will."

"Then where's your value? Sounds like we can take them with no real effort."

"I didn't say that. I said if you took out the hardcore fighters, the rest would probably walk away. But as long as the Mexicans are there, nobody would dare – they'd get a bullet in the back the first time they tried. So you'd still be up against two hundred, maybe two-fifty gunmen, and they'll be dug in, expecting you. Even up against thousands of yours, they'd do some damage. So you're going to have to do something unexpected. Do a sneak attack they won't see coming, you know? That's where I can help. I know their entire layout and where they'll have their main force. I can tell you how to get men into the city without being spotted, and how to sneak up on them from behind before they know what hit them. Instead of hundreds of your troops dead, it could be only a few, you know? That's what I'm offering."

Elliot stabbed a chunk of rabbit with his fork and ate it, taking his time to chew carefully. He sat back after he swallowed and considered the gangbanger for several moments before speaking.

"What I see is a prisoner who's trying to sell a story. You haven't given me any reason to believe you."

"Here's my deal. I help you get into Dallas and take out the cartel, and you let me go with as many guns and as much ammo as I can carry. And in return, you save who knows how many of your men?"

Wink and Elliot exchanged a glance. "Who's in charge in Dallas?"

"Roman was the main man, but he bought it during the ambush. So it would be his brother, Bernard. He thinks he's a badass, but he isn't his brother, who was straight up hard, you know? Roman was old school. Bernard's younger, and he's got more of a temper. I've heard stories. He's mean, but he's not a soldier like Roman was, and he isn't a leader. He always stood in his brother's shadow."

"But he's competent?"

Conejo made a face. "He could hurt you, if that's what you're asking."

"How do you know the cartel won't send reinforcements from Houston?"

Conejo shook his head. "If they were going to do that, they would have for the ambush. They didn't. Besides which, how would they even know what happened yet? I'm the only one who got away that I know of. So who would tell them?"

"Let's assume I believe you. And let's further assume I was interested in what you're selling. You're going to have to be far more specific than you've been. I'll need to know everything. You have to prove you know what you claim."

"I can deliver. I'm not worried."

Elliot took another bite of stew. "I'll entertain a little more of this. Tell me specifically how you would advise us to penetrate their defenses. Walk me through step by step. How large a force, how we make it into town unobserved, where we would have to hit to accomplish what you're suggesting. Generalities won't cut it. If you're going to be of value, you're going to have to convince me you're real, and right now I'm not convinced."

"If I do, you'll honor your agreement and let me go?"

"I didn't get where I am by breaking my word. If you're of genuine help and you haven't misled me, I'll give you what you want. But if you're running a scam, you'll wish you'd never been born."

"I need some kind of guarantee."

Wink snorted. "How about you either tell the man everything you told me, or I take you out back and break your legs, and then we can try again?"

Conejo swallowed hard. "I could use some food. This is going to take a while."

Elliot gave his assent, and Wink rose and moved to the tent flap. "I'll deal with the grub. Spill the beans, because if you haven't by the time I get back with your dinner, you'll be walking on sticks the rest of your miserable life. You were Crew, so you know my reputation."

Wink stepped outside, and Elliot forked more stew into his mouth and washed it down with a canteen full of water. "You heard the man. Tell me exactly how we're to get past their defenses, tell me what we can expect in terms of armaments, where they'll make their stand – the works. Convince me I'm not wasting my time with you, and if you prove valuable, you'll have what you ask."

Chapter 13

Lake Texoma, Oklahoma

Lucas regained consciousness to pain in his skull like he'd been dropped headfirst off a cliff, and he barely managed to stop himself from moaning in agony. He focused on his breathing and, when he felt like he had himself under control, cracked his eyes open.

He was still in the woods, leaned against a tree trunk with his hands and feet bound, but morning light was filtering through the treetops. A group of fifteen men sat around a fire, talking in low tones. Lucas tried to twist his neck far enough so he could see more, but stopped when a voice called out from behind him.

"He's awake!"

Several of the men by the fire looked up, and three of them joined the speaker and stared down at Lucas.

"What were you doing in our territory?" one of the men demanded.

Lucas blinked away the fuzziness in his vision and made out a muscular man with skin the color of burnished copper.

"Your territory? Coming to see Jarrow Logan." Lucas paused. "Why did you attack us on the bridge?"

"I ask the questions. What's your business with Jarrow?"

"I…my name's Lucas Shaw. Back before the virus, I did Jarrow a serious favor. Now I could use one."

"What favor?"

"His boy, Malcolm, got into it down in Texas. I got him a second chance when everyone else was out for blood. He said he owed me, and if I ever needed anything, to come see him."

The men exchanged dark looks. The muscular one stepped closer.

"Jarrow passed on three years ago." He paused. "I'm Drake. Malcolm's brother. If my father owed you, I'd say you waited too long."

Lucas sighed. "Why'd you kill my men? That how you operate out here now?"

"That wasn't us." Drake glanced at his companions. "Those were scavengers. We let them have a little territory on the other side of the bridge to act as a buffer — keeps the riffraff away. Anyone passing through is fair game if we don't give them a heads-up."

Lucas frowned. "Would've been nice to know. Those were good men they killed."

Drake shrugged.

Lucas sighed. "I still need help. Who do I talk to now that Jarrow's out of the picture?"

"Malcolm and I run the tribe. But I doubt you're going to get far. Texas was a long time ago."

"You haven't heard my offer."

Drake laughed. "It don't look like you're in much of a position to negotiate."

"Untie me and we'll talk. You might be surprised."

Drake regarded Lucas curiously. "What was it you were doing back in Texas that you helped my bro?"

"I was a Texas Ranger. He'd been framed for a murder. I was the only one who believed his story. To everyone else he was just some Indian drifter we could throw under the bus. But I listened to his story, and it made sense, so I dug around and found the real killer." Lucas shrugged. "Surprised you never heard tell of it."

Drake held Lucas's stare. "Didn't say that. I just wanted to hear it from you." He twisted to the man on his right. "Cut him loose and let's hear what he's got to say."

Lucas felt a knife sawing at the cord that bound his wrists, and then his hands were free. He clenched and unclenched his fingers as the blood returned, ignoring the discomfort, his eyes never leaving Drake. When his feet were loose, Drake helped him up and led him to the edge of the fire and offered him some water and jerky, which Lucas gratefully accepted.

"Sorry about your head," Drake said, when Lucas was done eating.

"Yeah." Lucas shrugged. "I need supplies for an army. Food to get us to Dallas."

Drake's eyebrows rose. "An army? How many men we talking?"

"Thousands."

Drake chuckled. "And this is the favor you were going to ask? That's a pretty tall order."

"I can pay for it. Assuming you have enough to make a dent."

"We're in good shape, so that isn't a problem. How you plan to pay for it? A few bullets won't cut it."

"Gold. Plenty of it."

Drake snorted. "We searched you. You don't have any. And I don't need to tell you that we don't extend credit."

"Not asking for any. The gold's back at the bridge. With a little help, I should be able to recover it."

"How much we talking?"

"Two hundred fifty ounces."

Drake's face grew serious. "That would buy a lot of grub."

"I figured."

"What kind of help you thinking you need?"

Lucas explained about having dropped the gold into the water. "So I'll need a couple of good divers. I would have been able to do it before you bashed my head in, but now…"

Drake nodded slowly. "That could happen. What else?"

"Need to keep the scavengers at bay."

"Shouldn't be a problem. Like I said, they don't mess with us."

"And finally, once we get the gold, I want to see if any of my men are still alive. Do the scavengers take prisoners?"

"Could be. There's only one way to find out."

"How good is your relationship with them?"

Drake grinned crookedly. "The day they step over the line, I can have three hundred men wipe them out in minutes. They'll do as we say."

"How many are there?"

"It varies. Usually around fifty, give or take."

Lucas grunted. "Okay, then. Let's head to the bridge and get this over with." He looked Drake up and down. "It'd be a decent show of faith to return my gear."

Drake frowned. "Once we've retrieved the gold."

Lucas understood his position. He could have been telling Drake a shaggy dog story in order to create an opportunity to escape. Lucas would have probably reacted the same way. But even so, he felt naked without his M4 or Kimber.

The group set off toward the lake. They arrived at its banks several hours later, the sun a fiery orb overhead. Lucas surveyed the bridge, and Drake edged alongside him.

"That's a long stretch. How you planning to find your gold?" Drake asked.

"I can get your men within a few yards of where I dropped it. It would have sunk straight down from there." Lucas hesitated. "Let's just hope it's not too muddy a bottom. Be a shame to have a small fortune lost in the muck."

Drake's gaze hardened as he stared at the bridge. "Shame for you if we can't find it."

"Then don't let that happen."

They walked together toward the towers, and Lucas looked ahead to where the bloated corpses of horses lay on the road. He squinted to make out any dead men, but there were none he could see.

Drake spit by his boots. "They would've taken anything of value your men had, and then tossed the bodies over the side so the next travelers don't get tipped off from the remains. They're probably going to head back and do the same with the horse skeletons once the buzzards have picked them clean. They'll have butchered the horses and taken the best meat. Nothing goes to waste with scavengers."

"I know. Had more than enough run-ins with their kind to know how they roll."

"We close to your spot?" Drake asked.

Lucas looked around and then walked to the side of the bridge and studied the underside.

Drake followed him over, hand on his holstered pistol, while the others waited with rifles at the ready in the center of the lanes.

Lucas pointed at the water's green surface, dimpled by a slight breeze. "Right there. About a yard from that piling in this direction."

Drake nodded and turned to his men. "All right, boys. Two best swimmers in the water. Now."

A pair of lean younger men broke off from the rest and walked to the edge. They placed their weapons on the asphalt and then stripped down until they were naked, their bronze skin glowing in the sun. Drake explained to them where they would be searching, and turned to Lucas.

"It's in a leather sack?"

"That's right. A little bigger than a canteen."

The men climbed over the railing and dove off with a whoop, their bodies carving graceful arcs through the air until they hit the water with a splash. Once in the lake, they treaded water and moved to where Lucas had indicated, and then flipped over and disappeared beneath the surface.

A half hour later, they were back on the bridge with Lucas's sack. Drake inspected the contents as they pulled their jeans and shirts back on, and after retrieving Lucas's weapons from his men, approached Lucas and offered them to him.

Lucas took the guns and then the gold. "Where you figure their camp is?"

"Somewhere on the far bank. It'll be out of sight, but close enough to the water for easy access. Why?"

"They may have my horse. Big stallion. Been with me forever."

"You remember I said there are usually fifty of 'em, right?"

"I do."

"Well, you're in no shape to tackle them right now. Let's go see Malcolm and talk turkey. If we have a deal, we can help you out with them. Like I said, they don't want a fight with us."

Lucas adjusted his flak jacket and nodded. "Fair enough."

"If we hurry, we can make it to town by sundown. Unless you got some reason to want to stick around out here and wait to see if they come back to finish the job."

"No, I need to sit down with your brother. But I'll hold you to helping me once we're done."

"All right. Let's make tracks. It's gonna be a long trek. No point dallying."

Drake set off back down the bridge, and Lucas followed, with the rest of the group trailing them. Lucas's head still felt like he'd wrestled a bear, but he ignored the dull throb and focused on avoiding passing out, each beat of his heart a spike of pain through his temples, reminding him that for all his troubles over the last twenty-four hours, he was still alive – which was more than he could say for his loyal but ultimately unlucky men.

Chapter 14

.

Oklahoma City, Oklahoma

Snake and Petey crouched behind a rubble pile, taking turns watching what had been an industrial supply store in the days before the collapse but was now just another in an endless string of partially ruined buildings, their windows broken out by looters in the early days of the troubles, many of the façades blackened by soot from fires. They'd spent all day scoping the place out, and had seen clusters of emaciated gunmen patrolling in a neighborhood policing effort they'd taken great pains to avoid.

Petey fiddled with his pistol's slide while Snake scanned the area, and leaned toward him after verifying that the gun was as clean as it was likely to get.

"You sure about this?" he whispered.

"Completely." Snake patted his flak vest, where he'd stashed the folded map, and then glanced at his watch. "Seems to be the locals come by about every forty-five minutes. At least this bunch."

"We gonna wait until dark?"

Snake shook his head. "No point. We'll need the daylight to work." He rose. "We should have a good half hour before they return."

"Unless they change their rounds," Petey said.

"They've got no reason to search the place. If they come back before we're done, we'll just lie low until they leave again."

Petey's expression was doubtful. "Hope you're right."

"I am."

When the street was clear, Snake darted across, and Petey trailed him at a jog. Inside the store, which looked like a grenade had detonated inside, Snake led him to the rear, where the offices had been, and pushed open a steel slab door half off its hinges. They entered a dark hallway and walked toward the rear exit, where they found a loading area with steel shelves along the walls and dozens of empty chemical containers and supply bags strewn across the concrete floor.

Snake leaned down and picked up a metal pry bar and then pointed to a doorway with a faded sign that identified it as the shipping office.

"There."

They picked their way through the debris, and Snake entered the room first. Light filtered through a barred, wire-reinforced window, and dust motes danced in the beams. Snake looked around the ransacked office and grinned when he spotted a large black metal safe. He moved to it, and Petey joined him. They considered the scarred exterior, as well as the door that had been pried open, and Petey frowned.

"Looks like they went at it with an axe for days. Whatever was in it's gone now."

Snake took in the dents and gouges and shrugged. "Probably. Doesn't matter." He moved to the safe and took three large steps to the right. He stopped, facing the wall, and his grin widened. "This is it."

Petey appeared confused. "What are you talking about?"

Snake leaned his rifle against the wall and began tapping on it with the pry bar. Halfway up, the sound changed from the solid thunk of cinderblock to something hollower, and Snake started chipping at the mortar with the bar. Three minutes later he'd revealed a long gray metal box that had been sealed into a cavity in the block, and he pried at it with the bar until it broke loose.

He removed what looked like a safe deposit box, set it on the floor, and opened it. Petey stepped closer as Snake withdrew a small black velvet sack and peered inside. He smiled and hefted it, and then removed a rolled-up document encased in a plastic sheath and unfurled it.

"What's that?" Petey asked.

Snake studied the document for a long beat and then replaced it in the sheath. "Another map for the location of a weapons cache."

"So we're going after it?"

"Not we. I am. I have another job for you."

Snake reached into the velvet sack and pulled out a handful of gold coins. Petey gave a low whistle when Snake counted off five and handed them to him.

"I want you to get a wagon. Some booze. The best stuff you can find."

Petey weighed the coins in his hand. "Why?"

"I need you to listen to me very carefully. We're going to have to split up for a while, but I'll find you."

Snake spoke in low tones for several minutes and then stopped and grabbed Petey's sleeve.

"You hear that?" he whispered.

"No. What?"

"Voices. Outside."

Both men froze and listened. Footsteps echoed from the front of the store – the distinctive sound of boots crunching on rubble. Snake edged from the office and out to the loading dock door and tried it. It was locked. He scowled and looked to Petey, who was framed in the office doorway, and signaled for him to take cover wherever he could. Petey dashed to a forklift in one of the shadowy corners, and Snake moved to the far side, where some broken pallets and empty drums were piled.

Three men entered, rifles at present arms, and Snake held his breath, waiting for them to make the first move.

"Who's in here?" one of them called.

Snake bit his tongue and hoped that Petey was savvy enough to stay quiet.

"This is protected turf. Show yourself or you'll be sorry," the man warned.

Snake rose from his hiding place, rifle in hand. "I don't want no problems, man. I was just scrounging to see if there's anything useful in here. I thought it was cool. Place is empty."

"It isn't. Just you in here?" the leader demanded.

"That's right. Okay, man. I'll just take off and leave you be."

One of the others shook his head. "What are you doing here, anyway?"

"Just passing through, man. Like I said. I don't need no grief."

"We don't like scavengers," the leader growled, brandishing his weapon. The men behind him did the same.

A deafening boom from Petey's pump 12-gauge exploded from the forklift, and the leader's head melted like hot wax as the double-aught buckshot shredded the skin from bone in a bloody spray. Snake tucked and rolled and was firing as he moved. A baritone detonation from Petey hit another gunman in the torso. Rounds ricocheted off the floor around Snake, and then several of his shots caught the third man in the throat, ending his life and the immediate threat.

Petey stepped from behind the forklift and Snake stood, his features twisted in frustration.

"Damn it! Now we're going to have fifty more like them on our ass in a heartbeat."

"It was either us or them. They were about a second from turning you into swiss cheese."

Snake shook his head. "Let's get out of here. We'll figure things out once we're clear."

Petey strode to where the dead men lay in a pool of crimson and quickly confiscated their magazines, and then followed Snake out the rear door and down the alley behind the stores, both men running as fast as their legs would carry them.

Chapter 15

Durant, Oklahoma

A neon glow illuminated the western horizon as the Choctaw party arrived in town. Children and women ran to greet the group, and Drake pulled Lucas aside, ignoring the concerned looks of the locals.

"We'll see Malcolm first thing and get your proposition out of the way," Drake said.

He led Lucas down a main street to what had once been the city hall, and nodded to a lone guard seated outside the main entrance on a folding steel chair, his AK resting against the wall beside him.

"He still here?" Drake asked.

The man looked Lucas up and down before frowning. "Yep." He pointed at Lucas's rifle. "Gonna need your weapons."

Lucas handed the rifle and pistol over. "See that nothing happens to them."

Malcolm was seated behind an expansive desk in a ground-floor office and looked up from something he was reading when Drake pushed through the door with Lucas. He sized Lucas up and drew back in surprise.

"You…"

Lucas tipped his hat. "That's right. Good to see you again."

Malcolm had aged thirty years over the decade since Lucas had brought him to his father, and his face was weathered and lined, his skin taut over high cheekbones, his chocolate eyes flinty and alert.

Gone was the twenty-three-year-old Lucas had known, replaced by a tired man who looked as though he'd seen too much of the world.

"Sorry to hear about your dad," Lucas continued.

Malcolm inspected Lucas without comment for several long beats and then looked to his brother. "Where did you find him?"

"Over by the lake," Drake answered. "Said he got you out of a bind back in the day?"

Malcolm grunted. "Yeah. Long time ago." He shifted his attention back to Lucas. "What brings you here?"

"I wanted to talk to you and your brother about buying supplies for my army."

"*Your* army?"

"That's right. I need a month's provisions for a large group." Lucas spelled out what he wanted.

Malcolm eyed him like he was insane. "Wait. Back up. How did you happen to come across an army that size?"

Lucas gave him a brief rundown on the events that had led him to Durant. When he finished, Malcolm was shaking his head.

"Unbelievable. You sure you haven't gone round the bend?"

"I'm dead serious. And I brought gold to prove it." Lucas set the satchel with the coins on the table.

Malcolm didn't move to inspect it. "Don't think we can help you with a month's worth. Maybe we could round up two weeks' worth. I mean, you're talking about most of our production."

Lucas nodded. "I know. It's a lot of food. I'll take as much as you can manage. Name your price."

The negotiation lasted less than twenty minutes, and by the time Lucas shook hands with the brothers, they'd agreed on a two-week supply, delivered to the army by the tribe, in exchange for 150 ounces of gold – more than Lucas had hoped to pay, but not unreasonable considering the Indians were the only game in town. It would take two days of long hours for them to prepare all the stock and load it, and it would clean out their entire trading surplus for the season, but Malcolm assured Lucas it would be done on time, and that they would be riding west shortly.

Lucas retrieved his weapons from the guard, and Drake showed him to a guesthouse at the edge of town. At the threshold, Lucas paused.

"I'm going to want to deal with the scavengers tomorrow if you can lend me a good horse and a few men."

"It'll take more than a few if they decide they don't want to cooperate. We get along well enough, but you're a wild card. Not sure how they'll react to being called out." Drake hesitated. "You're just after your horse, right? No…retribution?"

"If it were up to me, it'd be an eye for an eye. But seems like I don't have much choice but to do it your way."

"We don't want to go to war with them. They serve a purpose."

Lucas's frown hardened. "Maybe. But in this case it cost me some of the best men I've ever known."

"I'm sorry about that. I really am. If we'd known you were coming…"

Lucas left it there, seeing no reason to belabor the obvious, and entered the house, which was simply furnished and operated by an older woman who didn't speak to him other than to point out how to operate the facilities and pump water, and inform him that dinner would be venison stew and that he could serve himself out of a pot in the kitchen.

The following morning Lucas, Drake, and a dozen men rode to the bridge and crossed it at noon. The smell of woodsmoke led them to the camp, which was little more than a huddle of ragged tents deep in the trees beside a primitive corral made from roughhewn branches and saplings. A group of armed men with filthy clothes and grimy faces blocked their way when they drew near.

"Afternoon, Drake," a tall, reed-thin man called out.

"Hello, Mike," Drake replied.

"What brings you out here?"

Drake indicated Lucas. "My friend lost his horse on the bridge the other day. He wants it back."

Mike studied Lucas for a beat and toed a small rock from in front of him. "That so? What was he doing there?"

"I was coming to see Drake," Lucas said. "You bushwhacked us and killed my men."

Mike's expression grew thoughtful. "How'd we miss you?"

"You aren't as good as you thought." Lucas allowed his eyes to drift to the corral and then back to Mike.

"I see my horse."

Mike shook his head. "You mean you see my horse. But I might be willing to sell him if the price is right."

Lucas's cold smile never reached his eyes. The barrel of his M4 swung a few inches to his left and settled on Mike as he thumbed the firing selector to three-round burst.

"How does three rounds sound?" Lucas asked, his tone dangerously soft.

Mike snorted derisively. "If that's all he's worth to you–"

"I could go as high as thirty."

"Still way too low for such a fine animal."

"First three will take your head off. The next twenty-seven will take down about half your men, the way they're grouped. You think you can handle the others, Drake?"

Drake's voice was tight when he answered, "That wasn't what we agreed to."

Lucas stood impassively, keeping his rifle trained on the scavenger. "Situation changed."

Mike raised his rifle, as did his men.

Lucas cleared his throat. "You either give me my horse, as well as the ones you stole from my men, or so help me God, you'll die where you stand. Drake here tried to convince me not to kill you all, and I was fine with that, but you're making it hard not to break my promise, you scumbag." Lucas leaned over and spit. "So decide if today's the day you want to die. I'm fine either way."

"Mike, give the man what he wants. We'll work it out later," Drake said.

"I'm supposed to let this bastard walk into my camp and order me around?" Mike demanded. "That won't fly."

Lucas drew his Kimber with his free hand. "Might not need much more than this and the rifle, seeing how dumb your bunch looks."

Mike appealed to Drake. "You gonna back him on this?"

"Don't have any choice. He's Malcolm's buddy. He said to give him whatever he needs."

Lucas sensed Drake and his men spreading out, their horses' hooves thumping on the hard dirt. The tension was thick as ground fog as Lucas turned slightly in the saddle to present a smaller target, his unblinking gaze locked on Mike's.

"Please give me a reason to shoot you," Lucas growled.

"This is a no-win, Mike," Drake said, from Lucas's left. "Seriously. Just give him the horses."

Mike glared holes through Lucas, but slowly lowered his gun. "You know if he weren't here, you'd be dead."

"Tell yourself whatever you want," Lucas said. "Now get the horses. The stink here's making me sick."

Mike began to turn away from Lucas and then spun back and fired at him, crouching as he did so. Rounds snapped past Lucas's head, and he loosed a three-round burst that knocked Mike onto his back, and was sliding from the saddle and returning fire at the rest of the scavengers when Drake's Kalashnikov roared on full auto, joined instants later by those of his men.

Lucas's borrowed horse crumpled as scavenger fire peppered the beast, and Lucas threw himself behind it and used it for cover as he picked off several of the nearest scavengers. A shotgun boomed with measured cadence to his right, and then the fire from the scavengers stopped. Lucas peered from behind the horse and saw the surviving shooters with their hands in the air, along with those in the camp. At least a dozen men lay dead or gasping in pools of blood, including the leader, whose sightless eyes stared up at the treetops as though tracking the flight of his soul.

"It's over," Drake said to Lucas, and then shouted at the camp, "You boys keep your hands up. We're going to get this man's horses and leave you be, but make a move and it'll go badly."

Nobody budged, and Lucas pushed himself to his feet and glanced at Drake, who was sitting unharmed on his horse.

"Sorry about that," Lucas said. "You saw, though. He drew down first."

"I could argue you backed him into that corner, but what's done is done."

"He had a chance to do the right thing."

Drake gave a grim chuckle. "Expecting a scavenger to do that's like expecting a wolf to spare a sheep."

Lucas shrugged. "World's no poorer for less of them."

"We can agree on that."

"All your men okay?"

"Looks that way. Fortunately scavengers can't shoot worth a damn."

Lucas worked his way over to the corral and whistled. Tango cantered to him, and if a horse were capable of smiling, Lucas would have sworn he was grinning ear to ear. He pulled the gate section of the fencing open and Tango trotted out. Lucas scratched the top of his nose and whispered in his ear, "Stay here, boy. I want to get your friends."

Lucas pushed past the stallion and headed to where two horses he recognized were watching him. He made a snicking sound with his tongue, and they followed him to the gap. He walked to a log where a row of saddles, headgear, and saddlebags rested and found his, as well as two that were obviously his dead men's, and quickly saddled the horses.

He looked around and spotted a form slumped against a tree at the far side of the camp. His forehead creased as he approached the tree, and his pulse quickened when he spotted Sam, a filthy bandage soaked with blood and dotted with flies secured against his chest, his head hanging with a string of drool trickling from the corner of his mouth.

Lucas knelt beside him and raised his head. Sam's eyelids flitted open, revealing unfocused, feverish eyes.

"How bad you hurt?" Lucas asked, drawing his knife.

"Been…better," Sam rasped.

Lucas cut the cord that bound him to the tree and helped him to his feet. "We're getting out of here. Can you ride?"

"I'll manage."

Lucas supported Sam and led him to the horses and helped him into the saddle before climbing atop Tango and leading the pair to where Drake and his men waited.

"We done here?" Drake asked, surveying the camp.

Lucas nodded. "Got what I came for."

Drake looked over the dead and wounded and settled on Mike's corpse.

"I'd say in more ways than one."

"Some days everything works out. Today's one of them."

Drake didn't respond and instead called out to the camp, "You all saw what happened. We didn't come to attack you. We defended ourselves. If you know what's good for you, you'll bury your dead, stay out of our way, and we'll get along just fine. We don't want a fight with you, but we'll bring it hard if you take us on. Anyone has any questions, you know where to find me." He spurred his horse, spun him around, and galloped back toward the lake, Lucas and his men behind him, the only sound in the camp the groans of the wounded, few of whom would make it till nightfall.

"My friend is going to need some antibiotics and a doctor," Lucas said, when he pulled even with Drake.

"We got both. One of the best on bullet wounds." He craned his neck to look at Sam, who was barely staying in the saddle. "If he's salvageable, she can do it."

"Anything he needs. He's been with us a while. A good man."

Drake cracked a smile for the first time since they'd left town. "I'll put it on your tab. We'll do what we can."

"That's all I can ask."

"Make sure he doesn't drop before we make it back. I've seen venison ready for the fire that looked better than him."

Chapter 16

Dallas, Texas

The shantytown stretched like a tumor through the streets of downtown. Carcasses of abandoned vehicles had been draped with tarps and turned into bedrooms for the indigent who were too unbalanced for the inhabitants of the surrounding buildings to tolerate in their midst. A rank pall of smoke hung over the dwellings, and the gutters reeked of raw sewage too foul for even starving rats to approach. Nearly naked children ran barefoot along the crowded streets, grinning as they played, and a few obviously diseased prostitutes lounged by the intersections, their brightly festooned scrawny forms a caricature of streetwalkers of bygone days.

Gera led a column of men into the midst of the dwellings but remained mounted as a score of his men swung from the saddle and dispersed. He cupped his hands around his mouth and called out in a commanding voice, and the men and women stopped what they were doing and listened with obvious trepidation.

"We're going to need as many able-bodied men as we can muster. Everyone who comes will be fed three good meals a day and compensated fairly at the end of the month." He paused and surveyed the squalid scene. "That's for volunteers. If we don't get enough and we have to do this involuntarily, it'll be a lot rougher, and there'll be no compensation. So everyone best volunteer."

Gera's squad returned several minutes later, directing a group of emaciated men clad in filthy rags to a line of wagons at the rear of the armed column, and he mentally counted them as they shambled past. Some of the squad returned to the shanties to find more conscripts, and Gera's nose wrinkled as a light wind blew a stench in his direction. He turned to study the source, and frowned at the sight of the charred remains of a dog that had been impaled on a piece of rebar and grilled over a fire, with a sign advertising two handfuls of meat for a bullet. A girl, no more than ten, with an expressionless, soot-covered face and vacant eyes, sat under a lean-to beside the dead animal, humming tunelessly and rocking slightly.

More men arrived, this time at gunpoint, some of them angry, but most fearful. Gera squared his shoulders. "Congratulations, men. Climb aboard the wagons and let's get this show on the road."

"Where you taking them?" a woman with a bandana tied over her hair called from a beneath a sun-bleached tarp.

Gera glowered at her. "We're organizing a defense force. These men are going to be a part of it."

"Defense force?" she echoed. "Defend from what?"

"That's all I can say," he called over his shoulder. "All right, men. Move out."

Grumbling from the tents followed the group down the street, but Gera ignored it, his mind churning over the challenges he'd have to overcome to carry out his task. There were precious few fit men he could draft to form his defense force, which would be little more than cannon fodder sacrificed to the enemy when they attacked. He'd exhausted all sources and was now dragging the bottom of the barrel with the drug-addled, the mentally ill, the diseased and starving. It would be a miracle if the staging area he'd set up didn't become a death camp before the enemy even arrived, but that was the least of his concerns. He desperately needed more men, but there were none left, which put him at serious risk with Bernard, who was as mercurial as he could be violent, and didn't take disappointment well.

The group proceeded north and reunited with a larger collection of draftees who were being guarded in an industrial area east of

Carrollton. They spent the night there and then continued their forced march north until just before dark they arrived at the junction where the 35W and 35E freeways split – where a collection of tent barracks had been set up on the grounds of Apogee Stadium, and at least six hundred conscripts were already gathered.

Clumps of men ambled aimlessly within the tent city, which was enclosed by barbed wire. Armed guards patrolled the perimeter on horseback, lending the encampment the air of a prison camp rather than a military hub. Gera rode through the gates and led his charges inside, and then swung down from the saddle and handed the reins to a Hispanic youth, who led the horse off toward a huge warehouse that was being used as a stable.

Inside what passed for the command tent, Gera slumped into a camp chair and read a handwritten report. They had managed to collect eight hundred and sixty-seven men, thirty-three of whom were so ill they could barely walk, and the rest in varying stages of starvation from years of deprivation and diets that consisted mostly of rats and expired canned food. The idea of such a group posing any sort of military challenge to a disciplined force was laughable, but it wasn't Gera's role to question either Bernard or the cartel's wisdom. They wanted men capable of holding rifles, and that's what he had delivered. Whether they would fight on behalf of the cartel wasn't his concern – that was where Bernard would come into play as the ragtag army's commander.

The tent flap pulled back and Bernard entered, followed by a youth who remained silently by the entry.

"Well? How did we do?" Bernard asked, shaking Gera's hand.

Gera gave him the count and Bernard's expression darkened. "Dammit, I told you I need a thousand men, not a best effort. Go back out tomorrow and find another hundred. I don't care where or whether they can stand up straight. I need bodies."

"There isn't anyplace we haven't tried. We've hit everywhere. This is the best we could do."

Bernard waved Gera's statement away. "Then get boys. Anyone over thirteen. From a distance, they'll suit my purpose."

Gera blinked in disbelief. "That will cause serious problems. The mothers will go berserk."

Bernard laughed. "I trust you can handle a few women, my friend. Shoot a few and the rest will fall into line."

"You realize that these men will turn tail when the first shots are fired, don't you?"

"Not if we're waiting to gun them down if they do. Which I'll make clear. A few National Guard Brownings at their backs should convince them that cowardice is a lousy choice."

Bernard left, and Gera moved to a filing cabinet, unlocked it with a key on a lanyard around his neck, removed and uncorked a bottle of tequila, and took a deep pull. He would follow his master's orders, even when they made no sense to him. He grimaced at the burn of the fiery liquid as it slid down his throat, and considered going to the mess area for food before deciding to drink his dinner instead. An hour later he was snoring loudly and dreamlessly on a cot in the corner, the empty bottle in his arms cradled like a sick puppy.

Chapter 17

North of Marietta, Oklahoma

A guard came running to where Elliot, Luis, and Duke were sitting by a firepit, prepared for another night after a long day's march, watching as the sun sank into the western hills. Duke looked up from where he was whittling, and Elliot and Luis stood.

"What?" Elliot demanded.

"A column of wagons and armed men are headed toward us on the highway." The man swallowed. "Looks like Lucas is riding point."

Duke leapt to his feet. "He's back!"

They followed the guard to the road, and Lucas materialized out of the dusk at the head of a procession of rickety conveyances overloaded with supplies. He grinned when he saw his friends, and dropped from the saddle and led Tango over to them.

"Thought I'd never find you," he said, and wiped the road dust from his face with the back of his sleeve.

"You did it!" Elliot declared, shaking his hand.

"In drips and drabs. They'll be bringing more to us as we work our way to Dallas. I didn't want to wait until they'd collected everything we bought." Lucas paused. "Get a medic. Sam's wounded. He's on painkillers and antibiotics, but he needs checking. It's been a tough ride."

Luis spoke. "How bad?"

"Bad enough."

"I'll go fetch one," Luis said, and took off toward the main body of the camp.

Lucas watched him go before addressing Elliot and Duke.

"Anything I need to know about happen while I was gone?" he asked.

"Not really. But you showed up in the nick of time. We only have enough provisions to last through tomorrow."

"This should keep us going another week. They'll resupply us closer to Dallas. I gave them a rough estimate of how much time we're making per day, so they'll be waiting. The downside is that they only have enough to get us to Dallas. Their stores aren't bottomless."

Duke frowned. "Better than nothing. And once we take Dallas, we'll figure something out."

"Assuming we can take it," Elliot said. "It doesn't sound like we can afford a drawn-out siege."

"We shouldn't have to, if Conejo is telling the truth," Duke said.

Lucas appeared puzzled. "Who?"

Elliot sighed. "That's right. You were gone. We may have caught a substantial break."

Lucas whistled at a soldier and handed him Tango's reins. "See that he's fed and watered."

"Yes, sir," the man said, and led the stallion off toward where the other animals were grouped.

Lucas yawned. "Where are we set up?"

"Over there," Duke said, pointing at the command tent.

"I could use a hot meal," Lucas said.

"Then we'll kill two birds with one stone," Elliot replied. "This way."

When they were seated at a folding plastic table in the tent with bowls of stew in front of them, Elliot filled Lucas in on Conejo's story. He finished with his own belief in the gangbanger's account and sat back in silence, the only sound in the tent their chewing and slurping.

"Interesting," Lucas said when he was done with his stew. "Especially since you sound convinced. I want to meet this character as soon as possible."

"Wink has him. I'm sure that can be arranged."

"What happened to Sam and your men?" Duke asked Lucas.

Lucas's expression darkened. "Scavengers. They blindsided us. Trapped us on a bridge over the lake. Seems like their favorite spot. Pretty good one. I barely made it. Logan bought it holding them off."

"A shame. He was a good man," Elliot said.

"Yes, he was. Hopefully Sam will pull through. The Indian doctor said it would be touch and go for a week. Didn't want me to take him, but I couldn't just leave him there."

"Are their men headed back once the wagons are unloaded?" Duke asked.

Lucas nodded. "Yep. They'll return, load up again, and then meet up with us." He told them about the deal he'd made.

"Sounds like a bargain," Elliot agreed.

"Not a lot of negotiating room when it's the only game in town." Lucas paused. "How's morale? Any illnesses sweeping through the troops?"

Duke shook his head. "They're in good spirits. Bored, but that's to be expected. And everyone's sick of the same thing for dinner every night, but compared to what most have been through, that's like complaining about what the girl who kisses you looks like. And thank God, nothing significant on the sickness front. We've been lucky on this leg."

"Let's hope our luck holds." Lucas yawned and stood. "Think I'll see if I can't find Sierra and the kids. Been a while."

Elliot smiled. "An excellent idea. Get some rest, and we can discuss Conejo and how to proceed on the road. Lord knows we'll have enough time."

Lucas turned to Duke. "Do me a favor and check in on Sam, see how he's doing. He's been through a lot."

"Will do. Don't worry. We'll hold down the fort."

"Thanks."

Elliot pushed back from the table. "I'm glad you made it back. The troops need to see a real commander at the helm, not a broken-down fossil pretending to be one."

It was Lucas's turn to smile. "Hardly. But point taken. We need to prepare for Dallas, and everyone needs to be at the top of their game."

Elliot stood. "Focus is everything."

"You have any idea where Sierra is?" Lucas asked Duke.

"I suppose I could walk you over there."

"That's the spirit."

Chapter 18

North of Dallas, Texas

A harvest moon glowed in the night sky above the 35 freeway, bathing the area in a ghostly pallor as a half dozen men on horseback picked their way along a trail a hundred yards off the asphalt. A hot wind out of the east wrinkled the top of the tall grass around them, lending the fields the appearance of an ocean in relative calm. The air was dank with moisture from a squall that had dropped rain a few hours earlier, having blown through as quickly as it arrived, and the horses' hooves squished in mud as they plodded along, the only other sounds the night calls of amorous cicadas and the occasional hoot of an owl.

Duke led the patrol, which had ridden well ahead of the army to scout out the approach to Dallas and confirm that there was little in the way of resistance. It had been a week since Lucas had returned, and they'd met the Indians two nights earlier to replenish their stores, so they were ready for whatever battle they faced, even though Conejo had been insistent that there were few real fighters left in Dallas. Lucas had listened to his pitch but had expressed doubt afterwards, and had decided that it wouldn't hurt to verify the man's claims and not rush in headlong to discover the turncoat had painted the situation overly optimistically.

Duke sniffed the air and signaled for the men to stop. He cocked his head and listened, raised a finger to his lips, and then dropped down from the saddle and motioned for the others to do the same. He guided his horse forward, and after fifteen minutes, the southern sky grew brighter as they neared the junction of the 35 West and 35 East. He stopped short of the mammoth curved overpasses, which loomed impossibly large in the near distance, and raised his binoculars.

He adjusted the focus until he could make out fires and a sea of tents on the far side of the interchange, with men milling about. Duke leaned into the man closest to him and whispered, "Stay here. I'm going to get as close as possible and see what's going on there."

Duke left his horse with the others and jogged along the trail, M16 in one hand and binoculars in the other. He'd been riding all day, and it felt good to get out of the saddle to stretch his legs, even under the stressful circumstances, but every step over the uneven terrain served as a reminder that he wasn't young anymore. Coupled with the lack of cushion his boots afforded, by the time he'd approached the overpasses, his knees were throbbing like he'd run a mountain marathon.

The smell of smoke was stronger now, and the flames from dozens of fires dotted the grounds of a large encampment. He was getting ready to move closer, but stopped when he spotted a sentry ambling with a shouldered rifle on the other side of the junction. Duke crouched low and decided to collect as much information as he could from a safe distance, and glanced around for a spot where he wouldn't be seen if there were any more guards.

He spied a series of rungs that climbed one of the concrete highway supports, and made his way to them. After a brief inspection, he slipped his rifle strap over his shoulder and hauled himself up, the darkness beneath the freeway deeper due to the overpass blocking the moonlight. He paused halfway up and peered through the binoculars at the scene on the far side of the junction.

A huge sporting arena loomed in the darkness a third of a mile away. In the foreground, hundreds of men were sitting around fires, cleaning weapons. Duke did a rough estimate based on the number of tents, and swallowed hard. Conejo's assurances that Dallas didn't have many fighters was obviously wrong, because Duke counted at least eight hundred gunmen, along with plenty of mortars, anti-tank rockets, and .50-caliber machine guns on display.

He took in the scene until his arms and legs were aching from supporting himself, and when he was sure he hadn't missed anything, lowered himself back down the rungs and retraced his steps to where his men were waiting.

"Well?"

Duke cleared his throat. "There's a big force dug in with serious ordnance. Looks like they're expecting us. Not a good situation."

"How large?"

"Big enough so I would say we're going to lose a lot of men if we tackle them directly."

"So…now what?"

Duke walked to his horse, removed a canteen, and drank deeply before replacing it in a saddlebag. When he looked up, his expression was dark.

"Now we ride back and report on what's waiting. Figuring out how we want to deal with it's above my pay grade."

The men groaned, but Duke's expression ruled out any protest.

"Come on. Saddle up. Every second we're here increases the chances we're spotted."

He mounted up, and the others followed suit. Duke swung his horse around and they began the long trek back, his mind poring over the ramifications of a large, well-armed force waiting to engage the army, playing multiple possible scenarios through his imagination, with none of them ending well. He'd been so convinced by Conejo's assurances that he'd assumed there wouldn't be significant cartel resistance, but now he had to confront the certainty of a large group dug into an easily defended area, where the army's approach would be spotted from miles away.

Everything pointed to a bloodbath for the army.

The expected skirmish for Dallas had just morphed into a major battle – one with the odds heavily stacked against them.

Chapter 19

North of Dallas, Texas

The army had finished its day's march, and as dusk approached, the men were busy pitching tents in a sprawling field by the side of the highway. Horses were being watered and grazing on the plentiful grass, wagons were gathered near the mess area for unloading, and workers were digging latrine trenches along the periphery as a scattering of clouds drifted lazily overhead. Bats flitted through the cool gloaming in pursuit of insects, and birds winged their way home to nest in tall trees, safe from predators for another night.

Guards were positioned on both approaches of the freeway, with instructions to keep any travelers moving north from nearing the camp and to stop any traveling south, lest they spill the beans to Dallas on the army's size. Two carts had been pulled to the center of each double lane stretch of pavement, and four gunmen were lounging beside them, their horses free by the side of the road. A Browning .50-caliber machine gun rested on a tripod atop the larger cart, with a metal ammo can containing a belt of tracer rounds beside it.

One of the guards scanned the asphalt that stretched to Oklahoma City through a pair of dusty binoculars, and when he lowered them, he called over to the nearest man, spyglasses outstretched.

"Looks like we got company headed our way."

The second man took the glasses and peered through them and, after a few seconds, handed them back to the first guard and yelled to the others, "Heads up. We got incoming. Wagon, pair of horses. One rider I can make out."

A lanky young man with long matted hair moved to the machine gun, and the rest took up position behind the carts, using their bulk for cover. Several minutes later the wagon rolled into view, and the patrol leader called out in a loud voice, "Stop, and keep your hands where we can see them."

The man piloting the wagon slowly raised his hands, leaving his shotgun lying across his lap. "What's this all about?"

"Road's closed. Can't go any farther."

The man frowned. "What? Who the hell are you to tell me what to do?"

"State your business," the guard said. The one at the Browning adjusted his aim so the driver was looking down the big gun's barrel.

"I got me kind of a traveling trading post. Headed wherever the road takes me."

The guard's eyebrows went up. "Trading post? You got a wagon. Am I missing something?"

"I sell booze. Guns. Provisions. Anything I can get my hands on." The driver grinned vacantly. "What is this, anyway? You part of that army I heard about?"

"That's right. Why?"

The driver laughed. "I been looking for you."

"Why?"

"Business, of course. I figure you boys could use some of what I got. Wet your whistles, play some cards, maybe smoke some stale ten-year-old cigars. Whatever you want, if I got it, we can deal. I been riding day and night to catch up to you ever since you passed by Oklahoma City."

The guards exchanged glances. The leader visibly relaxed. "You can't go any farther."

"Why would I want to, now that I found you? I'll just set up near the camp and let everyone know I'm open for whatever comes my way."

"We can't authorize that."

The driver continued to grin. "I'm not asking for permission. Those your tents? I'll just stake a claim outside your camp and we'll see what happens, all right? No harm in that, is there?"

"We'll have to check with someone first." The lead guard lowered his rifle. "What's your name?"

"Petey. What's yours?"

"Miles."

"Well, Miles, let's get a move on, then. Take me to your leader. I ain't got all night."

Two hours later, Petey was set up and doing a brisk business in rotgut whiskey and tequila that would strip paint, as well as acting as dealer for a poker game with seven of the soldiers. The group played by torchlight until late in the night, and when Petey's final customer had staggered back to camp, Petey had gotten a good start on collecting information on the army's abilities and strength. Two of the players who had been with the force since Seattle had regaled Petey with tales of their exploits. Petey had been a good listener, ensuring that their glasses stayed filled, and he'd played the gracious host until the players were nodding off.

He drained the dregs from the glasses into a cup and swallowed it with a wince, and then unfurled a bedroll and spread it on the back of the wagon. He lay down and yawned and stared up at the tapestry of stars, his eyes heavy and his head spinning. As Snake had predicted, a rolling bar had been an in-demand camp follower, and he was now welcome to stick with the army as long as he felt like, gathering intelligence the entire time. Snake hadn't told Petey why the army was of such interest to him, but Petey didn't care. This was the best gig he could have found; far better than serving as Red's gofer, stuck in Oklahoma City with no prospects and nothing to show for it. Hell, at the rate he was going in just one night, his little sideline would turn out to be a lucrative proposition in its own right, with his wealth growing by leaps and bounds as he charged a premium in ammo for every swallow of hooch he sold.

He was still conflicted over swearing allegiance to Snake, but it had seemed the prudent thing to do, seeing as Snake had plentiful gold and seemed like a man with a plan. Red had been okay to work for, but it was boring. The idea of hitting the road and being part of something bigger appealed to Petey, and Snake's vision of a revitalized Crew regaining its standing as the lord of Texas was compelling.

"Beats the hell out of playing babysitter," he whispered to himself, and shut his eyes, visions of a position of power with the new Crew playing through his imagination until his breathing faded into a rumbling snore.

Chapter 20

North of Dallas, Texas

Lucas sat with Luis, Duke, Sam, and Elliot, studying a map by lamplight at a large folding table in the command tent. Their faces were grim, and Duke's eyes had discolored bags beneath them from having ridden most of the last two days without sleeping.

"You sure about the number?" Elliot asked.

Duke nodded. "Damned right. Close enough to a thousand that I could see, and armed to the teeth."

"Given their location, it's hardly likely that they aren't expecting us," Luis said, tapping the interchange with a forefinger.

"The question is…how?" Sam mused.

Lucas sighed. "A radio in Oklahoma. Or a fast rider. Does it really matter? It doesn't change that they're in place, and we have to go through them unless we detour around Dallas."

"If we try to take them on, we'll be walking into cannon fire," Duke said. "We could lose most of our men before it was over."

"We're obviously not going to do that," Elliot snapped.

"Then…what?"

Lucas chewed his lower lip. "Conejo had us half convinced that Dallas didn't have any real firepower. That's clearly wrong. However it happened, they got reinforcements. So now we need a new plan – one that doesn't involve suicide."

Duke gestured at the map. "We could bypass the junction and

take the 380 Truck route over to the 35E and avoid them entirely."

Lucas shook his head. "You have to assume that they have men watching all the approaches, and that they have radios. With a group as large as ours, even if we moved at night, they'd be onto us before we knew it, and would flank us and attack when we were most vulnerable."

"And there's the problem of provisions. Even if we went to half rations, we wouldn't be able to sustain ourselves for a long battle," Elliot said. "Our entire premise was based on surprising them and our attack being over within a day. That option's off the table."

Luis sat back. "Can we get the Indians to supply us with another week's worth of supplies? Seems like that would buy us more choices."

Lucas frowned. "Not a chance. We cleaned them out. Like it or not, to keep advancing on Houston, we need to take Dallas, and we don't have the stocks to engage in a protracted fight."

"Our men could go a few days without eating, if it came to that," Sam said. "God knows we've all done it."

"Starving troops don't fight as well as ones with full bellies. And they've been marching for months. Any reserves they had are long gone. It's a bad idea," Elliot said.

"Then what do we do?" Duke snapped, clearly exhausted.

Lucas sighed. "Get some sleep. I'll keep working at this. There's nothing to be gained by you dropping in your tracks."

"I'm fine," Duke protested.

"I need you at the top of your game, Duke. This ain't it," Lucas said. His tone softened. "Grab some shut-eye. That's an order."

Duke grumbled, but left the tent, and the rest continued their discussion late into the night. When the meeting finally broke up, a consensus had been reached, but nobody liked it, and Lucas remained in the command tent with Elliot after Luis and Sam departed for their bedrolls.

"I don't know, Lucas. What if Conejo's been lying all along?" Elliot asked.

"That's always been a risk. But it's better to find out now than to walk into a trap." He studied the map in front of him and shook his head. "We need to know whether what he proposed is still viable. A small group can slip through without giving away the plot. But an army of our size can't. So seems like the best we can do for now is hunker down and move cautiously."

"Burning more of our resources."

"You have a better alternative? Because right now I'm not seeing it."

It was Elliot's turn to exhale heavily. "Who are you thinking on sending?"

"I'm going to go."

Elliot shook his head. "Absolutely not. You almost got done in by the Indians. We can't risk losing you now, especially given the situation. We've got plenty of others as qualified to do this, and we both know it."

"What if I tell you I want to go?"

"I'd say your desires have to take second place to what's best for the army."

Lucas managed a tight, humorless smile. "Sierra would no doubt agree."

"Look, Dallas isn't the only ones with radios. If we stay put, we can erect a workable antenna for our shortwave, and we can send the group out with a two-way that we can receive at a considerable distance. So let some of your men do their job, you stay put, and once you have better intelligence, decide what to do. That way we won't burn time we don't have, and you won't endanger yourself for no reason." Elliot smiled. "Sierra isn't always wrong, Lucas."

Lucas held up his hands in surrender. "Right now I'm too tired to fight you on it."

"Which is why I pick my battles carefully. There's a lesson there."

Lucas laughed. "Point taken. So who would you suggest? I'm thinking Luis."

"Agreed. I'd say Sam as well if he wasn't wounded."

"He's mostly recovered. I could ask. He'd tell me straight if he could manage or not."

"Duke's burned out, but he's got a good nose."

"He's more resilient than you might think. Let's let him get a night's sleep and see if he's game. If so, I'd say Duke and Luis and however many men he wants."

Elliot rose. "Agreed. We'll fight this in the morning. I'm off. You'd be well advised to do the same. I'm sure Sierra wouldn't mind being woken up."

Lucas chuckled. "You working for her now? Lobbying job?"

"Hardly. Wish I had loving arms to go home to."

Lucas watched Elliot leave. The older man was right. He picked up the lantern and moved to the tent flap, brow furrowed in thought.

There were no good options, so they had to choose the least horrible and hope for the best. Which was a strategy that invited failure, Lucas knew.

But one he was powerless to do much about.

Chapter 21

The following evening, the army was within thirteen miles of the junction and had bivouacked in an area it could defend, with sufficient trenches and machine-gun nests from which it could fire. Mortars and rockets were being deployed in preparation for an enemy attack from the south, and the men had been instructed to be on battle footing until further notice.

Wink's group was putting the finishing touches on its area at the northern edge of the camp when Luis and Duke rode up with a large group of riders in tow. Duke and Luis dismounted while the rest remained in the saddle, and they approached Wink, who was sitting by a firepit, a bottle of rum in hand. Wink looked up at the pair.

"What can I do for you boys?" he asked with a frosty smile.

"We're here for your prisoner. Conejo," Duke replied.

Wink frowned. "Why?"

"Because Lucas said he wants us to bring him to him. Now where is he?"

Wink looked like he was going to protest, and then apparently reconsidered and shrugged. He turned his head and called out, "Shep? Go fetch Conejo. Be quick about it." Wink turned back to Duke and Luis and held up the bottle. "Want some? It's foul, but it'll warm your guts."

Duke shook his head. "Pass."

Luis did the same. "No, thanks. It's all yours."

Shep returned with a disheveled Conejo, who didn't look pleased. "What now?" he demanded.

"Lucas wants to see you."

"I told him everything I know."

Duke's expression was stony. "Then you'll get to tell him again."

Wink stood. "I'll come with you."

Luis frowned. "That isn't necessary."

"He's my prisoner."

Duke stared him down. "Not anymore. He's ours now."

Wink considered his bottle and then sat back down. "Have it your way. No skin off my ass."

Luis walked Conejo to a riderless horse. "Mount up."

Conejo blinked. "Why ride?"

"Because I said so."

Wink watched the group canter off and glanced at Shep, who stood motionless by the firepit.

"What do you make of that?" Wink asked.

"Since when does it take forty men to haul one lowlife across camp?"

Wink took another long pull on the bottle and set it down beside him. "Exactly."

When they arrived at the command tent, Duke led Conejo inside while Luis and the others waited in the saddle. Lucas looked up from the map he was studying when they entered, and leveled a cold stare at Conejo.

"You told us that Dallas was basically defenseless?" Lucas began. "Turns out that isn't the truth."

"No, I told you that there were only a couple of hundred competent cartel fighters. The rest are soft."

"Right. Another few hundred waste cases. But that's not what we're seeing. Care to explain where they got a thousand men from?"

Conejo's brow scrunched. "What are you talking about?"

"Recon patrol spotted a huge camp."

"Where?"

"By the 35 intersection, maybe ten miles from here. Looks like they're waiting for us."

Conejo was silent for several moments. When he spoke, his voice was low. "Probably reinforcements from Houston. The cartel must have changed its mind about making a stand in Dallas."

"Which changes everything," Lucas said.

"Not necessarily. The leaders will still be where I told you they'd be holed up. Take them out, and the reinforcements will be rudderless."

"Could be," Lucas agreed. "Which is why you're going to go with us. To make sure we get them."

Conejo's mouth dropped open, and then he recovered. "That wasn't the deal. I gave you everything. I never agreed–"

"Nobody's asking you. We'll still abide by our arrangement, but you're going to prove you told the truth. That way there won't be any finger-pointing after the fact. Instead of a few hundred, there's a thousand. Guess you could say I'm skeptical about the rest of your story now."

"Nothing should go wrong if you're careful. You'll see," Conejo protested.

Duke placed a large hand on Conejo's shoulder. "Hope so. If not, you'll be the first to get a bullet. Come on. We've got a ways to ride."

Conejo shook off Duke's hand and glared at Lucas. "I took you at your word."

"Prove that you told the truth and I'll honor it," Lucas said. "Now quit complaining. This is going to happen one way or the other, so either ride out under your own steam or hog-tied and lashed into the saddle. Your choice."

Conejo bit his tongue and allowed himself to be escorted from the tent. When he was astride his horse, he looked to Duke. "Gonna need a gun."

Duke chuckled, and Luis outright laughed. "Yeah. Sure. We'll get right on that."

"I need to be able to defend myself."

"From what? You have forty men guarding you. You're safer than in the womb." Duke twisted and spoke to his men. "He tries to make a break for it, put a bullet in him."

Duke spurred his horse forward, as did Luis, and then the group was riding toward the highway, the darkness enveloping them, the only evidence of their passage the dull thump of horseshoes on hard-packed dirt and a faint cloud of beige dust.

Chapter 22

Dallas, Texas

Eight men guided a pair of carts laden with wooden crates along an empty street in north Dallas, Bernard and Gera leading the way on horseback. Two mules with baleful expressions pulled the wagons, their hides rubbed raw from poorly maintained harnesses chafing for hours on end, their breathing a rasp from exertion. The wheels creaked with each rotation, the conveyances were overloaded almost beyond capacity, and the axles strained over the cracked and potholed pavement.

They had been underway since the prior morning, when their precious cargo had been loaded from a top-secret facility that officially didn't exist, adjacent to a university medical center in a nondescript windowless building that could have easily passed for a bank depository. Thirty of Bernard's most trusted henchmen had worked through the night to secure the crates, and when he and Gera had shown up at first light, they'd been ready to go for the forty-mile trip to the stadium.

They'd continued their trek after a restless night in the northern suburbs, anxious to make it to the camp by nightfall. An advance scout had sent word that the enemy army was less than a three-day ride from Dallas, and everyone in the party was aware of time working against them. It had taken longer than Bernard had planned for them to locate the mortar shells filled with mustard gas that

Houston had told him about, and he suspected something had gotten garbled in the translation. They had wasted a full day securing the correct shells and verifying they were still in serviceable shape, and Bernard now felt the clock ticking with every passing hour.

He'd ordered his men to ride ahead to the sporting arena, from the heights of which they could bombard the approaching army with deadly mortar fire while remaining safe from all but their heaviest artillery. Based on how Houston had described the gas, the army wouldn't have the ability to bring anything substantial to bear, and mopping up the survivors could be done with heavy machine guns from the top of the stadium without risking any of Bernard's valuable men.

The conscripts in the camp were expendable and would draw most of the fire. Bernard didn't care. They were for show, to slow the army down on its approach and ensure he had ample opportunity to lob as many gas projectiles into their midst as it took. An elaborate diversion, the camp would allow Bernard to fight a completely different type of battle than the army would have planned for – one where death rained from the heavens, and there would be no escaping the deadly clouds of poison that would quickly envelope their ranks.

At least that was the plan. Bernard still had to reach his destination and set up the mortars, test-fire them to establish range, and prepare for the onslaught he knew was coming. He wasn't afraid – he'd seen enough bloodshed to be inured to it – but the thought of thousands of battle-hardened men on approach sent an involuntary shiver up his spine. If for some reason this ruse didn't work…

He didn't want to entertain the thought.

Gera cleared his throat. "Won't be long now."

"Those mules look ready to drop."

Gera eyed the animals. "How long do you think we have before the army shows?"

"It'll be tight unless they've decided to play it safe – assuming their scouts spotted the camp," Bernard said.

"Which was the whole idea."

"Let's hope it worked. We don't want to underestimate them. They can still inflict a ton of damage, even if they're crippled."

Bernard had been justifiably doubtful about the strategy Houston had insisted he implement, but now that he had the gas, he was feeling more confident. He'd been briefed on what to expect and how it would disperse, and four of the crates contained gas masks so his most seasoned gunmen could counterattack once the mortars and the big Browning machine guns had done their damage. While no plan was perfect, he was now seeing the wisdom in what he'd initially dismissed as a desperation move.

The sun was setting when the bulk of Apogee Stadium loomed in the distance, its towering form dark against the fading light. Bernard's nose flared at the faint smell of woodsmoke that drifted from the camp near the base of the arena, and he urged his men to goad the mules to greater speed, anxious to be done with the trip.

When they arrived at the stadium, Bernard barked orders at the dozens of men who greeted them, instructing them to unload the carts as quickly as possible and transfer the crates to a holding area he'd set aside for the specific purpose of safeguarding the chemical weapons. An accidental discharge of mustard gas would be devastating, and it was up to him to ensure that didn't happen.

The stock he'd raided was the remnants of a US Army storage facility that had some of the last of the agent in the country. A particularly potent variety, it had been created by a clandestine government lab and earmarked for shipment to the Middle East, for use in deniable proxy wars in which the US was embroiled – in violation of international treaties the country was a party to. But then the virus had hit and the transfer shut down, leaving a small storage room filled with artillery shells and mortar projectiles containing the banned gas.

It was a particularly foul agent because the damage inflicted wasn't necessarily immediate and could take up to a day to present – typically as ulcerative blisters and respiratory distress culminating in agonizing death. Which was one of the reasons the conscript camp was critical to Houston's plan – the cartel needed a large enough force of putative fighters to keep the army from moving quickly, making it a sitting duck for a mortar attack that would maim or kill the majority of those it exposed to the gas. The more cautiously the army moved as it positioned to tackle the camp, the more damaging the exposure would be. Between fire from the admittedly unqualified conscripts in the camp and the .50-caliber rounds from the stadium's heights, the army would be frozen in place, leaving it completely vulnerable to the deadly toxin.

Bernard ascended the stairs to the top of the stadium and stood with Gera looking down at the tents that stretched from the parking lot to the junction. He grunted approval and glanced at Gera, his eyes hard as flint.

"See to it that the mortars and machine guns are positioned. I'm going to rest. You're welcome to join me for dinner when you've finished."

"That sounds great. I'll get to work," Gera said with a fatigued smile. Bernard had his entourage of sycophants and young boys waiting for him at the hospital near Lewisville Lake, which was known as Sodom among the men, although never within Bernard's earshot. That scene held no appeal for Gera, but he knew better than to refuse the invitation, and steeled himself for several hours of supervising before his first meal of the day, which if he was lucky would happen before the moon was high overhead.

"Do that. I'll see you later. I'm sure I'll be able to find something to wash whatever they cook down with."

Bernard did a final survey of the area and called over his shoulder to Gera as he descended the stairs, "Have the camp light more fires, and see to it that it's ringed with torches. I want it to be impossible to not make it out from miles away."

"Will do," Gera said, and then returned to the business of figuring out where to place the heavy machine guns and the mortars for the decisive battle to come.

Chapter 23

Duke and Luis rode ahead of the gunmen they'd selected for the sneak attack on the Dallas cartel headquarters, equipped with freshly solar charged night vision monocles and hunting crossbows in addition to their rifles. Conejo rode between them, his expression making clear his displeasure at being included in the scheme. They'd left the highway well before they reached the junction, and cut through suburban tracts with deserted ranch houses stretching as far as they could see. They rode slowly, wary of being spotted by a patrol, even though Conejo had assured them that it was unlikely there would be any that far afield.

He had described in detail the small hospital the cartel used as its base, well away from Dallas proper and hence easily defended compared to anything they could have chosen downtown. It was also close to plentiful fresh water in the nearby lake, which was a strong attraction in the hot summer months, when the downtown area was baking under the sun's relentless glare.

They reached railroad tracks in Denton and dismounted so Conejo could get his bearings and the horses could rest. He'd told them that there was a Y junction of tracks, one of which led along the western side of the hospital grounds, and so far his account had been accurate. Now, pacing in the dark under a moonless overcast sky, he seemed more agitated than at the camp, and Duke and Luis regarded him with concern.

"What're you so jumpy about?" Duke asked, his voice a low rasp.

"It's just weird to be out here at night. I can't see my own hand in front of my face."

They hadn't given him night vision goggles, partially because there was too little of the precious gear to spare, and because without them there was little chance he would try to escape, given the profundity of the darkness.

"But these are the right tracks?" Duke asked.

"They must be. I'm just trying to remember which branch goes by the hospital and which heads to Fort Worth."

Luis cleared his throat. "You've got five minutes. How far are we?"

"About six miles, give or take."

"Nobody lives around there?"

"Not really. Most everyone is on the lake or downtown. This is kind of the boonies, which is how the top guys in the cartel like it. Not like the Crew. We were always downtown…where the action was."

"Tell me again about who's in charge."

"Probably Bernard. He was next in line after his brother got killed. He's lazy, but he's a schemer and a snake. Smart; at least that's his rep. I never spent that much time around him."

"And that's it?"

"Maybe some lieutenants. Most of the best guys went to Oklahoma for the ambush, so this is more the B team that was left. That's why I don't see what the big deal is. You guys should be able to take them no problem."

"Obviously not the case with a thousand men waiting for us," Luis spat.

"I told you I don't know anything about that."

Duke exhaled heavily. "All right. Saddle up and let's ride."

Fifteen minutes later, Luis held up a hand and signaled to Duke and the men about an area ahead. Duke sidled close to him. "What is it?"

"Couple of men with guns. Rifles."

Duke studied the area where Luis had pointed for a moment before saying, "I see them."

"So?"

"We're invisible, but let's head into that neighborhood and cut them a wide berth." Luis leaned into Conejo. "What do you think?"

"Could be anybody. Couple of scavengers."

"Or a patrol," Luis whispered. "You know anything about this place?" he asked, indicating the houses.

"Not really. They're all kind of the same. Bunch of houses. Industrial farther along."

"Let's get off the tracks."

Duke guided his horse down an access-way and onto a residential street, weaving between vehicles rusting where they'd stalled. The men followed him, and he stiffened at an explosion of thunder that shook the ground beneath him. He urged his horse faster, his weapon sweeping the street, and grimaced when the first heavy drops of rain pattered against the pavement.

The rain quickly strengthened into a steady shower, and water streamed down the brim of his hat and the NV monocle as his steed plodded forward. Any threat of being spotted vanished as visibility dropped to a matter of a few yards. The street meandered past dark rows of homes, windows long ago sacrificed to looters in the early days of the collapse, some burned-out husks with only foundations remaining.

Half an hour later, Duke led the procession back onto the tracks and continued south until Conejo hissed a warning to him.

"The hospital should be coming up on your right soon."

Duke slowed and allowed the prisoner to catch up to him. Luis pulled abreast and wiped the rain from his face with the back of a gloved hand.

"All right. Time to find out if you've been telling the truth. Got any changes to your story you want to make before we do this?" Duke asked.

Conejo shook his head. "I told you everything I know."

"You'll be going in with us, so if you left anything out, you'll be the first to get popped."

"That wasn't my deal."

"It is now. Lead the way."

Conejo grumbled, but then peered ahead through the rain and pressed his horse forward. They veered away from the rails and toward a string of smaller outlying buildings, and then he cut away and led them off the railway and down an embankment to a storm drain. Water coursed from the grid, and he stopped by its side and pointed.

"That's drainage, but in a ways there's a section that connects to the sewage system. Once we're in that, we can make it to just under the hospital. There's an access hatch in the basement."

"How do you know all this?"

"One of my buddies helped set up the security for it."

"Then won't it be guarded?"

Conejo smirked. "You don't know the cartel. They're lazy. Ruthless, but they're basically criminals. So no. I'd say less than one in ten chance it is. Especially with their manpower shortage. They'll have better things to do than guard a basement nobody's ever tried to get through."

Luis returned his expression. "You'd better hope so."

The men dismounted and Duke gathered them around him. "Okay. We'll go in light – half of you. The rest wait here." He knew that if anything went wrong, they'd have to fight their way back to camp, so there was no point in risking all his troops. If Conejo was being truthful, twenty would be overkill. If he wasn't, Duke would need every bit of firepower he could muster to live to tell the tale.

Duke motioned to one of his gunmen. "Let me have your NV goggles."

The man handed them over, and Duke presented them to Conejo. "You know how to use these?"

"I can figure it out."

Two of the men pried open the rusted iron grate, and Duke and Luis followed Conejo into the chute, the rushing rainwater knee deep. He led them forty yards into the culvert and then stopped and pointed at a depression on his right.

"That's the manhole cover that leads into the sewer system," he explained. "Give me a hand with it."

The three of them wrestled the heavy metal disk out of the way, and Conejo looked down into the shaft.

"Looks dry."

He lowered himself into the hole, and Duke and Luis followed him down nine metal rungs and found themselves in a concrete tunnel barely four feet in diameter.

"This way," Conejo whispered, and then took off, the rest of the group behind him.

Eight minutes later they'd traversed the two hundred yards to the manhole that accessed the hospital basement, and Conejo spoke in a low voice. "We have to be really careful not to make any noise when we move the cover out of the way or it could tip off the guards."

"All right. This leads into an equipment room? How big?" Duke asked.

"Should be able to fit us all."

Duke tapped the hunting crossbow hanging from a shoulder strap. "Okay. Remember, everyone. Silent but deadly. Nobody uses their guns unless we're overwhelmed."

Duke climbed the rungs and pushed against the metal disk with his shoulder and managed to lift it the required two inches so he could slide it aside. The interior of the room was dark, and Duke crossed the span in four strides and stood by a steel door while the rest of the group ascended and joined him. Luis tapped him on the shoulder to indicate they were ready, and Duke eased the door open, revealing a long hallway.

Conejo whispered to him, "Stairwell at the end leads to the ground floor. They use the offices on the ground floor as their headquarters."

Duke nodded. "Follow me."

The group filed slowly along the corridor, careful to be as quiet as possible, crossbows cocked, loaded, and at the ready. The weapons had been Lucas's idea after Conejo had described the layout, and he'd commandeered them from the hunting squad, which used them to provision without scaring off everything in the vicinity whenever they made a kill. When they reached the end of the hallway, Duke indicated the fire door, and Luis inched it open.

Empty.

Duke leaned into him and murmured almost inaudibly, "Stick by the prisoner in case he tries to make a break for it."

"Got it."

Another door at the ground floor landing was cracked just enough so Duke could make out the glow of firelight from the other side. He signaled for the men to be ready, and then pulled it wide and slid into the lobby like a wraith. He didn't wait for his men, knowing they would be right behind him, and instead made his way to where Conejo had said the offices were, just off the lobby.

He scanned the area and spied four guards lounging outside under the overhang, huddled out of the rain. There were none inside, which was consistent with what Conejo had described, increasing Duke's confidence in the thug's veracity. He waited until Luis and the men were nearby, and whispered to them, "Spread out and be ready to tackle the guards when they enter. Luis, you, Conejo, and half the men come with me."

Luis relayed the order in a terse whisper, and ten of the troops broke off and took up position on either side of the lobby, sticking to the shadows. The guards were sitting with their backs to the entrance, any threat expected to come from the exterior, and Luis spotted a heavy machine gun on a tripod at the far end of the overhang, ringed with sandbags. He issued an instruction to the nearest gunman, who nodded – his priority would be to take out the machine gunner if he had the presence of mind to man his station and swivel the gun around.

Duke waited until Luis returned, and after taking a deep breath, pushed the double mirrored glass doors open while Luis and the men rushed through.

Six men were dozing on cots in the antechamber, and Luis skewered the first through the heart with his crossbow bolt as he sat up, reaching for his weapon. More quarrels whizzed through the air, and the other five guards were dispatched with no sound but the soft wet thwack of the bolts striking them and the groans, moans, and muted screams that accompanied their deaths.

Luis paused to free another bolt from the quiver strapped to his back, drew and cocked the bow again, and inserted it. His men did the same as Conejo watched with his mouth open, and then they were rushing through the door into the next room, bows at the ready.

Bernard was lying naked on an ornately carved king-sized bed with Miguel beside him. A single lantern lit the chamber, and a bowl of fruit and a bottle sat on a night table near the bed. Conejo stepped into the room beside Duke and Luis and pointed at the cartel boss.

"That's him!"

Bernard whipped a pistol from the night table and threw himself off the bed, firing blindly at the door as he did so. Duke loosed a bolt at him that drove through his throat, and he dropped the pistol and clawed at the shaft as his mouth worked in strangled horror. Duke watched him impassively as the color leached out of his face, and then walked over and kicked the gun away.

Luis was drawing a bead on Miguel when Conejo grabbed his sleeve. "No. I know him. He's harmless."

Luis was about to reply when gunfire erupted from the lobby as the guards responded to their master's shots. Duke slipped his crossbow strap over his shoulder and freed his M16, and the rest of the men followed his lead.

A firefight erupted in the lobby as the troops returned fire at the cartel guards, and then the big .50-machine gun began firing before abruptly stopping. A grenade detonated outside the lobby entrance, and the shooting ceased.

Duke dashed through the antechamber and surveyed the lobby, where six of his gunmen were still standing; the others lay on the floor, obviously dead. He took in the devastation with a frown, and then called out, "Keep your eyes peeled, and be ready to move out in one minute. Mission accomplished."

He returned to the bedchamber, where Conejo was speaking in

low tones with Miguel, who'd covered himself with a sheet. Duke approached.

"Where's the rest of the cartel command?" Duke demanded.

"That's what he was telling me. They're at the camp by the stadium."

"Why? I thought you said they'd all be here."

"They've got some kind of mustard gas. The camp's a ruse. Mostly just derelicts. To slow us on approach so they can gas us."

Luis's brow furrowed. "How does he know that?"

"He…overheard. I can vouch for him. He was tight with my crew before I left. He got pressed into this with Bernard…it was either do what he wanted or take a bullet to the head."

"I got no love for these scum," Miguel spat. "Anything I can do to help take them down, I'll do. I know all about what they have planned. Where they're keeping the gas."

Duke considered the youth before speaking. "Get dressed, then. You're coming with us." He looked to Conejo. "So are you."

"I'd just as soon leave now."

"I'm sure you would. But the job's only half done. I'd hate for you to get captured or something and tell them what we have planned."

Duke pushed past him and made for the door, leaving Conejo staring hate at his back.

Chapter 24

North of Dallas, Texas

Lucas walked through the darkness with Elliot, inspecting the wagons that contained the mortars and rockets, LED lanterns in hand.

"What's the story on this one?" Elliot asked one of the mechanics, indicating a wagon.

"Axle bearings aren't going to last much longer with the additional weight. We'll be lucky to make Dallas," the man replied.

"Can you source new ones there?"

"Should be able to."

"Can't we offload some of the gear to the other wagons?" Lucas asked.

"Negative. They're all in about the same shape."

A trooper came at a run from the area of the command tent. He stopped, winded, in front of Lucas, and struggled to catch his breath.

"What?" Lucas demanded.

"There's a transmission from Duke."

Lucas looked to Elliot. "Will you finish up here?"

"Of course."

Lucas followed the trooper back to where the shortwave radio was set up, running off a deep-cycle battery attached to a 335-watt solar panel and inverter. He sat at the set and pulled on a pair of headphones, and the operator handed him a microphone.

"Duke?" Lucas asked.

"Roger that. Got some G2 for you."

"Fire away."

Lucas listened as Duke described the situation with the mustard gas. When he was done, Lucas's expression had darkened.

Lucas keyed the transmit button. "He's positive about where it's located?"

"Seems that way."

"How far are you from the stadium?"

"Maybe five miles or so. Riding hard, we could be there in an hour and a half, tops."

Lucas checked his watch. "What's your strength?"

"Lost a half dozen."

"Damn."

"Not sure that'll be enough to pull off a stealth attack. I mean, it could be, but if we encounter any serious resistance…"

"Give me a second," Lucas said, and removed the map from his flak vest and unfolded it. He studied the area around the junction, and then keyed the mic.

"I can rendezvous with you a mile west of the stadium with reinforcements in two hours."

"I was going to suggest that."

"In the meantime, see if you can get enough info from your prisoners to come up with a strategy."

"Already working on it."

"Ask them what's around there. Some landmark we can find easily to meet."

"Stand by."

Lucas waited as a minute dragged by, and then Duke's voice returned to the headphones.

"There's a motel right off the 35 East. Desert Sands. He says you can't miss it from the freeway – right before you hit the 377 interchange. I'm guessing you'll know what that means."

"10-4. See you there."

Lucas pushed back from the radio and handed the operator the headphones. He thought for a moment and then marched to the command tent, where Sam was sitting with an inventory log.

"How's the wing?" Lucas asked.

"Mending. Could have been worse."

"You up for some action?"

"Been bored out of my mind. What's shaking?"

Lucas explained what he needed, and Sam rose. "I'll get the men ready. You think a couple of hundred will be enough?"

"If it's the right ones. I'll leave that to you. But they all need NV gear, or at least scopes. We move out in twenty."

"Then better not waste any time."

Sam departed, and Lucas called to one of the troopers standing guard. "Get Tango ready to ride."

"Yes, sir."

The man ran off, leaving Lucas to check his weapons and add extra magazines and grenades to his vest. When he was done, he returned to where Elliot was waiting and gave him a brief rundown of what he planned to do.

"I'll want some shoulder-fire rockets," he told the mechanics. "Where are they?"

"Over here. How many?"

"Fifteen or twenty would be good. Take them over to the horses."

"Will do."

Elliot pulled Lucas aside. "You're really going to lead this charge? Why not leave it to Duke?"

"Because he's good, but he isn't me, and the army's survival depends on us getting this right."

Elliot studied Lucas's face before sighing. "I'm not going to tell you what I think."

"Elliot, don't take this the wrong way, but it doesn't matter. I'm doing it." Lucas paused. "You're in command until I get back. Have the troops mobilize, and be ready to march in a few hours. We'll stay in touch by radio, but I want you a mile from the interchange when we hit them, so you can move on the camp once we're done."

"Frontal assault?"

"Hit them from both sides, as well as the front. But remember they're dug in, so go light on the frontal approach."

"Will do."

"Get a radio from the tent. I'll call in once I know more."

Sam was waiting with the men when Lucas arrived at the makeshift corral. He inspected the troops, confirmed the rockets had been delivered, and then climbed into the saddle before addressing the assembly.

"We're headed to meet up with Duke's group. From there, we'll be moving on the stadium by the enemy camp. We don't want to give away our position, so no talking from here on out. Pass the word along."

Lucas waited until everyone had confirmed they understood, and then directed Tango toward the highway, a compass in hand. It looked like he would be able to cut through a residential area, skirt the enemy camp by a wide margin, and make it to the rendezvous on time, even with the rain. That would take him off the main road, which was best given there had to be advance cartel scouts positioned on the approach.

They made it to the motel on time, and Lucas approached Duke and Luis, who were waiting out of the drizzle with Conejo and Miguel.

Conejo introduced Miguel, who told Lucas everything he knew about the gas and the plan to bombard the army with it. Lucas listened intently and then thanked him and huddled with Duke and Luis to discuss how to proceed. After ten minutes, they had what they felt was a workable plan, and Lucas issued orders to the men before mounting up and setting off in the direction of the stadium, troops in tow.

Chapter 25

The rain had lightened to a steady drizzle by the time Lucas could see the stadium. They'd agreed that the enemy wouldn't be expecting to be attacked from its rear, so they weren't surprised that there were no patrols working the southwest section in the rain, and they managed to get within a half mile without giving themselves away.

Lucas dismounted with the rest, and they left Conejo and Miguel and the horses with a skeleton crew headed by Sam and proceeded the rest of the way on foot. Any patrols they encountered they would handle with their crossbows. Lucas and Luis led the way, night vision goggles in place, each toting an anti-tank rocket in addition to their other weaponry.

A hundred yards from the stadium, Lucas pointed out a pair of slumbering guards beneath a tarp, and Luis and Duke crept forward until they were a stone's throw away. They each took the nearest man and fired simultaneously, killing them both instantly. Lucas moved forward and scouted the surroundings, and when he didn't see any other enemy gunmen, motioned for the troops to resume their approach to the stadium.

The men wended their way to the dark entrance. Lucas pointed to the right and motioned for Duke to take his contingent in that direction while he took half his group the other way. They'd agreed to leave a hundred men on the ground level to fight off any attack once the battle was joined, and those fighters deployed to seal off the primary access points.

Miguel had told them that the gas was going to be fired from the roof of the tall structure that housed the VIP suites and the administrative offices, as well as from the tallest section of the seating that rose over the northern side of the stadium. The cartel would be lobbing their payload over the camp at the army approaching from the north, so Lucas had a good idea of where the deadly mortars would be. He raised his two-way radio to his lips and murmured into it, and waited until he got two clicks in response before continuing toward the building with his contingent.

The rain had reduced visibility to the point he could barely make out the seating that Duke was to target, so he didn't concern himself with it and instead focused on the building. He saw several groups of guards sleeping in tents at the base, and motioned for his advance crew to take them out with their crossbows. Squads of six split off from the main force and crept toward them and, when they were within range, shot them point blank.

Almost all of them died within moments, but one managed to swing his AK-47 up and squeeze off two shots before succumbing to a second quarrel to the chest. The gunfire echoed off the stadium bleachers even with the rain, and Lucas sprang into action, running to the building entry and bounding up the stairs, followed by his men. He knew that his only edge now was speed of execution, because the majority of the enemy fighters who'd been chartered with the gas attack would probably be asleep. But the shots had started the clock on their rushing to their stations and mounting a defense, which would throw his entire plan into disarray.

He took the steps three at a time, the stomping of boots on concrete below him confirmation that his men were following, and when he reached the second level, he called out in a stage whisper, "Ten of you clear this level. The rest, follow me."

Lucas didn't wait for confirmation and continued higher. He issued the same order at each of the levels and, when he reached the top section, froze at the sound of shooting from below. A scrape from one of the doors sent him into a crouch, and he brought his M4 to bear, leveling it at the door and waiting, motionless.

The door cracked open and he held his fire. A rifle barrel poked through the gap, and he resisted the urge to squeeze the trigger. He could barely make out the sound of the men below him on the steps breathing as they waited, time seeming to stretch so seconds took forever. He knew that without night vision equipment, whoever was at the door couldn't see them, and he wanted to force the man to pull the door wide in order to enter before he fired.

More explosions rattled from the lower floors. The door opened farther, and a silhouette holding a rifle stepped onto the landing. Lucas fired a three-round burst into his torso, below the level a flak jacket would protect, and was in motion as the man dropped with a scream like a wounded animal. Another burst put him out of his misery, and then Lucas was firing at figures on the top floor who were running for cover in doorways. He tagged one, then another, and pulled back into the stairwell as a flurry of slugs pounded into the door and the concrete frame around it. He waited until there was a lull, and then pulled the pin on one of his grenades and tossed it through the doorway, grimacing at the sound of it skipping and rolling along the floor.

The explosion was deafening and sent a shower of glass out towards the playing field. Lucas and his men poured through the doorway, using the smoke and shock from the detonation for temporary cover. A few enemy gunmen did their best to fire into the darkness, but they were no match for Lucas's NV-equipped shooters, who made short work of them.

Lucas reached the far end of the space and waited as his men swept the chambers before giving the clear signal. When there were several dozen of them grouped behind him, he ascended the final stairs to the roof.

Only to find the door locked.

He thought for a moment and then retreated while freeing another grenade. "Everybody get out of the stairwell. I'm going to blow the door."

The troops reversed course, and when the steps were clear, Lucas wedged the grenade in between the lever handle and the door, freed the pin, and raced down the stairs, pulling the fire door closed behind him. It had just sealed when the grenade went off, buckling the fire door in the middle from the pressure and sending Lucas sprawling.

He shook off the stunned pressure in his head, struggled to his feet, and pried the door open. Lucas motioned to his men to accompany him and ascended the steps. The air was thick with smoke and dust. The upstairs door had been reduced to a couple of metal shards hanging from rusty hinges, and he peeked around the doorjamb only to pull back when bullets blew fragments of cement from the floor around him.

Lucas threw another grenade through the gap and, when it exploded, rolled out onto the roof and began picking off gunmen who were firing at him. Shots sounded from the stairwell, telling him that his men were now in the mix, and he crouched behind a housing and continued shooting at the enemy, trying to pin them down so his troops could make it onto the roof safely. His magazine ran dry and he ejected it and slapped another into place, and then cringed at the sound of one of the big machine guns coming into play.

He sneaked a glance around the housing, and saw that the big gun was at the other end of the long roof, surrounded by sandbags, which were protecting the shooter from his men's rounds. He did a quick calculation and then shrugged the rocket tube from his shoulder, clicked off the safety and cocked the firing mechanism, and leveled it at the nest and fired.

The projectile roared from the tube and flew straight at the nest, and when it exploded in an orange fireball, it blew two men and the big gun to pieces in a deafening blast. Lucas dropped the tube and continued the onslaught with his rifle, targeting gunmen who were shooting from behind housings as he was. He twisted and counted his men and saw that most of them were now on the roof, so he stopped firing and raised his radio to his lips.

"Elliot, you can hear we're taking care of this. Time to bring your men into play. Over."

"Roger that, Lucas. Consider it done."

"Good luck."

The gunfight on the roof lasted another few minutes, but the resistance was weak – they'd caught the cartel unawares and sleeping, so there was only a skeleton crew on the roof. Lucas could hear steady bursts of gunfire from where Duke and Luis were fighting it out with the enemy, but likewise few were in position at that early hour, so they made short work of them.

When there were no more cartel alive on the roof, Lucas barked at his men, "Swing those Brownings around and start hitting the camp with everything you have. But whatever you do, don't touch the mortars. They're filled with gas, and we don't want to contaminate the area for our men."

He was cut off by a series of explosions from the camp and smiled tightly to himself. True to his word, Elliot had brought the army's mortars to bear, and their first range-finding shells were landing at the perimeter of the camp. The Brownings on the roof began barking their staccato death song, cutting down shooters in the camp when they returned fire. Another barrage of mortar rounds boomed from the camp, these more on target, and then the Brownings from Duke's position joined the fray, pinning the camp under a deluge of bullets.

The cartel didn't stand a chance. All of their weaponry had been dug in assuming a frontal attack from the highway, and with the big machine guns hitting them from behind and the mortars raining destruction from above, there was no enemy for them to target that they could see. By the time Elliot's infantry began the final three-point assault, the camp was a killing field, with corpses strewn around the grounds, limbs twisted in agony, cut down as though by an invisible hand.

Twenty-five minutes after it started, the battle was over. Those who could flee from the camp had done so, and the remaining die-hard cartel fighters had been gunned to pieces from every angle. Lucas surveyed the carnage from his vantage point on the roof and shook his head. In spite of a lifetime of exposure to every possible sort of brutality, he never got over a sense of the tremendous waste of life that the war he was waging entailed nor the doubt he experienced after every battle that he was on the side of anything resembling right.

He watched the sun come up over the destroyed camp, and when his radio crackled, reminding him of his responsibilities, he sighed and returned to the stairwell, resigned to another endless day of picking up the pieces and doing damage control for an army he took no joy in leading.

Chapter 26

North of Dallas, Texas

Sierra watched Eve and Tim running along the paths between the tents, laughing in the sunlight, the little girl's hair streaming behind her like a flag, and smiled in spite of her annoyance at how distant Lucas had been lately. She hadn't seen him since yesterday, and their time together had been tense. The chasm between them seemed to grow daily, their long periods of silence as uncomfortable as they were frequent.

She knew he wasn't pleased that she was traveling with the army, and understood it was because of the danger to her and the kids that it posed, but she'd expected him to soften as he grew accustomed to it, and that had yet to happen. Now she was faced with a rift she wasn't sure how to mend, which left her feeling increasingly lost. And the situation with Eve wasn't helping. The uncertainty around her health, and whether or not she even had a future, worried Sierra daily.

Tim, on the other hand, was a rock, even though still a child. His horrific experiences had left him scarred yet as happy as a newly adopted puppy, content to have a day without pain and grateful for it. She could learn a lot from her child, she mused.

Sierra resolved to discuss her feelings with Lucas as soon as he was done with Dallas. He'd been preoccupied with the challenges of taking the city without losing too many men, and she understood. But there had to be time for him to pay attention to her needs and concerns, especially about Eve. She'd played the compliant partner, supporting her man while he slew dragons, but enough was enough. It was her life too, and she deserved and expected someone who would share it with her, not simply tolerate her to be in his. Their current arrangement, where she sneaked around to his tent whenever he had time, was a case in point that stuck in her craw. He felt it sent the wrong message to the men if their leader effectively lived with his family when they all had sacrificed being with theirs, so she'd been reduced to feeling like a by-the-hour hooker rather than his mate.

That state of affairs couldn't continue. She'd tried to raise the topic the night before, when he'd returned from the battle in Dallas after spending the day on what he termed "mop up," but he'd been in no mood to listen, which increasingly was the norm.

Not one she intended to allow to continue much longer.

"Eve! Tim! Come on. Time to eat," she called.

The children pretended not to hear her, and she had to walk over and block their way for them to acknowledge her.

"Aw, Mom…" Tim protested, but Sierra stared him down.

"Go wash your hands. I'll be waiting for you in the tent. And don't make me come back out to get you, either, or you'll wish you hadn't."

Eve smiled from behind Tim, who nodded glumly, and Sierra retraced her steps to the large tent she and the kids shared with Ruby. She pushed the flap aside and ducked inside, where there were four camping cots arranged along the sides and a folding picnic table in the center. She moved to one of the plastic storage containers in which she kept the dry goods she'd use as stock for a stew, and then stopped at the sight of an envelope on her bed.

Sierra frowned and stooped to pick it up, and looked it over before opening it with her thumb.

Inside was a note, which she read slowly and then reread before staring off into space for a long beat.

Her rumination was cut off by Eve entering the tent, the front of her summer dress wet from where she'd dried her hands.

"What's that?" Eve asked, her preternaturally blue eyes fixed on the envelope.

"This? Good news."

"News about what?"

"Never mind, sweetheart. I'll tell you later. Now, where's that boy?"

"He stopped to tell Ruby it was lunchtime."

"Oh. Okay." Sierra paused. "How are you feeling?"

Another beaming smile from Eve. "Fine. A little hungry."

"That's good. I'll see if I can't fix something especially tasty today." Sierra winked. "I talked one of the cooks out of a rabbit this morning."

Eve frowned. "Not a bunny!"

"It was going into the pot, sweetheart. Either we could eat it or the soldiers will. It was too late – there was nothing we could do to save it."

Eve's face relaxed. "Okay."

Ruby pushed into the tent with Tim, and Sierra hastily folded up the note and slipped it into her shirt. Ruby, her gray hair wild as ever, walked over to her cot and sat.

"Tim says you're making dinner. What can I do to help?" she asked.

Sierra looked around. "Can you maybe build a fire? Tim can help gather some wood."

"Of course. What's on the menu?" Ruby asked.

"Rabbit surprise!" Eve pealed.

Ruby made a delighted face and clapped her hands. "Oooh. That sounds amazing."

Sierra grinned at the older woman's antics. Ruby had been an invaluable help with the children, and both Tim and Eve seemed to love her like their own grandmother. She never tired of finding ways to amuse them, and was tireless and witty, which took a lot of pressure off Sierra when she wanted to be alone with Lucas – unfortunately, an all too rare event these days.

"Get it crackling while I prepare the stock," Sierra said. "I appreciate the help."

Ruby waved a hand. "Nonsense. It's the least I can do for another home-cooked gourmet meal!"

Sierra blushed at the compliment. Both women knew that given what she had to work with, it would be a miracle if the stew didn't turn out chewy and tasteless.

"Need anything else?" Ruby asked.

"No, I've got everything but the fire, thanks." Sierra looked to Eve. "Will you please go help your brother and Ruby scrounge for fuel and build a fire?"

"Okay," Eve said.

Ruby brushed off the front of her jeans and stood. "All righty, then. Let's go so Sierra can get to work!"

"Don't stray too far from camp," Sierra warned.

Ruby leaned down for her rifle. "Don't worry. I won't let an eagle swoop down and get them."

"That's a relief. I should be ready for the fire in about fifteen."

"It'll take at least that long to build it."

Sierra watched the kids leave with Ruby, and when they were gone, retrieved the note from the folds of her shirt and read it again, her mind working feverishly. She moved to the chest at the foot of her cot and opened it, and after moving the clothes inside to one side, slid the paper beneath them.

She straightened and looked around the tent, her expression thoughtful, and then walked back to the storage container containing the stew ingredients, humming softly to herself, a faint smile playing at the corners of her mouth.

Chapter 27

Dallas, Texas

The area around the command tent was bustling, with runners carrying orders to the field commanders in the wake of the cartel defeat in Dallas. Luis had taken several hundred of the best gunmen to clear any remaining cartel out of town, leaving Duke, Lucas, and Elliot to decide on the next steps. The army had lost only forty men in total, which was orders of magnitude less than they'd forecasted as a worst case, but that success had raised the next problem, which was the logistics of feeding the surviving troops.

"We spent half of yesterday talking to locals, and it's slim pickings," Duke said.

"Apparently our assumption that Dallas would have a lot of available food was overly optimistic," Elliot said.

"There has to be more than they're letting on. It was enough to support the cartel and, before them, the Crew, so we must be missing something," Lucas said.

"Maybe the reason they didn't want to put that much effort into defending it is that there isn't a lot of value here?" Duke asked.

"I don't buy it," Lucas said. "We're not getting the full story."

Duke shrugged. "Anything's possible, but I wouldn't hold my breath."

"We have enough to stay fed, but not to make it to Houston," Elliot said.

"I didn't ride all this way to get stuck in Dallas," Lucas said.

"Sounds like a bad country song. That makes two of us," Duke agreed.

Lucas ran a hand through his hair. "We need options."

A voice called out from outside the tent entrance. "Sir? Wink and a couple of prisoners are here to see you."

"Not now. We're busy," Duke snapped.

"They said it was important."

Duke frowned. "Did you not hear me?"

Silence from outside the tent, and then Wink threw the flap aside and entered with Conejo and Miguel.

Lucas scowled at the former Crew boss. "Maybe we weren't clear. We're in a meeting. Whatever you want needs to wait."

Wink shook his head. "Maybe not. The boys here heard about your predicament, and they have a proposal."

Lucas eyed Conejo. "Seems like you've got a 'proposal' for everything."

Conejo allowed a small smile. "I'm a deal maker. What can I say?"

"We don't have time for this," Duke snapped.

"That's right," Lucas said. "You did your part, so you're free to go. We'll honor our arrangement."

"You need food," Miguel blurted.

Conejo grinned. "We think we know where you can find some."

Elliot and Lucas exchanged a glance. Lucas considered the young Mexican and then shifted his attention back to Conejo.

"Okay," Lucas said. "You've interrupted us. State your piece."

Miguel cleared his throat and shifted from foot to foot. "I heard about a few ranches outside town that the cartel destroyed."

Duke glared at him. "So?"

Conejo cleared his throat. "So they had crops and hundreds of head of cattle. The cartel moved in and killed everyone, but the cows should still be there. And the crops might still be viable."

"That's right," Miguel said. "It's rained enough so they could be."

"Where are these ranches?" Lucas asked.

Conejo shrugged. "That's where the new deal comes in."

Lucas's eyebrows rose. "The new deal," he echoed.

"Right. We'll take you to the ranches, but we want something in return."

Duke snorted. "I'll just bet you do."

Conejo stayed calm. "I delivered like I said I would, right? So you'd do worse than to listen to me this time. Or your men can slowly starve. Your choice."

"What do you want?" Elliot asked.

Conejo held Lucas's stare. "Gold."

Lucas looked at him without reacting. "Excuse me?"

Wink stepped forward. "I heard about what you did with the Indians. So we know you got gold."

"What's your interest in this?" Lucas demanded.

Wink's smile was tight. "Just trying to help both parties get their needs met."

"In exchange for…?" Duke asked.

Wink held out his hands. "A cut. I figure I'll need some resources to encourage loyalty after we take Houston. Everyone understands gold."

"We? I must have missed you in the Dallas fight," Duke said.

Wink shrugged. "Nobody invited us."

"Maybe because nobody trusts you," Duke volleyed.

Lucas cut in. "So you want gold. How much?"

Conejo shook his head. "That's not all." He looked to Miguel. "We want to stay with the army. Sort of as consultants."

"Consultants," Elliot repeated.

"That's right. We can negotiate with the locals – here and in Houston. Miguel speaks fluent Spanish. Mine's good enough to get what I need. But we're not one of the troops. I'm Texas born and bred, so I can make arrangements you guys might not be able to."

Lucas pursed his lips. "I'm from Texas, too."

"Ditto," Duke said.

"But you're the top command. You can't spend time rooting out the best deals. We can."

Lucas sat back. "I asked you a question. How much gold do you want?"

Wink's brow creased. "A percentage of whatever they lead you to. We can negotiate the value of a head of cattle or whatever. But a cut, paid in gold."

The men went back and forth for several minutes, and Lucas finally agreed a ten percent "finder's fee" was reasonable, with their demand to stay with the army and act as its provisioning team taken under advisement based on how they did in finding the cattle. When they left, Duke was visibly annoyed.

"Not sure why you're letting that Wink character call the shots," he said.

"Because he thinks he's going to run Houston again, and I want him on our side. So I'll entertain a little insubordination," Lucas said. "As to the cost, they have to deliver to get anything. And if they can, it's worth it." He paused. "It isn't like we don't have enough gold. And you can't eat it."

Elliot spread his hands. "It's not an unfair proposal, in truth."

"Hey, it's your money," Duke said. "I just think that if we'd continued to nose around, we'd have run into someone else who knows about the ranches eventually."

"Probably," Lucas conceded. "But time isn't on our side. We all know the chances of Houston not getting word about Dallas are nil. So every day we stay parked here is another day they have to prepare."

"Judging by our reception here, they're already ahead of us," Duke observed.

"That may be. But we have to feed the men, so I have no problem with the deal. I'm actually surprised you do, being a trader and all."

Duke exhaled. "It's not that. I just don't like negotiating from a position of weakness."

Elliot sighed as well. "I think you mean you dislike Wink."

"That too."

Lucas held up a hand. "I'm not asking you to marry him. Look, Duke, round up some men who can handle themselves on a horse and have experience with cattle, and see where this takes us. If we don't find anything, we're out nothing. But if we do, we just solved one of our biggest problems, okay?"

Duke stood. "I'm game. When do you want me to go?"

"No time like the present," Lucas said. "I'll stay here with Elliot and try to figure out how to nail down Dallas so it's under some sort of democratic control."

"Ever the optimist," Duke quipped.

Lucas gave him a pained expression before turning back to Elliot. "What's the alternative?"

Chapter 28

Sierra approached Ruby at the fire, after the kids were sleeping, with a cup of herbal tea she'd blended. She offered the older woman the cup and smiled.

"Can you watch the kids for a while?"

Ruby took an appreciative sip and nodded. "Of course. How long will you be?"

"A few hours. I'm going to see if I can find Lucas."

Ruby gave her a knowing look. "It hasn't been easy with him so occupied, has it?"

Sierra looked away. "I know he's got to do what he has to."

"I remember those feelings from when Terry and I…well, that's not really why it didn't work out with us, in the end." She was silent for a moment and gazed off to the left, lost in thought. "But I know what it's like, is what I'm trying to say. You knew what you were getting into with Lucas. But still, even though you understand it, it leaves you on your own most of the time. And that's hard. It's okay to admit that. But you'll also remember it's part of the reason he didn't want you to come. To spare you all this."

Sierra looked at the floor. "It's still better than sitting in Provo wondering if he'll ever come back."

Ruby smiled sympathetically. "The devil you know."

"What about you?" Sierra asked. "Holding up?"

"Oh, sure. I'm living on borrowed time, and I know it. That's one of the benefits of being old. You don't kid yourself. That I made it this far is a shock." She paused. "I still feel twenty inside, although I have to admit most days my body doesn't agree with my mind. Enjoy yourself while you can."

"I'll try. It's hard when you're doing forced marches and living with thousands of unwashed killers."

"Don't I know."

Sierra ambled off in the direction of Lucas's tent and, when she was out of sight of the fire, made a left and continued to the perimeter. A patrol spotted her and approached, and the officer in charge looked her up and down.

"Where do you think you're going?"

"I was…just wanted to go for a walk."

"Nobody leaves the camp. Commander's orders while we're in enemy territory."

"I'm sure that's true, but I'm not in the army, so that doesn't apply to me."

"I've seen you. You're traveling with us, which means you're subject to the rules. Sorry."

Sierra's expression hardened. "I don't think you understand…"

"Take it up with the commander. That call's above my pay grade. Sorry, but nobody leaves the camp until I hear otherwise."

Sierra turned away, fuming, but bit her tongue. Fighting with the obstinate jerk wasn't going to get her anywhere, she could tell, and she didn't need to make any enemies out of Lucas's men. She retreated and wandered along the edges of the camp, staying far enough from where the tents ended to avoid drawing another confrontation. When she was sure that nobody was nearby, she made another try and was fifty yards outside the camp when a voice called out from her right.

"Halt. Stay where you are."

She froze, not wanting to be shot by a trigger-happy guard, and waited while another patrol, this one a two-man, approached with their weapons at present arms.

Sierra plastered a wide smile on her face and held her hands to her sides. "I'm unarmed, so you boys can relax."

When the men drew near, she saw they were young, maybe early twenties, and looked as nervous as she felt.

"What are you doing out here?" one of them asked.

Sierra decided to try a different approach, given how green they were. "Running an errand for my husband. You know him. Lucas – your commander?"

The men looked at each other. "It really isn't safe to be out after dark. Our orders are that nobody leaves or enters the camp."

"I'm sure he knew what his orders were when he sent me. He told me to just tell anyone I came across who I am, and suggest to them that they check with him if there's a problem." Her smile widened. "I'm sure I'm safe out here with all you soldiers prowling around. Otherwise what's the point?"

The first guard looked unsure, so she pressed her advantage.

"Look, if you want to follow me around, I don't mind. But I'm sure Lucas knew what he was doing when he told me it wouldn't be an issue. So do you want to come with me and hear it from his lips, or will my word do?"

"It's just that our orders…"

"Apply to the soldiers. But I'm not a soldier. I'm your commander's wife. You really want to bug him? He was sure nobody would doubt my word, but…I don't mind, but we need to be quick about it. He's super busy and won't be happy I was stopped."

"Where are you going, exactly?"

"He sent me to pick up some things from the trader who's camped on the perimeter. What's his name? Petey?"

The young man's expression relaxed. "Oh, yeah. Sure. Well, you're a ways from him. He's over on the other side, about two hundred yards from the camp. Over near the highway."

"No problem. It feels good to stretch my legs after being cooped up. Thanks for the directions. Carry on keeping the world safe!"

They all laughed, and Sierra strode off into the darkness, not wanting to linger and see whether the guards had second thoughts. She picked up her pace and beelined towards the ruins of a ranch house and, once the camp and its patrols were well behind her, turned and made for the highway.

She reached the trader's wagon five minutes later and called out softly, "Petey?"

Nothing. She tried again. "Petey? You here?"

A figure emerged from the dark. "Sierra, right? That you?"

"It is. I got your note."

Petey drew nearer. "I'm glad. I was afraid you wouldn't show."

"You said you know people who–"

Petey's right hand lashed out, and the homemade blackjack in his hand swatted Sierra in the head with a dull thwack.

She dropped like a sack of potatoes. He knelt by her, took her pulse to assure himself she was still alive, and then bound her ankles and wrists and gagged her with a dirty rag and some cord. When he was done, he stood back with his hands on his hips and inspected her inert form and, after glancing around, walked back to the wagon, leaving her lying battered and unconscious in the dirt.

Chapter 29

A thin beam of sunshine sliced through a crack in the tent flap, and Ruby's eyes batted open. She groaned slightly and stopped herself – she couldn't allow herself to feel the aches and pains of more than six decades on the planet or she'd never get out of bed. She allowed herself one yawn and then stretched before rolling to the side and glancing at the kids, who were still asleep.

Ruby looked over to Sierra's cot, which was empty and obviously hadn't been slept in. She chewed her lip while she mulled over what to make of that. Sierra had never stayed out all night before. When she went to see Lucas, she was always back before dawn. Perhaps she had succeeded in mending some fences?

Ruby yawned again and considered sleeping for another few minutes, but gave up on the idea as noise from the other tents signaled the start of a new day. Tim stirred and sat up and prodded Eve with his toe. She frowned and tried to swat it away, and then was awake as well, her little face wrinkled on one side from the folded towel she used as a pillow.

"Where's my mom?" Tim asked.

"She must have gone out early," Ruby said. "Don't worry. I'll get you fed."

"Did she come home last night?" Eve asked.

"I just woke up. I assume so," Ruby hedged.

Eve gave her a skeptical look, but Ruby ignored it and pushed herself to her feet. "Alrighty then! Let's get our clothes on and find some water to brush our teeth."

She jotted out a quick note for Sierra, telling her where they went, and led the kids to the water source and, after they finished their morning ablutions, took them to the mess tent for breakfast. Ruby didn't want to break into Sierra's food stores if she could help it, and she was on good terms with one of the cooks, so a little of the army's rations falling onto the kids' trays wouldn't be a problem.

While the children were eating, she approached a guard she knew.

"Hey, could you do me a favor and watch the kids for a few minutes? I have to run an errand."

"Sure."

Ruby left the mess area and stopped by the tent again, but her note was still on Sierra's bed. She next went in search of Lucas, but the guards at the command center indicated he'd taken off with Elliot earlier and wouldn't be back for several hours.

"Was Sierra with him?" Ruby asked.

The guards shook their heads. "No, ma'am. Just Lucas and Elliot."

Ruby's frown deepened as she returned to the tent. What was Sierra up to? It didn't sound like she'd been with Lucas all night. She could be a loose cannon, but she'd never done this before…

Ruby decided to make a lap around the area in case Sierra had gone in search of something outside the camp. Ruby made it as far as the perimeter when she was stopped by a patrol, who told her she couldn't leave.

"Authorized personnel only. Sorry. Until further notice."

Ruby eyed the young men. "I'm looking for someone who might have tried to leave yesterday evening or during the night."

"That shouldn't have been possible. We've been patrolling heavily."

"Just you?"

"No. We're on eight-hour shifts."

"How would I find whoever was working last night?"

"You'd have to wait till they report back for duty this evening. They're all sleeping now."

"Can you wake them up?"

"Sorry. They aren't in a centralized location. And we're talking nearly a hundred men."

Ruby thanked them and walked away, muttering an oath under her breath. Her stomach was tightening along with her throat – a reliable sign that something was badly wrong. She circled back to the command tent and left word with the guards to have Lucas find her whenever he returned, and then retraced her steps to the mess tent and collected the children.

"Where's Mom?" Eve asked.

"I don't know, sweetheart. But I plan to find out."

"Why would she leave us?" Tim demanded.

"We don't know that she did," Ruby said. "Don't worry. I'm checking with everyone. We'll find her."

Eve shook her head. "I don't believe you."

"Oh, darling, of course we will. She's around here somewhere."

"Maybe she's hiding," Eve countered. "Because she doesn't want to be found."

Ruby appeared to consider the idea. "Well, why would that be?"

"Maybe she's angry," Eve continued. "Sometimes she gets that way. Real angry."

"Hush, sweetie. I don't think that's the case. Really." She paused. "Now who wants to help me gather some wood so that when she comes back, we can build a fire?"

Tim threw her a sour look. "There isn't much left. We've used it all."

"Don't be so defeatist. Where there's a will, there's a way."

Ruby held out her hand and Eve took it, but Tim turned away, his eyes moist. Ruby swallowed hard at the sight, understanding his unease, and wished she could think of something to say to reassure them without uttering an outright lie. When she couldn't, she just swung Eve's arm and pasted what smile she could on her face, vowing to do her best not to show how upset she was getting, and cursing Sierra silently for putting her in this impossible situation in the first place.

That evening, with Sierra still missing and Lucas still somewhere in Dallas with Elliot, Ruby enlisted Sam's help, and they gathered the guards who had been on patrol the prior night. An older sergeant stepped forward when Sam was finished asking whether anyone had seen her.

"We did. She was trying to leave the camp. We told her no way. Turned her back."

A younger man sighed and spoke up. "She got by us. But she told us Lucas had approved her leaving."

Ruby glared at the man. "Did she say where she was going?"

"Yes. To get some things from the trader who's been following the camp. Petey."

"And you let her go?"

The man flushed. "She said we could ask Lucas. Have you talked to him? Maybe he knows what's going on."

Sam thanked the men for their cooperation and walked with Ruby back to the tent. "What do you think happened?" he asked, his expression dour.

Ruby took a long time to answer. When she did, her tone was defeated. "I don't know, but whatever it is, it isn't good. Would you please get me whenever Lucas returns? I don't care what time it is. Please."

"Of course." He hesitated. "Hope it all turns out fine."

Ruby stared off into the distance, and when she answered, her voice was almost inaudible. "Me too."

Chapter 30

North of Dallas, Texas

Petey led the nag carrying Sierra beneath a grove of trees and stopped in the late afternoon shade. His horse had started limping after misstepping that morning, and he knew he would need to allow the animal to rest if he was going to make it back to Oklahoma City without having to walk. Sierra had regained consciousness shortly after they'd gotten underway the prior night on the two horses that had drawn Petey's wagon, and she'd struggled for hours until she'd worn herself out.

Now she was sullen and quiet. The dried blood that had traced lines from her hairline had turned a deep brown, and the area beneath her eyes was discolored from lack of sleep and a slight concussion.

Petey had unbound her feet so she could sit in the saddle once the sun had come up, and warned her that if she tried anything, he would put a bullet in her, no warnings or second chances. To underscore the threat, he'd tied a rope from her horse's bridle to his saddle and kept her within five yards of him, his rifle in hand at all times. She'd apparently gotten the message and had been silent the entire trip, even after he'd removed the gag so she could drink some water whenever they stopped to rest.

He dropped from the saddle and pointed his rifle at her. "Get down."

She looked around. "You're going to have to help like you did earlier. I can't with my hands tied like this."

"Remember what I said. Any smart moves and I'll plug you." He laughed harshly and considered her. "Still might, if you know what I mean. But we can talk about that later."

"Lucas will cut you to pieces and feed you to the ants."

"Yeah. I'm shakin' in my boots." He helped her down and walked to the trees. "We'll stop here for a few hours. Get some sleep. We'll be riding through the night."

"Where are you taking me?"

"Got a friend who's dyin' to meet you. Told him all about you on the radio. He can't wait."

"Wait. Who?"

"You'll find out soon enough. Now git over by that tree and shut your face hole, or I'll gag you again."

Petey had a solar-powered shortwave set in the wagon. He'd told Snake about the battle in Dallas and that there was no easy way for him to get to Lucas, and Snake had suggested going after Sierra instead, leaving plenty of evidence as to where he was headed, which would force Lucas to come for her. It was a sound plan, he supposed, and way less risky than trying for Lucas when he was surrounded by an army. What Snake did with Lucas once he'd lured him into a trap was his business. Maybe he'd thank Lucas for ridding Dallas of the cartel before he killed him? He didn't understand why Snake didn't just wait until Lucas and the cartel had exhausted their armies in Houston and then deal with him, but in the end it wasn't Petey's concern. Snake was the boss, and he had a plan that he hadn't shared with Petey beyond retaking Houston and establishing the Crew there again.

Petey was beat, having been up for thirty-six hours straight, so the idea of catching some shut-eye was not only appealing but necessary if he was going to avoid making any stupid mistakes. Fatigue could be as big a killer as a water moccasin, and it was cool and quiet in the grove, the wind gentle and soothing.

He watered the horses and then tied them on long tethers so they could feed themselves on the plentiful grass, and then moved to Sierra and cinched her to the tree with some rope. After checking to make sure she was secure, he walked over and lowered himself against a tree trunk, his AK resting in his lap. He looked over at Sierra and gave her his best glare.

"Get some sleep. Or don't. It don't matter to me either way, but you'll feel better for it if you do."

"My head's throbbing and I'm seeing double sometimes. I think something's wrong."

"That's a shame. Now shut up or I'll clobber you again. Got no interest in your personal problems."

"Where are you taking me?"

"You'll find out in due time. Now shut your face and let me rest."

Petey was snoring within five minutes, and Sierra looked around her area for anything that could help her escape. There was nothing but a softball-sized stone and a few small rocks by her booted feet. She slid down as far as she could manage and dragged one of the loose rocks towards her with her heel and, when it was by her hip, contorted until she had it in her hands.

She ran her thumb along the edge, her eyes never leaving Petey. It wasn't razor sharp, but the jagged edge along one side where it had broken off from the larger stone was rough. Maybe rough enough to abrade the rope with enough time.

Sierra twisted her arms until the rock was against the rope securing her to the tree, and began scraping it against it. The rope was tough and her fingers were sore before it started to fray just a little, but the sensation of the rope beginning to give filled her with renewed energy, and she continued to rub, watching Petey for any signs of him awakening, sweat dripping off the tip of her nose onto the hard red dirt beneath her.

After an hour of exertion, she felt the rope give, and she flexed her arms. It was loose but still secured. She tried again, and it was sufficiently slack that she was able to slide down the trunk and out from under the binding, winding up flat on her back on the ground.

Sierra took several deep calming breaths and rolled over onto her stomach. Petey was still dozing, his snores loud enough to be heard from the highway. She forced herself to her feet and debated what to do. Petey stirred when a fly landed on his cheek. He swatted it away, and Sierra held her breath, frozen in place. When he resumed snoring, she choked back the bile that had risen in her throat and considered her next move.

Her eyes fell on the big stone, and she knelt and picked it up. It was heavy, but she hardly noticed as she crept towards her captor. She was a yard away when the fly returned, and she closed the distance in a blink and brought the rock down on his skull – which would have been a mortal blow had he not moved just before impact in response to the fly alighting on his nose.

Petey let out a bellow as blood streamed into his eyes, and Sierra hit him with the rock again, this time on the side of the head as he twisted away. The stone slipped from her grasp, and she grabbed his AK as his hands flew to his head in an attempt to wipe away the blood, and took off at a run towards the horses.

Petey sputtered with rage and struggled to his feet, using the tree for support. Sierra was at the horses and fumbling with the firing selector on the AK with her bound hands. It clicked into single fire, and she squeezed off three shots, none of which hit him. She ducked behind her horse as Petey swung his pistol up and fired seven shots at her, squinting to focus through the haze of dizziness and blood.

Three of the rounds hit the horse, and the animal collapsed. She lifted the rifle and began shooting again, and then cried out when one of Petey's rounds knocked her backward. The AK fell from her grasp when she thudded against the ground, and she reached for it as she fought to stay conscious, only to succumb to a numbing darkness that quickly descended upon her.

Petey staggered toward her with his pistol, his face contorted with rage, and wiped the blood from his forehead with the back of his sleeve. He stepped past the horse and stood over her, shaking with fury, and kicked her in the side.

She didn't move. He kicked her again and then dropped to feel her pulse at her throat.

There was none.

He stood slowly, the ground beneath him swaying like the deck of a fishing boat hit by a wave, and blinked away crimson.

"Shit. Shit, shit, shit."

He looked around, his expression wild, and moaned when he probed his skull wound.

"Shit," he repeated, this time less angry, and then stumbled away, his head spinning as he tried to figure out how badly hurt he was…and what the hell he was going to do now.

Chapter 31

Lucas called out to Ruby from outside her tent, a lantern in hand. She emerged and he faced her with a concerned expression.

"Sam told me what happened," he said.

Ruby placed an arm on his shoulder. "Let's go for a walk. I don't want to wake the kids."

They moved away from the tent, and Ruby gave him a sympathetic glance. "I'm so sorry, Lucas."

"Me too. Sam said she disappeared after going to look for the trader's wagon. We rode over there just now, and everything's still there…except his horses and him."

"I don't know what to think."

"Neither do I, but anything that comes to mind isn't good." Lucas paused. "Did she say anything to you before she took off? Anything that would explain this?"

Ruby shook her head. "No. Although…Tim said she was reading a letter or a note yesterday. Not sure if that helps any."

"Did she say what was in it?"

"No, Lucas. She was as tight-lipped as ever."

He made an exasperated sound. "That sounds like Sierra." He looked away. "Ruby, I want to ask you to do a huge favor for me."

"Anything, Lucas. You should know that by now."

"Stay with the kids and watch them. Don't let anything happen to them."

"Do I need to ask where you're going?"

"I have to find her. The longer I wait, the colder the trail will get."

"I kind of figured. No way you'll send someone else to track them?"

"Not a chance."

"Didn't think so. And yes, of course I'll watch the kids. Don't worry about them. Just do what you have to do and find Sierra."

"Thanks, Ruby. I won't forget it."

"You leaving tonight?"

"No reason to give them any more of a lead than they already have."

Lucas walked Ruby back to her tent and then stalked to the command tent, where Elliot and Sam were waiting for him. They both looked up expectantly, and he met their gazes.

"I'm headed out. Elliot, you run the show while I'm gone. Once Dallas is secure and we have provisions, make for Houston. I don't want to delay moving on the cartel."

Elliot nodded. "Will do. Did Ruby have anything helpful for you?"

"No." Lucas collected his weapons. "I need to get going."

Sam's eyebrows rose. "Just you? What about backup?"

Lucas shook his head. "They'd just slow me down."

Elliot understood that Lucas meant to ride all night without sleep – as long as it took to find Sierra – and didn't need company, or anyone who might make a mistake that could give him away. He stood and offered his hand.

"Good luck, my friend."

Lucas took it and shook. "Appreciate it." He looked to Sam. "I'll take a two-way. Have someone monitor the emergency band."

"Will do, Lucas."

Lucas left them and carried his weapons to where Tango was waiting nearby, saddled and ready. He slid his M4 into the scabbard and checked the saddlebags for the night vision goggles he'd requisitioned, and confirmed he had sufficient food and water to last several days. He had no idea why Sierra had run off with the trader or where they were headed, but he'd find them if it was the last thing he did.

He rode to the perimeter, where a waiting patrol pointed him to the trader's wagon. He removed his hat and slid the NV goggles into place and, after switching them on, fit the hat back on his head and directed Tango to the wagon. When he arrived, he dismounted and slowly circled it until he spotted two sets of hoofprints leading away, toward the highway. Lucas saddled up and followed them until they turned onto the well-worn trail that paralleled the road north, and spurred the stallion forward, his lips a thin line.

He dismounted periodically to verify the prints didn't veer off the trail, which was easy because the rain had washed away the army's tracks and nobody had passed since the downpour. Lucas allowed Tango to rest the minimum amount of time he could, and kept him at a trot in order to narrow the distance between him and his quarry.

The following morning he spied dozens of buzzards circling over a grove of trees in the near distance, and slipped his M4 from the scabbard and switched the firing selector to three-round burst. His mouth was suddenly dry and his tongue felt like sandpaper while he approached, and his gut twisted in a knot as he followed the tracks from the trail to the trees.

Tango whinnied as he drew near, and Lucas reined him slower until he spotted the horse carcass the carrion birds were feasting on. When he dropped from the saddle, they took flight with a noisy flapping of wings, and one screeched at him in protest as it soared with its fellows into the sky. Lucas's nose twitched as he drew near the horse, and he frowned when he saw the bullet holes in the bloated dead animal's hide.

His gaze turned back to the trees, and he studied the grass and dirt beneath them, stopping when he saw drops of dried blood. He knelt and eyed a rock, and then picked it up and studied it. There was a trace of rust color and a few hairs stuck to one side.

He stood and looked around the grove, and his breath caught in his throat when he spotted a skid mark in the dirt near the horse's corpse – much like a body being dragged by the feet might make.

Lucas followed the track behind the trees. A strangled cry burst from him and he dropped to his knees at the sight of Sierra, partially covered with rocks, in a shallow depression caused by runoff.

Lucas scraped some of the rocks away, but stopped when he saw the bullet wound in her chest. He touched her cold alabaster skin and shuddered, and a streak of tears tumbled down his face. He sobbed quietly for a time and then forced himself to his feet, his expression dark.

He gathered more rocks and covered her body so the buzzards couldn't get to her, and stood with his hat in hand and offered a soft prayer before finishing with a hoarse whisper.

"I'll get the bastard if it's the last thing I ever do," he said, his eyes ablaze. "And then I'll be back for you, Sierra."

He wedged his hat back on his head and retrieved his M4 and then jogged to where Tango was munching grass at the far side of the grove. The vultures had returned to pick at the horse, but he ignored them — everyone was entitled to a meal, no matter how grisly, the wheel of life completing another pointless turn.

Lucas climbed back onto Tango and patted his neck. "I know you're tired, big guy, but I need you to keep going."

Tango snorted as though he understood and made his way back to the trail, where only one set of prints continued north. Lucas spit to the side and snapped the reins, and the stallion surged forward while Lucas scanned the distant horizon with murderous intent.

Chapter 32

Nightfall had come several hours before the orange glow of flames drew Lucas's attention to the ruins of a truck stop several hundred yards up the highway. He slowed Tango from the trot the horse had maintained for hours, flipped the night vision goggles out of the way, powered on his NV rifle scope, and raised the M4. He scanned the wreckage that clogged the pit stop and settled the crosshairs on a figure seated near the fire, back against a stripped truck, rifle beside him.

Lucas left Tango free to graze and moved cautiously towards the buildings, sweeping the structures with the rifle scope in case there were more men. When he was within fifty yards, he settled the scope on the seated figure again and compared his face to the description he'd gotten from the troops who'd frequented Petey's rolling trading post.

A blood-soaked bandanna encircled the man's head, and he had his eyes closed. Other than that and the four days' growth, he could have been anyone, although he more or less matched the descriptions – of course, seventy percent of the Caucasian men who'd survived the virus did as well, so it wasn't a lock.

Lucas crept closer, and when he was within rock-throwing distance, he noted a horse tied to a pole near what had been the truck stop convenience store, one of its front legs wrapped with cloth. Lucas slowed his breathing and closed the distance to the seated man and, when he was close enough to spit on him, called out, his M4 steady on the man's head.

"Petey, end of the line."

The man stirred and one eye snapped open. He reached for his rifle, but Lucas shook his head.

"Give me a reason to shoot you. Please."

Petey's hand dropped back in his lap, and his bloodshot eye glared at Lucas, but he didn't speak.

Lucas stood immobile. "Toss your pistol over here. Draw it with your thumb and index finger only."

Petey fumbled with his holster for a few moments and then exhaled.

"Sorry, boss. Seems like my hand ain't workin' right."

"Use your other. Nice and slow, or I'll take a kneecap off for target practice."

"You're gonna kill me anyway. What's the difference?"

Petey's speech was slurred, and Lucas could see that half his face was sagging and his right eye wouldn't open. Drool ran from the corner of his mouth, lending him the appearance of a demented demon.

"Difference is whether I make the next hour the worst in your miserable life, or you go quick. Now toss the pistol here."

Petey reached across with his other hand and did as instructed. When the pistol was on the ground in front of him, Lucas stooped cautiously, scooped it up, and stuffed it in his flak jacket.

"Now the AK," Lucas said.

"Afraid you gotta get that. Like I said, having a hard time moving."

Lucas approached Petey and kicked the AK to the side. It bounced on the pavement and lay well out of his reach. Lucas stood over him and regarded Petey.

"Why did you kill my woman?" he asked, his voice so quietly menacing it radiated danger.

"Didn't mean to. She brained me with a rock and started shooting. I had no choice."

Lucas considered Petey's story and contrasted it against the scene at the grove. It made a kind of sense, he supposed, but he barely was able to control a blind rage that descended over him as he imagined the drama playing out. Lucas drew a shaky breath, blinked away the anger, and forced himself to remain calm.

"Why'd you take her?"

"Now there's a story. Just business."

"Business? What – to sell her?"

"She was a looker, but nah. I was told to bring her to my boss." He coughed and spat a pink chunk of tissue on the pavement. "I was just following orders."

"Who's your boss, and why did he want her?"

"Pretty sure he didn't give two shits about her. It was you he's after. She was to get you to come to him. Leverage. Decoy. Bait in the trap."

"Who's your boss? I'm not going to ask again."

"Snake. Used to head up the Crew."

"Snake," Lucas repeated.

"I see you've heard of him."

"Where is he?"

"Oklahoma City. Waiting on me."

"Why?"

"Like I said, he wants your ass something fierce."

Lucas digested the information. "You look pretty bad."

"I told you everything I know. You gonna end it, do it quick, like you promised."

"I should leave you to drown in your own blood."

"I suppose you could. But it won't bring her back. And I told you, I didn't mean to kill her."

"Two little kids depend on her for everything. Now they've got no mother."

"I'm sorry, boss. Really am. We all gotta pick our sides, though, and I was on the opposite one. That's all. It happens."

Lucas took in Petey's sagging face and noted the spreading stain in his crotch. Sierra had done serious damage to him with the stone. He considered killing him right there, but that was his fury talking.

Logically, he'd be better served keeping him alive and pumping him for as much information as he could about Snake's whereabouts, his allies, anything that could help Lucas bring him down for good.

Lucas whistled and Tango galloped over. He removed a length of rope from his saddlebag and approached Petey, who was obviously struggling to remain conscious. Petey looked at the rope and barked a harsh laugh.

"You gonna hang me?"

"Nothing would make me happier. But no. I'm going to tie you up so you can't run off. We'll ride in the morning."

"Where?"

"Oklahoma City, you said. This Snake's got such a hard-on for me, seems a shame to disappoint him."

"You lost your mind?"

"Could be.

Lucas bound him to the wreckage, removed his gear from Tango, and found a spot where he could doze with a view of the highway as well as Petey. When he finally drifted off, his dreams were ugly, Sierra's last stand against Petey playing in an endless loop in his head, her death scream the closing moment before it started all over again. Each time Lucas tried to intercede and save her, he was unable to move, as though encased in lead, forced to watch her die over and over in graphic detail.

When the sun finally rose over the distant flatlands, Lucas was soaked through with sweat in spite of the early morning chill. He felt like he'd barely slept minutes, even though his mechanical watch insisted it had been five and a half hours. He yawned and pushed himself to his feet and went to relieve himself before returning to where Petey sat silently.

One look at the miscreant told Lucas he'd died during the night; his complexion was ashen, his wide eye completely bloodshot from the fatal bashing Sierra had inflicted. Lucas searched him, confiscated everything of value, and then retrieved his rope. He considered burying the man, but decided to leave him to the scavengers.

"At least something will get some use out of you," he snarled by way of eulogy, and went to inspect Petey's remaining horse.

The sun was high overhead when he reached the grove of trees again, and he gagged as he uncovered Sierra and slung her over Petey's horse. He didn't want to think of her as a decomposing collection of carbon and water. He would have buried her properly where she lay, but he wanted closure for the kids and for Ruby, and he knew that a story about burying her wouldn't be a substitute for making peace with her passing at a service where she was put to rest. He knew from experience he only had hours before she started coming apart, but he resolved himself to try, and set off south again, intent on reaching the army before he rested, and damn the consequences.

Chapter 33

Lucas stood, hat in hand, at the head of a grave he'd insisted upon digging himself. Eve and Tim wept beside Ruby, whose eyes were welling with moisture as Lucas delivered his parting words to Sierra, who rested in the grave, ensconced in a body bag so the children wouldn't be subjected to the sight of her remains.

"Sierra, you were a loving partner and an honorable woman. You deserved better than me. I always knew that and counted myself lucky at the blindness you showed in putting up with me." Lucas swallowed tightly and cleared his throat. "You were a loving mother who will be sorely missed and forever remembered."

Elliot and Lucas exchanged a glance, and the older man stepped forward. "The road to Eden is twisted and bumpy, especially in troubled times like these. Sierra, you were an inspiration and a guiding light to all who crossed your path. An extraordinary spirit who met every challenge headlong and didn't flinch. Rest in peace."

Lucas looked next to Ruby, who wiped away tears and struggled to speak. "You did everything to find your son and bring him to safety, and to keep Eve safe. I can think of no better proof that you were an amazing, strong woman who battled adversity and came out ahead. I'm sure you're in a better place now. Rest in peace forever."

She knelt and grabbed a handful of dirt to toss into the grave. Eve and Tim did the same, their plaintive sobbing like the cries of a trapped animal, and Elliot joined them. When they'd dropped the dirt into the grave, Ruby and Elliot led them away, and Lucas tossed in his own handful, retrieved his shovel, and began scooping in mounds of it, his expression stony. Sam and Luis stood back and watched – they'd offered to help with the grave, but Lucas had refused, and they knew better than to interrupt his self-inflicted ordeal now.

When he was finished, he inhaled deeply and straightened. "Meet me at the command tent in an hour," he said to his men. "I have to take care of some things."

They didn't ask what, and he didn't offer. Instead he walked off, shovel on his shoulder. He trailed Ruby to the family's tent, and when he arrived, he took her aside after hugging the children.

"Ruby, you've already done so much, I hate to ask."

"You're going to find Snake and finish him, aren't you?"

Lucas had filled her in on the broad strokes of Petey's confession earlier.

"I need you to watch the kids while I'm gone."

She nodded. "I know you well enough. Of course I will. But…what if something goes wrong and you don't come back?"

Lucas frowned. "Hell, Ruby, that could happen any day of the week."

"Still. We both know you're not bulletproof."

"I expect you'll figure things out. Between you and Elliot, I have faith."

"When are you leaving?"

"Soon as I put my house in order. Later today."

Ruby sighed and put a hand on his forearm. "I'll be sorry to see you go."

"I have to do this, Ruby."

"I know."

Lucas entered the tent, where Eve and Timmy were huddled, and sat on one of the cots. "I'm going to leave for a while. But I'll be back. I want you to mind Ruby and behave, do you understand?"

Tim bobbed his head mutely. Eve fixed him with her piercing blue eyes. "You promise you'll come back?"

"Absolutely, sweetheart."

"How long will you be gone?"

"I don't know. A couple of weeks. Maybe three."

"And then what?" Tim asked.

"Then I'll be back and we'll figure things out from there."

"Are you going to get whoever did this to Mom?" Tim continued.

"I already did. But he wasn't working alone."

Tim nodded again, as though the answer made complete sense and he approved.

Lucas took Eve's tiny hand in his. "Be good to Ruby and Tim."

Eve's upper lip trembled. "I'm always good."

"I know."

Lucas left them to their grief and made his way to the command tent. When he was nearly there, a cry went up from the periphery of the camp, and he walked over to see what was happening.

A cloud of dust approached from the direction of Dallas, and hundreds of cattle swam into view. Duke rode along the perimeter of the herd with his men, driving the animals like pros, hats in the air in greeting as they neared. Duke broke off and beelined for Lucas, who waited for him by the edge of the camp. Duke dismounted and handed his reins to a trooper and walked over to Lucas.

"I hate to say it, but that pair delivered," he said, indicating Conejo and Miguel. "You're going to be into them some serious weight." Duke stopped talking and studied Lucas's face. "What happened?"

"Sierra." Lucas gave him an abridged summary.

When he'd finished, Duke shook his head. "Sorry, Lucas. What a blow."

"Yeah. Well, I'm going to be leaving you and Elliot in charge. I'm riding north to finish this once and for all."

"You mean we, right? No way I'm letting you do this alone."

"I need you here to help Elliot, Duke. Otherwise we'd do it together in a blink."

"Help him what? Babysit the troops? Please."

"We can't afford to lose any time. We need a government set up for Dallas, the cattle slaughtered and cured for the march, and preparations made for Houston. Which means we need our best minds on it. Between you, Elliot, and Luis and Sam, you should be good. But you each bring your own skills and perspectives, and we can't afford to lose any one of you."

"How the hell are you thinking you'll find Snake in Oklahoma City? Sounds like a needle in a haystack. And he'll probably have a bunch of killers with him. Cowards travel in packs."

"I'll find him like I did for years. I was a Texas Ranger, remember? It's one of the things I was good at." Lucas stared off into the middle distance. "Maybe that's all I've ever been."

"You're the commander of this army, Lucas. Much as I know revenge sounds—"

"I'm not asking, Duke. That's how it's going to be. I've already talked to Elliot. I want you to make preparations to march on Houston, and I want you to leave as soon as you have a government installed here. Pick whoever wants to govern the place, meet with the locals, leave a large enough group behind to enforce authority, and get moving."

"What about you?"

"I'll catch up. Tango can make better time than any horse I know."

"And if you haven't by the time we're in range of Houston?"

"Then you come up with a strategy and attack. Wink knows the place cold. He'll help out of self-interest. Promise him whatever you need to. Between all of you, you'll come up with something that'll work."

"Damn it, Lucas. At least take some men."

"The bigger the crowd, the harder it is to be invisible." Lucas looked away. "This is something I have to do myself."

"Lucas, you have the biggest army in the country at your disposal. If you want, we can march on Oklahoma City with a thousand men and turn Snake into a stain on the sidewalk."

"Assuming he didn't bolt. And assuming we could feed them all the way there – and back. And that it didn't weaken the Houston attack force." Lucas shook his head. "If I need help, I can put the bite on Tyler. Look, I've thought this through. No other way makes sense, buddy. Just me against him. It'll be over, one way or the other."

Duke exhaled heavily. "You'll need to pack extra provisions. Take two horses. And plenty of weapons and gold."

"Wouldn't think of doing anything but." Lucas's smile was sad. "Negotiate with Conejo and arrive at a fair price for the cattle. Don't try to stiff him. I'll leave most of my gold in your care."

Duke laughed drily. "I should take off the moment you're out of sight."

"That's why you're in charge. I know you'll see this through to the end. Work with Elliot. Craft a plan. We've discussed it often enough, but be ready to change if anything's different than what we thought. If I'm lucky, I'll be back with you before you reach Houston. But I don't want you to wait for me. Understood?"

Duke nodded. "You're going to have to make amazing time."

Lucas rubbed the stubble on his chin with a tired hand. "Tango can manage thirty-five to forty miles per day standing on his head, so I can be in Oklahoma City in four days or less. Now let's hash out anything else we need to finalize with Elliot. I want to ride within the hour."

Chapter 34

Oklahoma City, Oklahoma

Moonlight bathed the exterior of a boxy two-story faux French revival home on a large lot near the outskirts of the city in a neighborhood that had been one of the best before the virus, now largely deserted except for squatters, scavengers, and the feral gangs that preyed upon them. A pair of gunmen sat on a bench by the main entry, watching the gate that provided the only egress from the walled compound, a lantern flickering beside them.

Inside, Snake was lounging on an Italian leather sofa with an emaciated teenage girl with hollow cheeks and lank hair beside him. A meth pipe fashioned from a light bulb lay on the coffee table in front of them. Snake shifted and reached for a bottle of rum. The girl scratched her ribs and grunted, her eyes shut, and Snake smiled to himself. Now that he had plentiful gold, he was one of the most prosperous men in the city; anything he wanted was his for the taking as long as he stayed out of the way of the military governor the army had left in charge. Bodyguards, whores, drugs, liquor – nothing was out of reach. He contrasted his life over the last few weeks to being on the trail with a gunshot wound, and blinked in wonder.

A knock at the front doors interrupted his reverie, and he looked up at the double slabs of Honduran mahogany with a frown.

"What?"

One of the doors swung inward, and two rough-looking men in

worn jeans and black leather vests entered. Snake pushed the girl aside and rose unsteadily to greet them.

"Goat! Liam! You made it!" he exclaimed, his voice colored by the meth he'd smoked earlier.

"We did," Liam said. "We practically ran here when word reached us."

"Well, have a seat," Snake said, indicating a dining table with six chairs around it in an adjacent area. "Rum? Something stronger?"

Goat grinned like a newborn. "Been forever since I had some decent rum."

Snake fished the bottle from the table and paused to glance at the girl before bringing the liquor to the dining room.

"Never said it was decent. But it's rum," he said.

He sat down across from them and slid the bottle to Goat, who took a long pull before handing it to Liam with a burp. Liam took a smaller swig, made a face, and pushed the bottle back to Snake.

"Someone make that in their tub?" he asked.

Snake chuckled. "Could be. Tastes like motor oil, but it does the job." He eyed them. "So how have you been getting by?"

"It ain't like the old days, when we ran things," Goat said. "Back then the Crew was God. But we're okay, I guess."

"Doing this and that," Liam added. "Whatever to make ends meet."

Snake could guess that the ex-Crew enforcers were terrorizing anyone they came across and stealing what they could. A far cry from when they'd ruled the roost.

"You managed okay with the cartel?" Snake asked.

"We kept out of their way. Which was easy." Liam paused. "How about you? We heard about Houston and what they did."

"Surprised you made it out," Goat chimed in.

"Takes more than a few burrito slingers to keep me down." Snake grinned. "I decided to bow out and wait for the right chance to boot them for good. Which looks like it's going to be soon."

"Yeah? How? I heard tell there were thousands of Zetas there now."

Snake's smile widened. "Doesn't much matter. There are going to be a lot fewer soon enough." He winked at the men conspiratorially. "That army that passed through here? They're headed to Houston. By the time they get done with each other, it'll be chaos. That's when I plan to hit and take the city back for the Crew."

Goat regarded Snake as though he'd announced he could levitate. Liam's expression was unreadable. "How? We're all in, but how are we going to do that? Even if they both lost most of their men, we're still talking thousands. Right now I see the three of us and some hired muscle."

"You need to have a little faith," Snake said, his eyes glittering from the last of the speed buzz. "I have a plan. A secret weapon."

Liam shook his head. "I figured you must. I'm all ears."

Snake offered more rum, and the men drank deeply before setting the bottle down. Snake sat back in his chair, his face confident. He spoke for five solid minutes, and when he was done, a sheen of sweat was glistening on his forehead in spite of the relative cool inside the house.

Liam and Goat exchanged a long look. Liam sat forward, with a thoughtful expression.

"That could work if everything went right. But you're going to need men, too. To establish order once the cartel and army are defeated. Where are you going to get them from?"

"There are still Crew who are loyal to me. Like you two. We won't need that many to start. If the army does its job, it'll wipe out most of the cartel, and the rest of them will be running back to Mexico faster than you can spell tequila. If the cartel wins, the army will be destroyed, and the cartel will be weakened enough that a well-timed strike would take most of them out. Either way, whoever wins the fight will be a shadow of what they are now, and they'll probably be concentrated in one or two areas they can defend. That will make destroying them relatively easy."

"Okay. But…how do we get there without being stopped by the army? Do we pretend we want to join?"

"That's one possibility. Another is that we round up as many ex-Crew as we can here and head toward Houston. Then we pick up some more in Dallas – there's bound to be some who went underground when the cartel moved in, or who pretended to switch sides. And I work the radio and put word out to loyalists down around Houston, so we have men there waiting for the final battle." Snake paused and licked his lips. "And I have another puzzle piece that will make it all come together."

Snake told them about his Illuminati contact, and the group's promise to help him once he'd dealt with Lucas.

Goat looked confused. "Right. But how can you deal with Lucas if he's commanding the army?"

"Good question," Snake acknowledged. "What if I told you that he was going to come to me? Here?"

Liam blinked rapidly. "Why would he do that?"

Snake explained about Petey and his kidnapping Sierra.

"That's…brilliant," Liam acknowledged. "But how do we know he won't turn the army around to rescue her instead?"

"Simple: food. Petey knows their situation. They can't make it back here with what they have. So he'll have to choose between rescuing her himself or continuing to Houston. Knowing what we do about him, he won't risk his entire force. He'll come to us, maybe with a small group. That's his style." Snake went on to tell them about the intel Petey had gathered from befriending the troops – about Lucas, how he operated, his history of lone-wolf missions.

An hour later, the bottle was empty and Liam and Goat convinced. They embraced Snake and swore their loyalty and committed to recruiting as many of their former Crew as they could find to act as the new commanders of the gang once they retook Houston.

When they left, Snake stuck another crystalline rock of meth into the pipe and lit it, holding the smoke in as long as he could. When he finally exhaled, his lips and eyes were twitching. He smacked the slumbering teen on the ass with enough force to rattle her teeth. She yelped and rolled off the sofa, and he grinned wolfishly and held out the pipe.

"Little pick-me-up, and then it's time to earn your keep again. Get busy or I'll carve my name in your face."

Chapter 35

Lucas stopped at the grove where Sierra had met her fate, and allowed Tango to rest while he walked slowly around the area, his mind a blank. The fallen horse's skeleton had been picked clean by the carrion birds and other scavengers, and the bones were bleached in the sun, white as a freshly painted picket fence. He studied the spot where Sierra had been shot, and then moved to the trees and examined the trunk that Petey had been leaning against when she'd delivered the blow that had ultimately killed him. The leaves overhead shivered slightly, the only sounds the whisper of the wind and an occasional bird cry. The setting would have been idyllic were it not for his mate having been murdered a stone's throw away.

He took a deep breath, sat near where Petey had met his fate, and shook his head. It was all so pointless – the struggle to survive, to prevail against long odds, with nothing as a reward but another day's hardship. It seemed so distant from the life he'd led before the collapse, when he'd been younger, more idealistic, and possessed of purpose and certainty. Now there was nothing but moral relativism, of rationalizing an existence ruled by the law of the jungle, of pushing away doubts that could get a man killed, of doing what had to be done no matter who got hurt.

Perhaps it had always been that way, and the thin veneer of civilization had only served to mask the beast lurking right below the surface, waiting to rampage; a function of millennia of evolution and genetics; a survival drive that ensured that only the most ruthless and dispassionate persevered.

Lucas closed his eyes, suddenly tired at a level far deeper than the fatigue from days without sleep. He'd failed to keep those he cared about safe, and he felt sick because of it – sick of the constant killing, sick of the pointlessness of it all, sick of what he'd become. A young woman had died for no other reason than she'd been important to Lucas. He was as responsible for her death by virtue of his existence as Petey or Snake.

He understood that wasn't true at an intellectual level, but it felt all too real, and he couldn't shake the feeling of foreboding that intensified with each mile under his belt as he made his way to Oklahoma City. Perhaps he'd finally run out of luck, and this would be the end of the line.

"Not before I've cut your black heart out," he whispered, imagining Snake's expression as the light went out of his eyes.

Lucas had no doubt he would find and kill Snake. He was exceptionally skilled at doing so, and this was intensely personal. But when he had, what would be accomplished other than the momentary satisfaction of revenge? Nothing would change. Sierra would still be dead, the kids would still be without a mother, and he without a mate.

He closed his eyes and let the breeze cool him, and within moments had drifted off. He dreamed that Sierra was with him, her mouth working wordlessly, begging for him to help her. Her arms were outstretched, and a bloody wound in her chest stained her shirt as she mouthed his name, eyes wide in terror and pain…and silent accusation.

Eventually the dream faded, replaced by the relief of nothingness.

When Lucas jolted awake, he checked the time and saw that he'd slept for over an hour. He swore under his breath, annoyed by the careless episode. If raiders or scavengers had been in the vicinity and come upon him, he'd have been a sitting duck. A lapse that could have cost him everything.

He groaned quietly as he forced himself to stand, and the dream came flooding back into his psyche. Would Sierra still be alive if he'd kept his promise and stayed in Provo? By breaking his word, was he not a primary reason she was dead? If he hadn't left to lead an army he hadn't wanted to command, would she have had any reason to follow?

He pushed the thoughts away. Beating himself up over the decisions he'd made served no good purpose and would lessen his resolve. Whether he liked it or not, he'd chosen, and now he had to live with his choice. He had thousands of men depending on him for leadership, and he couldn't fail them. Just going off to finish his business with Snake was letting them down. He wouldn't allow himself to further sabotage his mission with recriminations.

He whistled for Tango. "Okay, big guy. Let's make tracks."

The stallion stood motionless while Lucas mounted him, and then took off at a trot – a pace he'd been comfortably maintaining all night and much of the day. Lucas settled into the saddle, accustomed to the bouncing from the horse's gait, and considered his next move. He had no real plan, other than to touch base with the men they'd left in Oklahoma City to maintain order, and begin asking around. Snake would stick out there, being a stranger. At least, that was Lucas's hope.

Once he located him, he didn't need a strategy other than to blow the miscreant's head off. But only once he knew why Snake had been so hell-bent on trapping him.

Determined enough to invade Lucas's inner sanctum and kidnap his woman.

An action that would determine the outcome of the scumbag's short life.

As to what Lucas would do once he'd finished his task, he really had no idea. A part of him wanted to ride away and keep going, leaving the army and its crusade behind. But a vision of Eve and Tim quickly extinguished that fantasy. Lucas might have felt inclined to abandon the troops to their fate, but he couldn't do that to the kids. Like it or not, he was the only father they had, and he wouldn't dishonor Sierra's memory by running from his obligations.

Lucas leaned forward and patted Tango's neck.

"Hell of a mess we're in, isn't it?" he said.

Tango shook his mane without slowing. Lucas adjusted himself in the saddle and tilted the brim of his hat forward to shield himself from the afternoon sun.

"No question we're in the swamp now, boy. No question at all."

Chapter 36

Dallas, Texas

Low clouds drifted across the Texas sky as Elliot and Duke sat in one of the central plazas, facing several hundred locals who had gathered to hear the conquering army's plans for the city. The throng was glum and largely malnourished, almost entirely female and elderly, the fit males having been conscripted by the cartel and mostly slaughtered during the battle.

Tension hung in the air like humidity, and the heavily armed troops that were providing crowd control were jumpy, alert for threats from the throng as well as anyone external who might have attempted to use the assembly as an opportunity to attack the army's senior command.

Luis and Sam stood to the side, gazing out over the gathering, weapons on conspicuous display. Elliot was in the process of explaining how the new government was going to work, but it was obvious that the mob didn't believe him.

"We're going to install a military governor who'll keep order, enforce rules, and create a police force so everyone's safe. Once you have a working government, he'll step down and leave you to manage your own affairs. I want to stress that unlike the Crew or the cartel, this is not an occupation. We have no interest in preying on you like those groups did. Our objective is to return Dallas to democratic rule, for and by its citizens."

A woman near the front rolled her eyes. "So you butchered our men, and now you're going to run the place. Doesn't sound much different than the others."

"The key is that we're not going to steal the fruits of your labor or terrorize you. We aren't here to do anything but provide a framework for a local government."

"But you got all the men with guns. Seems legit to me."

Elliot smiled, keeping composed. "I can understand why you're suspicious. You have every right to be. But you'll find in time that I'm not misleading you. The army will be moving out shortly, and we'll leave a hundred men to help you organize and protect yourselves against the usual threats. But it's your city, and you're going to be responsible for its operation. Not us. We're just a stopgap."

"Fine words," another, older woman called from the middle of the group. "Who's going to be running the show?"

"Good question. Sam here will be the temporary governor. He's fair and evenhanded and wants nothing more than to rejoin the troops once things have stabilized here."

Elliot nodded to Sam, who walked over to him and waved.

He cleared his throat and, when he began talking, was so soft-spoken the audience had to strain to hear – a deliberate mechanism to ensure everyone paid attention and viewed him as the polar opposite of the warlords they were used to.

"One of the main reasons that the Crew and the cartel were able to take over Dallas without much of a fight is there was no organized defense force. It was every man for himself. As long as you live like that, you'll be easy pickings for any group that wants to rule you. Part of my job is to ensure that doesn't happen again. So my first order of business will be to set up a militia and a police force. The message I'm sending is simple: behave like decent human beings and you'll have no trouble with me. But if you're going to steal, rape, murder, extort, I'm going to come down on you with the full weight of my troops. There will be a rule of law, one way or another." He paused and allowed that to sink in before continuing.

"I'm not going to confiscate your guns or dictate how you go about your business. The laws will be simple. Kill someone, for whatever reason other than provable self-defense, and you'll be tried by a jury of your peers and executed. Same goes for rape. As to the rest, I'll work with whoever you decide will be your representative council, and the penalties will be whatever you feel are appropriate. But there won't be any vigilantism. No tribal infighting. You want to live in Dallas, you're living in a civilized area where you can't behave like animals. That's the message. As Elliot said, once you've got things under control, my men and I will bow out and leave you to it." He looked out over the group. "Any questions?"

The woman in front called out, "Who picks who's going to run things once you're gone?"

"You do. By a vote. We'll elect a council. That's worked well in other areas we've freed."

"Who gets to be the judge when someone misbehaves?"

"Whoever you decide you want. I'll suggest a framework, but it's up to you in the end."

Sam patiently answered questions for another half hour and then adjourned the meeting. Elliot took center stage again with some closing comments.

"Go tell everyone what you heard here today. The only way this will work is if you all take responsibility and pull together. Divided, you're the food for whatever predators feel like taking over. Together you're a community, and as one you get to determine your future."

The crowd dispersed, and Duke and Sam moved to where Elliot was waiting.

"We should be ready to move out in forty-eight hours or so," Duke confirmed. "Looks like you're going to have your work cut out for you," he said to Sam.

"You picked up on that, huh?" Sam said, the irony clear in his tone.

"It's only natural they'd be distrustful," Elliot said.

"We did just murder most of their able-bodied men," Duke agreed. "That would give anyone pause."

"I'll give it my best shot," Sam affirmed. "That's all I can do."

Elliot nodded. "Agreed. In the end, it's their town, so they need to deal with it. Do your best."

"Hate to miss all the fun in Houston," Sam said.

"Not sure fun's the word I'd use," Duke countered.

Sam looked away. "You know, I was thinking about Lucas. Since I'm going to be here for a while, it might not be a terrible idea to send a party after him. Just in case he needs help."

Duke frowned. "He was clear on that. Doesn't want anyone else involved. And we still have men up in Oklahoma if he does. I'd say focus on your job here and let him do his there."

"Just seems…wrong…to leave him in the wind like that."

"That's how he wanted it."

Sam shook his head. "We all know he probably wasn't thinking straight. Not that I blame him. Who would be?"

"He's a big boy. He knows what he's doing." Duke looked to Elliot. "It's your call when we roll south."

"If we're ready in two days, Lucas was adamant that he doesn't want us to delay. So ready the troops." Elliot smiled at Sam. "Good luck with the locals."

"Thanks. If you want to leave someone else in charge, I wouldn't fight you on it."

"No, you're the right man for the job. I'm sure you'll knock it out of the park."

Sam looked over his shoulder at the few stragglers from the assembly. "Hope you're right. They didn't seem too impressed."

"They'll come around."

Elliot, Luis, and Duke left, leaving Sam to talk with the women who'd stayed to speak with him. When they were out of earshot, Luis leaned into Duke.

"You think he'll be able to pull it off?"

Duke shrugged. "Not our problem. But he's a good organizer, so I don't see why not." He smiled. "And judging by the way a few of those young ladies were looking at him, it may not be as rough a duty as walking into the Zetas' machine-gun fire."

Luis sighed. "Maybe I should have volunteered."

Duke clapped Luis on the back. "Too late now, *amigo.*"

Chapter 37

South of Oklahoma City, Oklahoma

Shots rang out in the distance ahead, and Lucas slowed Tango and leaned forward to minimize himself as a target. More shots, and Lucas frowned – the first had been rifle fire, the second the lower-pitched boom of a shotgun. The pop-pop of pistols followed, and Lucas withdrew his M4 from its scabbard and urged Tango toward the shooting, which appeared to be coming from a ranch house off the highway a quarter mile ahead.

Morning had broken several hours before, and Lucas had gotten a few hours of sleep before dawn, but had awoken with the calls of birds as the sun rose. He'd been riding at night and some of the day, pushing Tango as hard as he dared without blowing him out, and had covered a decent amount of ground, but even the indefatigable stallion had slowed as the journey wore on, the cumulative effect of the multiple trips in the last weeks having taken a toll on his stamina.

When he was a hundred yards from the ranch house, Lucas guided Tango beneath a tall oak tree and leapt from the saddle, gun in hand. He hurriedly lashed the horse to the tree and made his way the rest of the distance to the house on foot, staying low in the tall yellowish grass, his eyes glued to the structure. He drew nearer and spotted five horses tied to the wooden post fence that encircled the grounds. As he closed on the rear of the house, a scream reached him – a woman's or girl's, by the timbre.

Lucas crept forward and reached the rear door and, after quickly debating moving around the house or through it, decided on the latter and eased the rear screen door open. He walked stealthily through the kitchen, leading with his rifle, and after poking his head into the bedrooms to confirm they were empty, continued to the living room, where the front door yawned open – blocked by the leg of a dead man lying on his back in a lake of blood, two wounds in his chest the obvious cause of death.

Lucas stepped over the man's torso and surveyed the scene outside. Four rangy men with filthy long hair and unkempt beards were standing around the body of a young man, the shotgun beside him doubtless the source of the earlier shots, laughing as one urinated on him. A woman struggled in the grip of one of the men, and a boy, maybe twelve or thirteen, did the same nearby where a fifth scavenger held his arms.

Lucas drew a deep breath and considered the odds. Five against one, but he had the element of surprise. The problem being the two hostages. He had little doubt he could take the five with as many well-timed bursts, but not without hitting one or both of the civilians.

A little voice in his head warned him that this wasn't his fight, and that the smartest thing he could do was to walk away and let the ugly little drama play itself out. But the vision of Sierra that swam into focus banished the warning, and Lucas flipped his firing selector to three-round burst and pulled back into the shadows to find the best place from which to shoot. The door looked to be cheap hollow core and wouldn't provide any meaningful cover, and he didn't want to count on nailing all five before they returned fire.

He moved to one of the open windows and was settling into position when another shot rang out from the front yard, and the boy screamed in horror. Lucas ignored the histrionics and knelt, steadying his rifle, and took in the scene outside.

"What did you have to go and do that for?" one of the men bellowed at the one who'd just shot the woman in the stomach.

"The bitch bit me."

"You ruined her for everybody, you idiot."

"Nah. She'll stay warm for a while. You'll get your shot."

The man holding the boy looked over at the house and had begun to shout a warning when Lucas's first burst blew through his skull, taking the back of it off in a shower of bone and blood. The boy froze in place as the man dropped, and Lucas was already firing again, this time drilling the one who'd shot the woman. Wounds blossomed across his chest, and then Lucas shifted to the other three, loosing burst after burst as they struggled to bring their weapons to bear on the house.

Two of the men crumpled in as many seconds, but the final one dropped to the ground as he fired at the window, and chunks of sheetrock blew into the living room inches from where Lucas was crouched. Lucas got off another burst, one of which winged the man in the arm, and then a pistol shot tore through the man's throat, killing him as a spray of bright red arterial blood arced through the air.

Lucas swung his gun back to where the boy stood with his captor's pistol in hand, and then called out, "Drop it. You're okay. I'm not here to hurt you."

A range of conflicting imperatives played across the boy's face, and then he dropped the pistol beside him and ran to the woman, who was gasping her last breaths.

"Ma!" he cried, and buried his head in her chest as Lucas stepped from the house and approached.

The boy looked up at Lucas, tears streaming down his cheeks, and then back to the woman. She fought to say something, and then groaned and lay still.

The boy's shoulders shuddered as he cradled the woman in his arms. Lucas stepped away and checked the corpses of the attackers. One was still alive, trembling with shock, and Lucas unceremoniously shot him in the head. The boy jolted at the report as though he'd touched a live wire, and Lucas returned to where he sat and shouldered his rifle.

"You got a shovel around here?" Lucas asked.

The boy looked at Lucas like he was mad. "What? Why?"

"Got to bury your kin before we leave. These animals can get picked clean where they fell, far as I'm concerned."

The boy slowly pushed himself to his feet. Lucas reassessed his earlier guess about his age. He was more like eleven. "What's your name?" Lucas asked.

The boy fixed him with a bleak stare. "Ansel."

"Ansel, sorry about your family. I got here fast as I could. But now it's time to bury them and say our prayers, and then move in case there are more where these scum came from."

Ansel nodded curtly and shambled to a shed. He returned with a pick and shovel and handed the shovel to Lucas.

An hour later, the dead had been buried and Lucas had said a few words over their mass grave. Ansel was stoic as Lucas spoke, and Lucas suspected he would be permanently damaged by the experience, but there was little to be done about it.

"Grab one of the horses and pack everything you want to take with you," Lucas instructed. "Bedroll, a tent if you have one, clothes, guns and ammo. Any matches and food. Canteen. You have any drinking water?"

Ansel nodded again. "We got a well."

"Good. I'll water the horses while you pack. You have fifteen minutes."

"Where we going?"

"North to Oklahoma City."

Ansel stared at him for a long beat. "Got an aunt up there."

"There's some luck. But hurry up. We can talk about it on the ride."

Ansel walked off, and Lucas gathered all the scavengers' ammo and weapons and anything of utility he found in the house. He would chain their horses together and lead them to town, and when he found someone to trade them to, would do so and give the proceeds to the boy. It wasn't any sort of consolation for losing his family in a matter of minutes, but the new reality everyone inhabited was brutal and senseless and curt, and the only thing Lucas could do now was to try to give him a stake to start with, and find his aunt, assuming the boy knew where to look.

That Lucas's arrival with a youngster and a string of ponies might provide cover to anyone watching had scarcely entered his mind, although he registered it almost unconsciously and instantly recognized the benefit.

Ansel returned carrying a backpack and a ratty suitcase, and Lucas helped him select a horse and pack his bags. Next came the weapons, and when they were ready to leave, Lucas took a final look around the homestead.

"You know how to ride?" Lucas asked. He hadn't seen any horses but the scavengers', so he couldn't be sure.

"I been on one before," Ansel replied.

Based on the boy's use of the pistol, he didn't have to ask about his familiarity with firearms.

"All right, then. Let's move. Got a long way to go before we're there," Lucas said.

"Mister, what's your name?" Ansel asked.

"Lucas."

"Lucas, thanks for helping."

"Just wish I could have done more."

When Ansel met his gaze, his face held the sorrow of the world. "Me too."

Chapter 38

Houston, Texas

Julio paced in the hotel conference room he'd set up as his command center while his lieutenants watched in silence. They'd received a radio communication from one of their surviving men in Dallas, who'd informed them of Bernard's inglorious defeat and the army's departure for Houston. While unsurprised that Dallas had fallen, Julio was still clearly shaken, and his demeanor was anxious as he considered the cartel's next steps as Lucas's army bore down on them.

A knock at the door disrupted Julio's ruminations, and a guard poked his head in.

"Guy named Lorne says he needs to talk to you," the guard said.

Julio's expression transformed from pensive to angry at the mention of the name. "He's here? Where?"

"Waiting downstairs."

"Bring him up." Julio eyed his men. "I'm going to need the room."

"Is this the guy from…?" one of the men began.

"The less you know, the better," Julio snapped. "Give me half an hour."

The lieutenants filed out, and moments later the guard returned with Lorne, who looked as composed as though he'd just woken up from a nap. The guard departed, and Lorne waved a greeting to Julio.

"So you've heard," Lorne said, pulling up a seat and sitting.

"Obviously you knew about this before we did."

"Yes. It was most distressing that your men were unable to execute the plan. It would have saved us all a lot of bother."

"I don't know the details. It doesn't matter."

"The summary is that most of your men were killed in a matter of minutes. Almost an instant replay of the disastrous ambush. It seems you didn't assign your best or brightest, and now Houston will pay the price."

"What's it to you? This is my problem, not yours. And it was your plan in Dallas that failed, not mine."

Lorne shrugged. "Perhaps. But that isn't how I heard it."

Julio glowered at him. "So why are you here?"

"To offer my services."

"Your services? Another plan that's impossible to execute?"

Lorne ignored the barb. "I can help you with strategy and tactics."

"I don't need your help. We're unbeatable here. This isn't Dallas. We've got fuel; we've got artillery; we've got thousands of hardened fighters. We'll manage."

"If I were you, I'd want every advantage. That may not be enough."

"I'd watch my mouth if I were you. That's what I'd do."

Lorne sighed. "We both want the same thing. To stop the army. The reason I'm here is to help you however I can. It didn't just occur to me. I've been ordered to do so. I'd just as soon sail to Cuba as be here, so there's no love lost."

"You can leave whenever you want."

"And be…reprimanded…when you lose Houston? I think not."

"Fine. So surprise me. What's your proposal?"

"I first need to understand your total strength and how quickly you can get reinforcements from Mexico."

"We're not going to need any. We have over four thousand fighters. Tanks. Howitzers. They can stop anything. Some ragtag army is no match."

"You've underestimated their effectiveness twice now. Both times didn't go well."

Julio flushed and made a visible effort to control his temper. When he next spoke, his voice was a hiss.

"You forget who you're talking to."

"Not at all. I'm simply trying to avert a disaster. I have nothing but your best interests in mind. We'll need to put aside any egos if we're to work together effectively. That's a luxury you can't afford."

Julio whipped his pistol free and leveled it at Lorne's head. "Enough of your insolence," he spat. "Nobody talks to me like that."

Lorne's voice was steady. "If you shoot me because you're throwing a temper tantrum, you'll have sealed your fate."

"Get out. Now. And don't come back. You owe me your life, because you're seconds away from losing it."

Lorne shook his head. "My superiors won't be pleased."

The blast of Julio's .45 in the enclosed room was as loud as a cannon. A hole appeared in the center of Lorne's forehead, and he tumbled backward onto the floor. Julio walked over and spat on him as six armed guards burst through the door with their weapons drawn. Julio looked at them and indicated the dead man.

"Get rid of this. It's stinking up the room."

The guards hauled Lorne's corpse away, and Julio returned to pacing, his brow knit and his face still twisted with rage. How dare this messenger boy insult him? And what of his mysterious group? So far they'd been of only limited help, for all their self-important promises. He didn't need anyone looking over his shoulder and implying he was incompetent. He'd been in charge of the Zetas for decades and had ruled northern Mexico successfully before and after the virus. That hadn't been accidental, and to imply he had no idea what he was doing could only result in one response.

He didn't trouble himself with how the Illuminati might react. They were as distant a threat as he could imagine, incapable of projecting power, other than the story of their battleship – but two could play that game as petroleum refining improved.

Julio spun and called to the guards, "Get the men back in here. We're losing time."

When his lieutenants were seated, the group avoiding any comment on the bloody pool on the ground and the chair in their midst, Julio spoke slowly, as though to a class of slow children.

"I want defenses mounted on the northern approaches. Tanks, artillery, mortars, rockets, the whole nine yards. I don't want this army to get within ten miles of our base or the refinery. So do whatever it takes, but I want a plan within twenty-four hours. We have maybe ten days before they're here. Let's not waste them."

The group left Julio to his ruminations, and he stayed until one of his subordinates asked him about lunch. As he walked downstairs to where his cook had prepared one of his favorite dishes, he shrugged off any lingering doubts about his rash action with Lorne.

"You picked the wrong man to try to bully," he muttered. "I haven't survived this long to be lectured like a child. Not by you. Not anyone."

If the guards noticed the one-sided conversation, they didn't show it, except by an exchange of furtive glances once Julio was out of sight. They knew better than to land on their master's wrong side, and the dead messenger was all the proof they needed that he wasn't feeling charitable at the moment.

Chapter 39

Lucas led Ansel and the string of horses down a main street towards the building Tyler had set up as the army's provisional headquarters. Two days on the trail with the boy had convinced Lucas that he'd survive, even if scarred by the experience of seeing his family murdered in front of him. There was nothing Lucas could do about that, and he understood the boy's sullen silence when they pitched their tents every night, long after dark and well off the road. Lucas had little to offer the boy in terms of conversation or advice, and Ansel seemed fine with that, keeping to himself, preferring to mourn in silence.

They drew near the headquarters, and three sentries behind a cinderblock checkpoint stopped them.

"Can't go any farther," the leader said.

Lucas smiled, amused that he hadn't been recognized by his own men. "Appreciate that, but I've got business with Tyler."

The leader appeared confused by Lucas's use of Tyler's name, and one of the other guards called to him, "That's Lucas. He can pass."

The leader's face changed to one of embarrassment and mild surprise, and he saluted. "Oh. Sorry, sir. I wasn't…"

Lucas shook off the apology. "Don't sweat it. He there?"

"Yes, sir."

"Good."

Lucas continued to the building and, when he dropped from the saddle, looked to Ansel. "Stay here and mind the horses."

"Why did he get all weird? That guard? Salute and all? They know you…"

"Long story. I'll be back shortly." Lucas glanced at the gunman who was stationed just inside the entry. "Where is he?"

"Up the stairs. First room on the right."

"Thanks."

Lucas knocked on the door, and Tyler looked up from the documents on his desk.

"Yes?"

Lucas entered, and Tyler bolted to his feet. "Sir! This is…unexpected."

"Please. Sit."

"Is everything okay with the troops?"

"Yes. We took Dallas, and we're marching on Houston as we speak. But that's not why I'm here."

Tyler blinked in confusion. "Then…?"

"I'm looking for a man. He used to run the Crew in Houston. Complete lowlife named Snake. I've got reason to believe he's in Oklahoma City."

"Snake? Here?"

"I'm guessing this is news to you?"

"Well, yeah. How do you know? What's he doing here?"

Lucas gave a short synopsis of his encounter with Petey and his trek north, leaving out Sierra's murder. When he finished, Tyler was shaking his head.

"Haven't heard about him or seen him."

"That's a shame, but I thought I'd check in and ask." Lucas paused. "How are things going?"

Tyler shrugged. "We've had a few run-ins with some gangs that tried to take over once the army left, but nothing we couldn't handle."

"Lose any men?"

"Negative. Two wounded, but they'll recover. We've been concentrating on cleaning up the downtown area and consolidating here. The locals have been cooperative so far. We're working with them, and every day more are coming forward. We'll have a police force within another week. Mostly locals, supervised by our men."

"That's good." Lucas thought for a moment. "Where would you start to look if you wanted to find this Snake?"

Tyler thought for a moment. "West side. That's still a no-man's land where all the lowlifes hang out. It's on our list of places to clean up, but right now it's a no-go zone for us. Too dangerous. Don't need anyone taking potshots at our patrols. But we'll get to it once downtown is under our control."

"Sounds like a good place to start."

Tyler looked him over. "I don't think I'd risk it, sir."

Lucas held his stare. "Not sure I have a choice." He hesitated. "I picked up a boy on the ride up. Lost his family. I'd appreciate it if you'd help him find his aunt here in town."

"Of course. Do you know what area she's in?"

"I'm assuming he does." Lucas took several steps to the door and then turned towards Tyler. "Where's the nearest trading post?"

"Um, about six blocks away."

"I'll leave the boy with you. I need to take care of some business before I get started on Snake. Will you bring him up and watch him?"

"I'll come down."

Tyler and Lucas exited the building, and Lucas approached Ansel and introduced him to Tyler. "Stay here for a bit and see to it that Tango's tended to. I'll be back," Lucas instructed the boy.

Ansel dismounted. "Where you going?"

Lucas laid a hand briefly on his shoulder. "Got a few things to do. Take care of Tango, and stay out of Tyler's way."

Lucas had a hushed discussion with Tyler and, when he understood where the trading post was, led the string of animals there on foot. He arrived at the shop, which had the usual muscle guarding it, and quickly did a trade of the horses, guns, and ammo for a number of silver coins that could be easily hidden and stored in shoes, even if the boy was searched – something bullets weren't suited for.

Upon his return, he presented Ansel with the coins and warned him to keep them secret, even from his aunt. Ansel nodded and looked Lucas in the eyes.

"You leaving?" he asked.

"I have things that need taking care of. Tyler will help you find your aunt. Good luck, Ansel."

"Is it true you're some kind of general?"

That stopped Lucas. His smile was sad. "Not much of one, depending on who you talk to. And it's hush-hush I'm in town, okay? Not a word to anyone."

"You're on some kind of secret mission?"

"Something like that." Lucas ruffled the boy's hair, and then walked to where Tango was waiting. "Take care of yourself, Ansel. Things will get better with time."

"Um, thanks, Lucas."

Lucas saddled up and waved over his shoulder, unwilling to let the boy see his eyes moistening, and set out towards the west end of town, his long trail coat flapping against his legs.

Chapter 40

The watering hole on the western reach of Oklahoma City was nearly deserted in the late afternoon as Lucas nursed a shot of locally distilled moonshine at the bar. The few occupied tables were filled with trail bums and criminals with filthy clothes and unkempt hair, drinking the cheapest rotgut they could get. All had networks of gin blossoms on their weathered faces and the plodding movements of the perennially addled, and gave off a stink of failure and desperation as palpable as oil smoke.

Lucas surveyed the clientele and took another sip of his drink. This was the tenth such place he'd been to since he'd begun his search eight days before, and he was no closer to finding Snake than when he'd started. Patrons weren't interested in talking, especially to a stranger, and most of them weren't local anyway – everyone seemed to be just passing through.

The bartender was a stout woman who looked like she could have been a pro wrestler, and Lucas assumed that business was good if she was able to maintain the diet to support her bulk. He'd watched her dust bottles and avoid eye contact for the better part of an hour, and was ready to make his move before trying his luck with the customers.

He finished his drink and lifted a finger.

She approached with the bottle and raised an eyebrow. "'Nother one?"

"You bet. Not like I've got anything better to do."

"Tell me about it."

"You own this joint?" Lucas tried.

She nodded. "Going on three years. Be careful what you wish for, right?"

"Looks to do a decent business."

"I get by."

"You happy to see the cartel go?"

She smiled slightly. "One less mouth to feed. Can't say as that's not a blessing."

"Same as the ones before, right? The Crew? They took a cut too?"

She gave him a wary look. "What do you think?"

"They aren't so bad. Spent time in Dallas around them, and some in Houston. I've seen worse. Trust me on that."

"No thanks. Been there, done that, got the T-shirt."

Lucas tried a smile. "You get many of them in here?"

"Used to. They pretty much all cleared out when the cartel came in."

"So none around anymore?"

"A few old school stuck around. But they don't come in here. They mostly hang out at another place."

She poured him another shot, and he placed some rounds on the table. She pocketed them without looking.

"I'm Lucas, by the way. Pleased to meet you."

"Likewise. Thelma. Everyone calls me Ma."

Lucas grinned again. "All right, Ma." He took a pull of his fresh drink. "Who makes this stuff?"

"I've got a local source." She winked.

"Tastes like turpentine. But in a good way."

"You aren't far off. I think he sells the better stuff for paint thinner."

They both laughed.

Lucas shook his head. "Yep. But it sure does warm you up."

"Customer's always right."

"You said the old-school bunch hangs out somewhere else? Where's that?"

Her face hardened. "Why? They're nothing but trouble. A man could get himself killed in some of the rat holes around here."

Lucas looked around before leaning forward on the bar. "I'll let you in on a little secret. I'm looking for one of them. Bad hombre."

She took his measure and set the bottle down. "I'd steer clear. There's still enough of them around here to cause a lot of grief."

"That may be, but I can do my share of it, too."

"You got a beef with this guy?"

"You could say that, Ma. Let's just say I owe him one."

She shrugged. "You ask around long enough, you'll find out they like a place called Red's. Owned by one of them. Rough place. They see you coming, you'll have a problem."

Lucas raised his glass. "Thanks. Easy to find?"

"Just follow the stink. It's pretty hard to miss. Up by the tracks, near the old station." She paused. "Watch yourself. I'd hate to lose a good customer."

"Will do."

Lucas finished his drink and sidled out to where Tango was tied. He flipped a bullet to the youth who was watching the horses, and when he caught it, paused before climbing into the saddle.

"What's the easiest way to get to Red's?"

The youth pointed to his right. "Up this street maybe four blocks, and then take a left on the big one. It's about, I don't know, half mile on the right." He grinned. "They got a sign," he added.

"They open this time of day?"

The youth made a face. "Beats me. But I hear it's more of a night kind of place."

"Thanks."

Lucas set off and found Red's with little trouble. As the boy had said, the sign was difficult to miss, but there were no horses tied in front, and a steel shutter was closed over the entryway. Lucas checked his watch and yawned, fatigued by the alcohol, and resolved to get some badly needed rest before returning to the bar and continuing the hunt. He'd been bouncing from boardinghouse to boardinghouse since arriving, never staying in the same place more than two nights, and had vacated his last place that day, so it was time to find somewhere new, preferably nearby. He turned Tango around and eyed the street and rode to where a man was sitting on the curb with a collection of scrounged junk laid out on a blanket.

"Help you?" the vendor asked.

"Looking for a room."

The man laughed, revealing a dearth of teeth. "That ain't no problem. Most buildings are deserted."

"I was hoping for someplace with a bed and some water so I can wash the dust off."

"Might give Emma's a try." He pointed down the street. "Keep headed thataway and you'll see it. Like an old-timey house. Looks haunted. On your left." He cackled again. "Used to be a whorehouse back in the day."

"Not anymore?"

"Ha. You never know. Tell them Leo sent you. I get a vig."

"Will do." Lucas hesitated. "That Red's place. Lot of Crew go in there?"

The vendor looked away, suddenly interested in his boots. "Wouldn't know anything about that. I mind my own business."

"Sure thing, Leo. Thanks. I'll give Emma the good word."

The boardinghouse was around a bend in the street and down another hundred yards. Lucas was glad to see a stable hand brushing a mare inside the gate, and tipped his hat as he rode up.

"Howdy. I'm looking for a room."

"We got those, mister. Bring your horse in and talk to the lady in the house."

"Will do. How much to brush, feed, and water him?"

The man named a price, and Lucas lowered himself from the saddle. "Deal. His name's Tango."

"How long you staying?"

Lucas removed his saddlebags and his rifle and moved to the house. "Till I leave."

The room was clean, the water warm enough and gravity-pressured from a roof cistern, and Lucas luxuriated on a real mattress for the first time in too long and drifted off to sleep quickly. When he awoke, it was dark out, and he swore when he checked the time before going downstairs.

He checked in on Tango and then set off on foot towards Red's, armed only with his pistol. The street was quiet, the only noise the sound of his boots on the pavement, and he scoped out the buildings around the guesthouse, noting they were all unoccupied, inasmuch as there were no lights visible in any of the windows.

Red's was a typical dive bar of the sort frequented by the worst of the worst, and he wasn't disappointed by the collection of hustlers, thugs, crooks, working girls, trail bums, and raiders. He drew little interest from the locals when he ordered a drink at the bar, and he slowly surveyed the customers, each a study in the uglier side of humanity that reminded him of how far he'd fallen from his days as a Texas Ranger.

He made small talk with the man next to him, a local who did "this and that" for a living and looked like he'd cut out your heart for the price of a drink. Lucas asked about the Crew days and whether any of the old guard were still around, but the man's interest in talking dried up suddenly, and he took off with his drink like he'd seen a ghost.

Lucas did the same with several others over the course of the evening, but got nowhere except to confirm his impression that the Crew's hold on the locals was still strong even if the gang no longer ran the town. After four hours and six shots of local brew, he decided to call it a night, having gotten nowhere. The bartender watched him weave his way to the door, and when Lucas had stepped outside, nodded to a table with three rough-looking younger men, who finished their drinks and moved to the exit, faces as sharp as hatchets and eyes dark as coal.

Chapter 41

Oklahoma City, Oklahoma

LED lanterns sat on the tarmac near a twin-engine Piper Navajo that had been gutted of all but the pilot seats. Abandoned planes hulked in the darkness around it, their paint faded from years of neglect, tires flat, many with their windows broken. A dozen men carried supplies to the plane as a man in dirty coveralls worked on one of the engines while a second, younger helper held a crank-powered flashlight so he could see.

Snake watched the scene from beneath a nearby hangar, jittery from an earlier meth hit. His lips twitched involuntarily as he fidgeted. He glanced up at the moon and crossed to the plane, walking hurriedly with the disjointed gait of an addict. The man with his hands in the engine looked up at him, his expression neutral, and then returned to the job while Snake hovered a few feet from him.

"Everything okay?" Snake asked.

The man stopped what he was doing and turned to Snake. "Yeah. Tightening down on some seals. The fuel eats through 'em too damn fast, so it's a constant battle to stay up on them."

"Why's that?"

"These engines were never meant to burn ethanol. But it's all we got."

"And that's safe?"

"Sure. The downside's a lot less power. But as long as we stay low and don't mind taking our time, it shouldn't be a problem. I modified them years ago, and I've had her up more than a few times. She'll do the job."

"Why did you strip the guts out of the plane?"

"Weight. We need to carry more fuel because the engines suck almost twice as much as if we were running avgas. And fuel weighs a bunch."

"Avgas?"

The man nodded. "100-LL. But they'll be fine running this."

Snake frowned. "Where do you get it?"

"A buddy of mine has a still. Mostly he makes moonshine. This is more expensive than booze, because he's after higher alcohol content and it takes for frigging ever to make it, but it costs what it costs. Plus, I take him up every now and then, so he gives me a break on it."

"Wait. So this is...booze?"

"Basically. But like 170 proof. It'd take the enamel off your teeth and burn a hole through your stomach if you drank much."

"What gave you the idea?"

"Oh, Piper tested using it on its piston engines before the collapse, so I knew it would work. Just a matter of changing a bunch of stuff." He paused. "Don't worry. It's stable. The engines run a hair rougher, and like I said, they don't make as much power, but we're not gonna be flying much over a couple of thousand feet, so we don't need all that much. But that's why I told your boys they have to be careful with what they load. It's why they had to weigh everything first."

Snake cut him off with a wave of his hand. "I get it. When will you be ready to fly?"

"Should be tomorrow, I'd think. I have to cut some more gasket material and replace a couple of these. Don't want to blow one on takeoff or on the way." The pilot scratched himself and held up a wrench. "Anything else?"

Snake shook his head. "No. Do what you have to do."

Snake returned to the hangar, where the security detail of ex-Crew fighters were gathered. All of them were old-school gangsters who'd done hard time and had either fled to Oklahoma City after the cartel had taken over Houston, or had been in Dallas and decided to move north rather than being slaughtered in a cartel purge. All had the prison-yard swagger and the icy stare of stone-cold killers, which they were, serving life sentences in most cases for murder.

A horse clattered across the tarmac and approached Snake. He eyed the rider expectantly.

"The guy you wanted us to keep an eye out for? Lucas? Man matches his description's been asking about you."

"Where?"

"Bars on the outskirts of town."

Snake smiled in grim satisfaction. "I knew he'd come. Where is he now?"

"At Red's."

"Anyone with him? Petey? Anyone else?"

"Not that I heard."

Snake looked to his men. "Time to saddle up. I've got some business to take care of."

The five bodyguards jogged to where the horses were tied. Snake followed them, smacking his lips in anticipation. Petey had gone dark, and Snake had no idea what had happened to him, but apparently his plan to draw Lucas to Oklahoma had worked, regardless.

The prospect of finally achieving his goal and being able to confirm with the Illuminati that Lucas was dead brought a smile to Snake's lips. While the gold had made his life more comfortable in Oklahoma, it was nothing like ruling over Texas, where he'd had anything he could imagine whenever he wanted it. With the Illuminati happy that he'd competently solved their Lucas problem, he would have the resources to take back Houston once and for all – and exact his revenge on those responsible for his fall from grace.

The men were mounted up when he reached the horses, and he climbed into the saddle with drug-fueled energy. Even after the collapse, when virtually nothing was available, meth was easily sourced, as was alcohol. It was a constant that the surviving population would want to blunt life's sharp edges with substances, and manufacturing Snake's drug of choice was relatively easy now that there were no cops to shut down the backyard labs.

The messenger rode up, and Snake's eyes locked on him. "Lead on. I don't want to lose him."

"We're maybe a half hour away."

"Ride hard and cut that in half."

The rider took off at a gallop, and Snake and his entourage lit out after him, the pounding of their hooves like thunder as they disappeared into the night.

Chapter 42

Lucas walked slowly back to Emma's, mind churning over how to proceed. What he'd been doing hadn't yielded any results, and he understood that continuing to do what wasn't working would likely turn out the same. The problem was that there weren't any other avenues to go down that he could think of, other than continuing to ask around and hoping for a lightning strike.

Perhaps he needed to offer a reward to some of the street people? The urchins who were an inevitable part of every metro area – the beggars and sidewalk vendors, the hookers and dealers?

The street was dark and stank of untreated sewage and rot, an inevitable result of the primitive living conditions the residents were forced to endure without power or running water. Most of the necessities that had been taken for granted had vanished with the collapse, and that was never more evident than in formerly bustling urban centers, which had reverted to medieval standards. Previously eradicated scourges like typhoid and cholera were now commonplace, and infection or one of those opportunistic diseases were responsible for more deaths than starvation.

Lucas reached an intersection where three cars were rotting in the middle of the street, and crossed, deep in thought. He was nearly at the other side when the hair on the back of his neck stood up at the sound of muffled footsteps down the block from him. He resisted the urge to look over his shoulder and instead picked up his pace, the deserted boulevard now a potential killing field if he'd attracted the attention of a scavenger gang. Tyler had warned him to steer clear of the area, but that hadn't been an option, and now Lucas was alone and out in the open, with only his Kimber for defense – a lousy situation under the best of circumstances.

He reached the end of the block and ducked down a smaller tributary, ears straining for sounds of pursuit. He stopped at a service alley behind a row of stores and slipped into the darkness, drawing his gun and silently chambering a round as he pressed himself into a doorway.

Seconds ticked by with his pulse thudding in his ears, and then he heard a scrape from the street, followed by a hushed curse. Lucas remained frozen in place, Kimber in hand, waiting to see whether his pursuers continued down the street or detoured into the alley.

He waited, motionless, for a half minute, and then another half minute.

Nobody entered the alley.

When he heard nothing more, he eased from the recess and peered along the pavement. The buildings blocked any moonlight, making it almost impossible to see, and he remained in place until he was sure he'd lost them.

Lucas took quiet steps back to the street and stopped again at the alley mouth. Nothing.

A hiss and a crash from within the alley startled him, and he turned, Kimber at the ready, ducking down into a crouch.

A pair of scrawny cats raced away, one of them with a rat in its mouth, the rodent still struggling in its jaws. Lucas exhaled softly at the sight and smiled at the perseverance of the hungry felines, who'd managed to survive even as most of humanity hadn't.

He was straightening when a blow to the back of his head knocked him forward. He tried to hold onto the pistol, but a brutal follow-on strike to his neck slammed him sideways, and the gun fell from his grip and skittered along the pavement.

Lucas fought to regain his footing, but a body slam knocked him to the ground. He sweep-kicked the legs out from one of his assailants, and the man went down hard with a pained grunt, but a kick to Lucas's ribs stopped his counterattack. Lucas landed a punch to another attacker's groin and was rewarded with a scream of pain. He managed to push himself to his feet as a third rushed him, and blocked his roundhouse swing and pummeled the figure in the stomach. The man's breath escaped with a loud whoosh, and Lucas dove for his pistol, hitting the asphalt and rolling. His fingers brushed it, but another boot to the ribs stopped him from grabbing it. He winced at the blow and then tried to protect his head as the boot continued pounding him.

He rolled onto his back and kicked at his attacker, but then one of the downed men got to his feet and joined his companion, and all Lucas could do was suffer the beating and try to avoid the worst of the blows. He lashed out when he could, and did some damage of his own, but then something slammed into his skull and he blacked out.

The men continued kicking him until a voice called out from the street, "What the hell do you think you're doing?"

The distinctive snick of a lever-action rifle cocking sounded off the building façades, and the snap of a cartridge being loaded in a pump-action shotgun accompanied it.

The men exchanged a glance, and then the biggest of them whispered to the others, "Run for it."

They took off down the alley, leaving Lucas lying prone on the ground, blood trickling from his savaged mouth and cuts on his cheekbones, his hat crumpled beside him.

Two men walked cautiously into the alley, leading with the guns. When they spotted Lucas, the taller of the pair whistled softly and murmured to his friend, "Make sure they cleared out. I'll see if he's still alive."

Chapter 43

North of Houston, Texas

The evening air was heavy with moisture as Duke scanned the buildings on the outskirts of Houston with his binoculars. He was hidden behind a large truck that was resting on its side, its front fender crushed from where a bigger vehicle had collided with it. Elliot did the same from beside him, looking for evidence of where the cartel had dug in its defenses so the army could target them with mortar bombardment.

"It's so spread out it'll be impossible to figure out where they all are," Elliot said.

"We always knew it wasn't going to be easy," Duke said, continuing to look at the area ahead. "But I see a couple of likely culprits we can hit with the mortars."

"It's hard to make anything out. Looks quiet to me. Maybe we should send out patrols to try to isolate their defenses? They can mark the range and send up flares."

Duke lowered the binoculars. "That's not a bad idea."

"Every now and then I have a good one."

The army had averaged better time than planned, the terrain relatively easy to navigate, and was now huddled on the northern edge of the Houston suburbs, with Luis to the east commanding a contingent of a thousand fighters and Duke heading up the main force with Elliot. The mortar squad was with the main body, over a

197

hundred gunners and loaders, ready to begin firing whenever targets were identified.

Duke and Elliot retraced their steps to the command tent, where their officers were gathered, awaiting instructions.

"Let's send out four-man patrols to identify targets for the mortars," Duke said. "Twenty patrols, separated by a hundred and fifty yards. That should give us a reasonable spread. We'll move the mortar squads forward as the patrols advance, but keep them a safe distance back. Let's say a thousand yards behind. Use flares and two-ways to confirm targeting." Duke looked at his watch. "I want the patrols ready in ten minutes."

The officers dispersed to relay the orders, leaving Elliot and Duke to consider their next step.

"Probably makes sense to soften them up before we send in the infantry," Duke said. "But this is going to be a long process. If I were them, I'd have set up multiple fronts to defend. With the number of buildings, it'll be like needles in a haystack."

Elliot drummed his fingers absently. "We're talking days. At a minimum. And if they've decided to do a hit-and-run campaign, maybe weeks."

"Agreed. All we can do is be ready for whatever they hit us with." Duke raised a radio to his lips and keyed the transmit button. "Luis, you in position?"

The handset crackled and Luis's voice answered, "10-4."

Duke explained what they were doing, and advised Luis to stand by until given the order to move forward in a pincer formation. He acknowledged, and Duke clipped the radio back onto his flak jacket.

"I don't like how quiet it is," Elliot said. "They have to know we're here."

"We have to assume so. God knows they've had enough time to figure out how they want to play it."

"It would be nice if Lucas were here. He's got an instinct for these kinds of things."

"Agreed. But he was clear: we're not to wait. Besides, there aren't that many ways to engage."

The officers returned with the patrols, and after confirming radio protocols, they left, heading towards Houston like ants in high grass. Twenty minutes later the mortar squads followed, moving slowly and cautiously through the residential neighborhoods north of the George Bush Airport, every home a potential booby trap or ambush waiting to happen.

An hour crawled by, and then another, and Duke and Elliot traced the patrols' progress on a paper map based on radio position reports.

"This is taking forever. Maybe they've hunkered down in the downtown area or by the refinery? Figured we'd wear ourselves out searching the outlying areas?" Elliot asked.

"Could be. But it would be a bad move, tactically. It'd make it easier for us to tie them down."

A flare lit the sky from several miles away, and the radio screeched with chatter. Moments later the distant pop of gunfire shattered the still of the night, and Duke nodded calmly.

"Looks like we found them. Let's get going," he said, and they jogged to where a trooper was waiting with their horses.

They rode along the highway, and a few minutes went by before the deep boom of mortar shells exploding joined the gunfire. The shooting intensified as they neared until it was a steady roar of heavy machine guns and rifle fire, punctuated by mortar shells detonating.

One of the captains radioed Duke and requested troops be moved forward from the camp. Duke gave the order, and a thousand men mobilized on foot as Luis confirmed that his group was on the move, headed towards the airport and ready to swing west when signaled. The radio traffic was frenzied as patrols engaged the enemy and called in mortar strikes, and Elliot winced with each explosion and long rattle of a big Browning in the near distance. Explosions lit the night ahead as they reached the first mortar crew, the loaders passing shells forward and the gunners watching the impacts through binoculars, and then the radio squawked and an alarmed voice called out, "Crap. I've got four...no, five tanks rolling up the highway. We're going to need some rockets. Hope the troops have some."

One of the field commanders responded from the army, "Roger

that. Thanks for the heads-up."

Elliot looked to Duke. "You want to try to get closer?"

Duke shook his head. "Nothing we can do from up there other than get shot to pieces. Let's see how they do." He toggled the radio back on. "Luis, do you read?"

"Yes."

"You can probably see where the action's happening better than I can from here. Feel free to engage at will."

"You got it."

The next hour was a nonstop barrage of reports from the front lines, where the fighting was furious despite the mortar shelling. The tanks had veered off the highway as they'd neared, and had separated and plunged into the fray, their machine guns mowing down the army troops as they advanced. The patrols were decimated and pinned down like sitting ducks, helpless against the motorized attack.

Luis's voice interrupted the chatter from the battle with bad news of his own.

"We're taking heavy fire from the tanks. And there has to be a couple of thousand cartel spread out here. We're losing more than we're taking down."

"We can send more troops to you," Duke countered.

"Negative. This is turning unwinnable. Request permission to fall back."

Duke glanced at Elliot, who was working his own radio on the tactical channel, receiving a report from the main group. When he lowered the handheld, his face was white.

"Looks like they're too heavily fortified to tackle. We've lost hundreds."

Duke swore. "Order a retreat. This isn't going anywhere but ugly."

Elliot was raising the radio to his lips when a whistle from overhead announced the arrival of the first artillery shells. A geyser of dirt and pavement soared into the air fifty yards behind them as the howitzer shell exploded. More whistles followed, and Duke screamed instructions to the mortar crews to fall back lest they be decimated by the heavy artillery.

Elliot wheeled his panicked horse around as another blast deafened him, and then Duke was at his side and they were galloping north, away from the aborted offensive. The landscape around them became a fiery hell as houses, fields, and vehicles erupted in flames. They rode as fast as the horses could manage, the death from the sky transforming the surroundings into smoking ruins.

Two hours later they were back in the command tent, assessing the damage and taking reports from their officers.

"We took out two of the tanks with rockets, but the others got away, which means they're still out there."

"They didn't pursue us, which makes sense – they killed five for every one we managed to hit."

Luis entered the tent, his face darkened with dirt but his eyes flashing anger. "They cut us apart. They must have had spotters we didn't see, because they were able to land too many hits."

"What's the damage?" Duke asked.

"Out of the thousand? Three hundred and sixty dead, another fifty-seven wounded."

Elliot exhaled sharply. "Christ. That's nearly half your men."

Luis raised his hands helplessly. "I know. We did some damage, but it wasn't worth it. We didn't stand a chance against the big guns and tanks. And unless something changes, I can't see how anything is going to go any better the next attack."

By the time all the reports were in, fully eighteen hundred of their troops had been killed or incapacitated – a staggering number for the relatively short battle. Although the cartel had taken casualties of its own, the toll on the army was like nothing they'd ever seen, and the officers were visibly shaken by the outcome.

Duke rose and tapped the map with his forefinger. "I want patrols making it impossible for the enemy to launch a reprisal attack. Expect them, just like they expected us, and be ready to chop them to pieces if they try. Let them see what an offensive against a dug-in force is like. In the meantime, let's tend to the wounded, and we'll come up with another plan."

Luis shook his head and wiped the grime from his face with his hand. "There's too many of them to do this again, and they're too well equipped. We need to switch up our approach, or the next try may be our last."

"Agreed. Get some rest, but keep enough of your men on alert to fend off a counteroffensive. We'll meet again in the morning."

Luis left with the rest of the officers, and Duke sat heavily at the table across from Elliot.

"We're going to have a serious problem with the men if this keeps up. They didn't sign up to get butchered en masse," Elliot said.

"I know, Elliot. Let me think some, okay? There has to be something else we can try other than throwing our men into machine-gun fire."

Elliot nodded. "I'm all ears. Because it's just a matter of time until they refuse to follow orders and hightail it out of here."

Chapter 44

Julio glared at his lieutenants as he listened to their summaries of the first engagement, their tones subdued. When they finished, he slammed his hand down on the table and pushed to his feet.

"How the hell did we lose half our tanks and so many of our men? I thought we'd spent the last week ensuring they could withstand anything these idiots threw at us!" he snarled.

Jaime, one of his top men, spoke up. "We did. But their mortars did more damage than we'd allowed for. We had no way of knowing how many they had, much less how efficient they were. As to the tanks, they had anti-tank rockets. Still, we did a lot of damage. They lost thousands."

"A third of our best men are dead. We can't withstand another…victory…like that. You assured me that our armor would be decisive. I'd say you overstated its effectiveness, no?"

"We knew the army was capable from our experience in Dallas. And yes, it appears we may have underestimated them somewhat. But the good news is that we dealt a serious blow to their ranks. Their men are rotting in the fields."

"*We* underestimated nothing. You did," Julio said, his tone dangerously quiet.

Jaime looked down. "We still have enough men to defeat them if we strike when they're not expecting it. They're still licking their wounds."

Julio regarded Jaime like he was a variety of unfamiliar insect.

"We have reinforcements arriving in a few days from Mexico," Julio snapped. "Why risk the rest of our men? Let the gringos expend themselves attacking us. If we leave the safety of the areas we've fortified, we're courting problems."

"Normally I would agree. And that's probably what they're expecting – a lull after a big battle while everyone regroups. It's the exact reason we should strike immediately, before they've had a chance to even treat their wounded."

Julio considered the proposal and looked over the gathered men. He fixed his eyes on the closest one. "What do you think, eh?"

"Attacking now is risky. But it could work."

"That isn't much of an opinion. What if you were running things? What would be your choice?"

The man's expression clouded. "I would probably attack. As you said, we'll have more men in a couple of days, so we can afford to be wrong and still wind up winning."

Julio considered his words for a moment and then looked to the next lieutenant. "And you, Edgar? What do you say?"

"It's a bold plan, no doubt. But I think you have an excellent point. If we stay in place, we have the defender's advantage, in that we're picking where we want to fight. If we do it Jaime's way, we lose that."

Jaime cleared his throat. "But we gain the element of surprise."

"Assuming we can move thousands of men undetected."

"Why wouldn't we be able to? We still have, what, three hours until dawn? We could attack at sunrise, when they're still half asleep. Nobody is watching the roads out of town after losing that many men. They have their hands full trying to salvage their wounded."

"You're guessing they'll be unprepared. I don't like guessing. We don't need another Dallas on our hands."

Julio sat at the head of the table as Jaime and Edgar argued, and poured himself a glass of water from a pitcher. He took a sip, made a face, and set it back down. "Can someone explain to me why our water tastes like metal? We sterilize it, don't we?"

"I believe it's the containers we boil it in," Edgar said.

Julio leaned back and considered the men. His gaze settled on Jaime, and his smile was frosty when he spoke.

"If we're going to do this, what will you need?"

"The tanks will make too much noise for a sneak attack, so I would have everyone approach on foot. Leave the horses at least two miles away. And I would come at them from the west and the east, not the south. We can circle around and hit them from both sides. Catch them in a crossfire."

"Why not simply send a patrol and hit them with the howitzers once we know exactly where their camp is?"

"Because it's too easy to move. We might destroy some of their supplies, but there's a limit to what artillery can accomplish against a mobile enemy."

Julio nodded. "I don't want to risk any of the men who are guarding the arms depot or the refinery. We'll need them in place should things not go as planned."

Jaime risked a small smile. "Of course. And in the highly unlikely event anything does go wrong, we could hit them with roaming attacks until the reinforcements arrive. Make them pay for every meter they advance."

Julio fixed Jaime with a hard stare. "You will lead the assault. And Jaime? If it goes poorly, it would be more honorable to die in battle than be shot for failure."

Jaime swallowed hard and met his eyes. "I understand."

"Good. Then gather your men and move immediately. Commandeer whatever resources you need. But don't come back with anything but good news. I won't have losers under my command."

"Of course, *jefe*. I think it's the right move."

Julio leveled a withering stare at him before turning away in dismissal.

"It'd better be."

Chapter 45

Snake dismounted in front of Red's and signaled to his entourage to stay in the saddle while he went inside. He pushed past the door security and made his way to the bar, where the bartender was waiting expectantly. He took a seat, looked around, and leaned forward as the man poured him a shot of tequila.

"You got any news?" Snake demanded.

"One of my boys told me your man got jumped. Left for dead."

Snake's eye twitched as he downed the shot in a swallow. "Who did it? I thought I was clear. He's mine."

The bartender shrugged. "I'm guessing the message got garbled. A few of the regulars decided to take him down. Too tempting to resist." He inclined his head at a man sitting at the end of the bar. "He knows the story."

Snake motioned to the man, who slid over beside him. "So?"

"I'll take you to him. I got a buddy who lives nearby. He saw the whole thing. He'll meet us there."

Snake pushed the shot glass away in disgust. "I'm not looking to make new friends. Where is it?"

"Not far."

"Then let's go."

The man led the group to the alley, where a skinny figure with long hair and a stringy goatee was waiting in the shadows. They dismounted, and Snake approached him.

"What happened? Where is he?" Snake demanded.

"Don't sweat it. Couple of neighborhood-watch types stopped it before he got killed. They took him to a boardinghouse down the street. He's there now."

"What's your name?"

"Nash."

Snake put a hand on his shoulder and squeezed. "Show me, Nash."

Nash winced at the pressure, and when Snake relaxed his grip, he licked his lips. "I watched when they carried him inside. I know what room he's in, too. That oughtta be worth something, right?"

"It will be once you take us there."

"That's all I wanted to hear."

Snake looked around impatiently. "Nash, are we going to stay here all night, or are you going to show me?"

"Let's go."

Nash led them down the street to Emma's, where he pointed to a second-story window that glowed from the light of a lantern. "That's where he is."

"You're sure?"

"Absolutely."

Snake dropped from his horse, and the others did the same. He handed the reins to Nash and the man from the bar. "Watch the animals for us."

Nash exchanged a look with his friend, then spoke to Snake. "When do we get paid?"

"After we confirm you told the truth. Don't worry, you'll get what's coming to you."

Snake pointed to the boardinghouse's entrance and the stable area. "Two of you guard the back exit. The others, come with me."

A pair of gunmen peeled off and went to the rear of the building as Snake led the remaining three up the steps to the front porch. He tried the door and, finding it locked, gestured to his men. The largest stepped back and then kicked it with all his might, shattering it and knocking it inward. Snake pushed him aside and dashed into the darkened interior and then up the stairs to the second floor, his guards close behind him. He reached the landing, drew his pistol, and made his way to Lucas's room, where he twisted the knob and then stood aside and whispered to his men, "Locked. Get it over with."

The big man slammed his boot into the door, and it burst inward. Snake darted into the room with his pistol and rushed to the bed, his men in tow, and fired twice into the form beneath the blanket, a demonic grin on his face. The smile transformed into a frown when he threw the covers aside and found himself staring at nothing but pillows arranged to resemble a body.

The window shattered, and a bullet thwacked into the chest of the guard beside Snake. He dropped his rifle and clutched at the wound, and then another shot downed a second guard as Snake and the remaining gunman hit the floor, ignoring the shards of broken glass littering the floorboards.

Gunshots exploded from outside as Snake's guards in the rear engaged the shooter from the side of the house. Snake dog-crawled to the door and murmured to his surviving guard, "This is a trap. We need to find the back door and get out of here."

They exited the room and stood and then ran to the stairway and took the steps two at a time. At the ground floor, Snake hurried to the rear of the building, ignoring the shocked faces that greeted him from the doorways along the corridor, and burst through the back door, brandishing his pistol.

Gunfire from the side of the house continued, and when his guards had expended their magazines and there was a pause in the shooting, he called to them.

"Come on. Let's go."

The two men slapped new magazines into their rifles and began working their way to Snake around the corner. Multiple shots rang out from a building across the street, and one of the pair crumpled to the dirt with blood streaming from his gaping mouth. The other made it to safety, and Snake indicated a wall that enclosed the grounds. "Help me over that. He's got us pinned down here."

They sprinted to the wall, and the two guards heaved Snake up. He clambered over the wall, and one of them helped the other up. The guard returned the favor and pulled his companion to the top, and they dropped to the other side and hit the ground running after Snake, who was already halfway to the rear of the home that occupied the lot, pistol swinging wildly as he ran.

Lucas changed magazines and peered through his night vision scope at the side of the boardinghouse, where the body of the downed guard lay facedown on the cobblestone path that ringed it. He waited and, when nobody else appeared, descended the steps to the lobby of the office building where he'd lain in wait. His left eye was swollen partially shut, blood crusted his forehead beneath his hat as well as his cheek, and his ribs and kidneys felt like he'd wrestled a grizzly; but he was alive. And hell-bent on finishing the fight now.

He looked out at the street and then darted across to the boardinghouse, staying low, his M4 ready for battle, his savaged features determined. When he got to Emma's, he edged along the side of the house and, when he reached the back, spotted the trampled ground beneath the wall and ran to it, ignoring the pain from his side, focused on tracking the survivors wherever they went.

Chapter 46

Houston, Texas

A radio crackled to life in the command tent where Duke, Elliot, and Luis were slumbering on army cots. Duke reached for it as the others groaned.

"Command," a voice said. "Inbound enemy troops headed your way. Estimate contact in…ten minutes, tops."

"Size of the force?"

"Large. At least a thousand, maybe more."

"Composition?"

"Infantry."

"No tanks or horse-drawn artillery?"

"Negative."

"Roger that."

Duke switched on the solar-powered LED lantern and pulled on his boots as the others did the same, and then radioed his field commanders to alert them to the threat. They responded immediately, and within minutes the camp was bustling as men rushed to man the defenses they'd prepared for just such an eventuality.

Luis watched from the tent and then turned to Duke. "We should get the mortar squads ready to hit them when they're a hundred or so yards out."

Duke nodded. "Good thinking. Might as well make it as damaging as possible for them."

"I'm going to order every Browning we have set up. Now," Elliot suggested.

Duke frowned. "I suppose there's no point in conserving ammo at this point. Do it."

Elliot jogged off toward the wagons, and Luis bolted to where the mortars were lined up, pointing at the sky. Men hurried to follow their orders, and by the time the first enemy was sighted from the camp, everything was in position.

"Wait until they get close enough that they can't escape," Duke whispered into his radio. "We'll lead with the mortars; at which point, open fire. I want this one and done, not an hour-long battle. Clear?"

The officers acknowledged, and Duke and Elliot watched through binoculars as the enemy neared like an army of ants, creeping slowly through the grounds of ruined houses as they advanced. When they were thronged at the edge of the homes closest to the darkened camp, Duke spoke softly into the radio.

"Mortars, fire. Machine guns, fire when the first shells explode."

A dozen projectiles shot into the air, and seven seconds later, the houses exploded in blasts of siding and human flesh. The heavy .50-caliber machine guns opened up from the camp nests and mowed down the cartel shooters who charged straight at them, urged forward by the hundreds of men behind them who were being shredded to pieces by the mortars. The fully jacketed slugs sliced through the walls of the sheetrock and plywood homes, sawing everything in their wake. Roofs and walls collapsed under their relentless streams of bullets as another volley of mortar rounds lit the predawn, exploding through the neighborhood.

"Move the next volley two hundred yards away, and then the next two fifty," Luis ordered the gunners, who hurriedly adjusted the sights and lowered the trajectory slightly to comply. Another dozen shells destroyed the next rows of homes, and then the next, and the next, as the mortars extended their devastation farther and farther from the camp, catching any enemy that was trying to fall back in an organized manner.

Duke lowered his binoculars and called to his commanders again.

"Finish up with the big guns, and send out the troops to mop up. Use the grenade launchers as much as possible. I want as few casualties in our ranks as we can manage."

Several minutes later, a wave of troops charged toward the houses through the haze of smoke that hung in the darkness. Running gun battles began as they engaged with enemy gunmen who'd managed to hang back or had retreated before the mortar inundation had reached them. Luis brought up the rear with several Browning squads, two men lugging the heavy guns, and another pair hauling ammo cans filled with ammunition belts. They trotted to a three-story building at the edge of the residential neighborhood where one of their spotters had hidden, and mounted the stairway to the top floor.

They hurriedly set the guns on tripods, and Luis scanned the area beyond for targets. He saw a cluster of enemy shooters near the parking lot of a strip mall, and indicated to the night-vision-equipped gunners where to direct their fire. They locked and loaded the big guns and began hammering the enemy position at a rate of hundreds of rounds per minute. Luis watched through the spyglasses as the enemy attempted to scatter, but most were brought down by the streams of lead. The onslaught was over in under a minute, leaving at least thirty that Luis could see lying dead on the pavement.

When the area within their range was clear of enemy, they repeated their maneuver at another building, and then another. At the point the sun was rising, it was obvious that the enemy force had been gutted, and the only remaining shoot-outs were with isolated pockets that the troops were taking out with grenades and rifle fire.

Luis returned to the camp as the sun hung low in the sky, wending through corpses that littered the neighborhoods around it. When he reached the command tent, many of the officers were already there, reporting their casualties to Duke and Elliot. Luis entered the tent and took a seat on a camp chair in the corner and listened as the grim accounting continued. When the last officer was finished, Duke cleared his throat and looked to Elliot, who straightened and addressed the men.

"Good job, all. Looks like we lost eighty-seven men, with another thirty-two wounded. A rough estimate places the number of cartel casualties in the high hundreds, so we took down eight to ten for every man we lost. Still, we can expect additional attacks at any time, as we don't know how many more men they have to throw at us, so we need to stay on high alert for the duration."

"Have we got a new plan for how to take the city?" one of the captains asked, his voice ragged from fatigue.

"We're working on it," Elliot said, his tone making clear he didn't want to discuss it any further.

"We're sitting ducks if we just wait for them to attack," another observed.

Duke nodded. "Agreed. To that end, I want to move the camp another mile north and fortify it. We passed a mall on the way in. That looked like it would be ideal, with nests on the roof and spotters in the surrounding cell towers."

"Move?" one of the officers echoed.

"We'll need to anyway, unless anyone wants to smell a thousand dead decomposing. So we might as well establish a hardened defendable base while we strategize. No point in sitting out in the open. And after this, we can't assume they won't bombard our current location with artillery fire. I certainly would if I had limitless howitzers to bring to bear."

The men grumbled but agreed, and departed to issue the order to break camp to the exhausted men.

Elliot eyed Duke and Luis when they were alone, and shook his head.

"We're playing defense. We need an offensive plan, or it's just a matter of time until they get lucky with another attack."

"Agreed," Duke said, "but there isn't much we can do right now, so let's focus on getting somewhere safe first, and then we can go back to figuring out how to take Houston. Prepare to move in an hour."

"It'll endanger many of the wounded to be moved again," Elliot said.

"True," Luis said.

Duke sighed. "Everyone in this tent knows that the wounded are largely going to die no matter what we do. We don't have adequate antibiotics to stop most of the infections that they'll develop, and our surgery is pretty basic, so let's not pretend. We'll do everything we can, but we're going to lose the majority. We can't take actions based on the survival of the walking dead. Sorry for being harsh, but it's the truth. So plan on moving out, and do the best you can to see to the transport of the wounded. Luis, if you can spearhead that effort, I'd appreciate it."

Luis nodded, but his expression was dour. "You may be right, but I don't have to like it."

"I wish I wasn't, my friend. I wish I wasn't."

Chapter 47

Lucas studied the street in front of the house that backed onto Emma's, noting the clear footprints in the coating of dirt that seemed to cover every inch of the city. The prints set off to the west, and Lucas followed them to the next intersection, where they looped back toward the boardinghouse main street. He paused occasionally to scan the area with his night vision scope and quickly realized that the prints were headed back to the alley where he'd been waylaid.

He confirmed his impression when they stopped at a spot near the alley mouth, where a fresh mound of horse dung told him what they'd been in search of. He walked in concentric circles until he spotted three sets of hoofprints leading west again. Confident in what he was now tracking, he returned to the boardinghouse for Tango, who was wide awake from the gunfight and eager to be released from the confinement of the stable.

Lucas saddled the stallion, climbed atop his back, and directed him to the alley, where he picked up the trail. The tracks led straight along the street, away from Red's, so they had a different destination in mind. He lost them and had to double back when they made another turn, but quickly found them again and continued his pursuit, secure that he would eventually catch up with the three men and rid the world of their presence.

He knew he hadn't hit Snake because he'd seen him go to ground in the room. Lucas hadn't had a clear shot at him, and by the time he'd neutralized some of his muscle, Snake had disappeared from view. So one of the riders had to be the ex-Crew chief, and he'd soon get a chance to pay him back for the abduction and murder of Sierra.

He pushed the thought to the back of his mind. He needed all of his wits about him now, and the beating he'd endured hadn't helped. The last thing he wanted were his thoughts meandering away from the business at hand, so he exercised every bit of mental discipline he could muster to focus on tracking the miscreants through the night.

Another turn, and he paused at the corner and took a reading on the street ahead. The commercial area was transitioning to a residential neighborhood, which was potentially bad news for him, given that some of the houses could be occupied by occupants who might pose as much of a threat as his quarry.

It was still dark when he arrived at the outer perimeter of an airport, where the tracks disappeared onto the grounds. He dismounted and tied Tango to a tree by the edge of the tarmac and proceeded on foot, using his M4 scope to scan the buildings, most of which were hangars and maintenance sheds, by the look of them. The hoofprints led past the hangars toward the terminal.

Lucas stopped when he spied horses lashed to a passenger trolley by the main building. He ducked behind a barrel and surveyed the animals and swept the area with the rifle, searching for any other signs of life. His eye was drawn to a faint glow upstairs from one of the terminal windows, and after assuring himself that there was nobody guarding the doors on the ground level, he continued to the building, using the abandoned planes for cover.

He reached one of the steel doors and pressed his ear against it. After listening for a half minute, he tried the handle, only to find it locked. He moved to the next one and then the next, with no better luck. He looked along the long building and then made for a service ladder embedded in the wall, that led up past the second-floor passenger lounges to the roof.

Lucas pulled himself upward, grimacing at the spikes of agony from his ribs, and when he reached the roof, lay on it for a moment, breathing heavily, before getting to his feet and moving to the nearest access door.

Locked.

Lucas examined the jamb, leaned his rifle against the housing, and drew his knife. He worked at the top hinge pin, and after a painful two minutes, managed to free it. The other two proved more resistant, and he wasted the better part of twenty minutes prying them loose. When they were resting on the roof, he heaved at the door and lifted it clear, and then leaned it beside his M4 before grabbing the gun and entering the stairwell.

The door to the passenger lounge wasn't locked, and he eased it open, rifle in hand. The cavernous terminal was dark and silent, except for the glow he'd seen from outside, at the far end. He slid through the gap and crept toward the light, sticking to the shadows and staying low. Lucas was within fifty yards of the glow when a piece of debris crunched beneath his boot, loud as a pistol shot in the empty terminal, and he froze, his pulse hammering in his ears.

A gunman swung an AK around the edge of a storefront and swept the space with it, searching for a target. Lucas was grateful that he didn't have any NV gear, or he'd have been dead. As it was, the shooter's eyesight hadn't fully adjusted from light to pitch darkness, which gave Lucas just enough time to draw a bead on him and fire at his exposed face.

The round struck the man's upper dental plate and blew half the back of his head off as it mushroomed and tumbled through his skull, and he collapsed in a heap. Lucas was already in motion, closing the distance to the shop while cutting toward the windows across the passenger waiting area, where the seats would provide some cover. He was in the midst of a row of seats when another shooter popped from the doorway and began spraying the hall with bullets.

The gunman's magazine ran dry, and he ducked back into the safety of the store, giving Lucas a chance to continue moving to where he would have a clearer shot into the interior. The snap of the new magazine being seated and the rifle's bolt closing announced more undisciplined shooting to come, and Lucas lay flat on the seats so he couldn't be seen from the shooter's vantage point. When the man appeared at the edge of the slot, Lucas was able to fix the scope's reticule on his torso and get off two shots, both of which hit him in the side of the chest, where his flak vest didn't have any plates to protect him.

The man screamed and slumped to the floor, his rifle firing as he reflexively squeezed the trigger. Lucas used the deafening roar to close the distance still further, and he ignored the dying thug's shooting in favor of doing a methodical grid search of the visible area inside the shop. The shooter's rifle ran out of bullets and the terminal fell silent, leaving Lucas to watch and wait.

His ears were ringing like church bells as he remained motionless in the closest section of passenger seating, rifle aimed at the store. A scrape greeted him from deep inside, and then the light flickered out, plunging the area into complete darkness. Lucas pressed his eye to the night vision scope and watched the interior of the shop in the eerie greenish hue, thanking providence that he'd charged it before leaving camp and that the battery was still holding up almost two weeks later.

A figure dashed from the storefront and away from the dead men, pistol in hand. Lucas flicked his firing selector to burst mode and rattled off a three-round burst at him, but he was moving too fast and the shots missed, instead punching holes in the wall behind the runner. Lucas tried again, and this time at least one of the rounds hit home – the running man stumbled and then fell to the granite floor with a heavy thud.

Pistol shots pounded into the seats near Lucas, and he hurled himself to the side as a hole appeared where his head had been a nanosecond earlier. He resisted the impulse to return fire, and instead crawled along the floor until he had a better shot at the downed man. Lucas switched the firing selector to single shot and squeezed off a round that caught the man in the abdomen. An anguished cry echoed through the hall and trailed off to a gurgle, and Lucas struggled to his feet and closed on the downed figure, who was trying to reach the pistol he'd dropped when the second shot had hit him.

Lucas approached and stood over him, rifle leveled at his head. He took in the man's facial tattoos and shaved head, and he gave a grim smile.

"Well, well. You must be Snake," he whispered. Lucas regarded his bloody hands clenching his stomach, and the look of pain on his face. "That's gotta hurt. Probably almost as much as burying Sierra did."

Snake spat blood at Lucas's feet and tried to speak, but only managed a groan. Lucas kicked his pistol away and stared down at him. "That all of you, or you got some more shitbirds around here?"

Snake growled a physically impossible curse, and Lucas's tight smile faded.

"Heard being gut shot's the worst way to die. Can take hours to go, and it gets worse every minute." Lucas leaned down and picked up Snake's gun. "You aren't much to look at, are you? For all that, you'll die sitting in your own filth. Fitting."

Snake moaned under his breath, and this time when he spoke, Lucas had no problem making out his words.

"Kill me."

Lucas shook his head. "Nah. I'll let the devil decide when to take you to hell. You'll get no help from me. You earned your reward a thousand times over. Enjoy it."

Lucas backed away from Snake and moved to where the second gunman was struggling for breath. He toed the man's rifle away and knelt beside him.

"You could hang on for a while, or I could end this for you now. Depends on whether you talk or not. What were you doing here, at the airport?"

The man's eyes met Lucas's, and he whispered hoarsely, "Got a plane."

"A plane? Where?"

"Out on the runway. Twin prop. Pilot…lives in the…hangar. Going to…Houston…"

Lucas stood and shook his head. "It runs?"

The man's face twisted in agony, and he nodded weakly.

"Just the pilot, or does he have friends?"

The man blinked twice. "Alone, I think."

"Why Houston?"

The man haltingly explained Snake's plan. Lucas asked a couple of questions and, when he was satisfied, considered the wounded man for a long moment.

The man coughed, and blood colored his lips. His eyes locked on Lucas's again. "Do it. Please. Nuthin' more to tell."

Lucas's rifle barked once, and a hole materialized in the wounded man's forehead. Lucas looked back at Snake, who was curled in a fetal position, and then walked with heavy steps to the nearest stairway.

Out on the tarmac, Lucas scanned the abandoned jets until he spotted a smaller twin-engine prop plane to the side of the main runway. He jogged toward it and slowed as he approached, rifle at the ready. When he reached the plane, he looked past it to the hangars and saw movement at the door of one.

Lucas fired a warning shot that tore a chunk of pavement loose two feet from the figure by the hangar door, and called out, "Keep your hands where I can see them."

The man raised his hands slowly. "Got no beef with you."

Lucas stopped four yards from him. Seeing he was unarmed, he lowered his weapon. "You the pilot?"

The man kept his hands up. "That's right. Name's Clinton. What's it to you?"

"I'm afraid your friends aren't going to be able to make it."

Clinton regarded Lucas. "No friends of mine. Customers. That's all."

"You should be pickier about who you work for."

Clinton shrugged. "Not a ton of people looking to pay to fly anywhere."

Lucas smiled, but his face hurt, and he relaxed his expression to cause the least discomfort. "I might be a buyer. What were they going to pay?"

Clinton named a high figure, which Lucas wasted no time pretending to consider. "I'll match that. My differences with them shouldn't cut into your business. When can you leave?"

Clinton looked Lucas over. "Half in advance, half when we land."

"That's fair. When can you leave?" Lucas repeated.

"Should be able to take off this afternoon."

"Perfect. I'll be back in a few hours with payment."

Clinton's gaze lingered on Lucas's bruised and beaten face. "Am I going to have any problems with their...associates?"

Lucas shook his head. "You shouldn't. Anyone comes by and asks what happened, you have no idea. But the chances of that happening are pretty slim. No love lost for that kind. Air's cleaner for them being dead."

Lucas returned to Tango and rode him back into town. Tyler looked like he'd just woken up when Lucas arrived at headquarters. He was clearly surprised by Lucas's appearance, although he tried not to show it.

"Sir, what happened?"

"Fell out of bed. Look, I need one of your men to deliver my horse to Houston. If he can leave today, that would be good."

"No problem. But where are you headed?" Tyler asked.

"Same place. Just taking a shortcut."

He told Tyler about the plane. Tyler whistled softly. "Well, I'll be damned."

"Maybe. But in the meantime, radio Duke and let him know I'll be there by evening. Find out where he's camped."

Tyler went inside and came back out ten minutes later with a scrap of paper. "These are the coordinates off his map. He said to tell you they attacked, but it didn't go well."

"Did he elaborate?"

Tyler shook his head. "Didn't want to say too much on the radio. But he didn't sound happy."

"All right. Can you find someone to ride with me to the airport and bring Tango back here? He'll need to be fed and watered before leaving for Texas."

"Sure. I'd be honored. But…might want to have my medic clean and stitch you up. And you eaten anything? The cook made breakfast. Eggs, tortillas, beans."

"I suppose I could use both."

After they ate, the medic attended to Lucas, and then Tyler and a squad of five troops escorted Lucas back to the airport. It was midafternoon by the time they made it, and Clinton was performing some last minute checks when they arrived.

Lucas dismounted, handed Tyler Tango's reins, patted the big horse and whispered a goodbye to him, and then went to the pilot and counted out two gold coins. "You get the other two when we land."

Clinton balanced one of the coins on his finger and tapped the edge with the other. A high-pitched ringing emanated from it, and he nodded approvingly. "Mister, you got yourself a flight. Climb aboard and we'll get this show on the road. Just you?"

"That's right." Lucas looked in the rear of the plane at the bags Snake's men had placed there. "What is all that?"

"No idea. They didn't say, and I didn't look."

Lucas crawled in the cargo area and tried one of the zippers before realizing it was locked with a tie wrap. He drew his knife and sliced through it, opened it, checked inside briefly, and then re-zipped it. He did the same with the others and, when he was finished, hopped down. "That extra weight going to be a problem?"

"Shouldn't be. I allowed for eight more warm bodies, so we'll be well below the safety threshold." Clinton explained about the ethanol.

"How long will it take to get there?"

"Maybe three hours or so, depending on whether we get a headwind. We'll be flying low, like no more than two thousand feet, and slow, on account of the fuel."

"So make it by nightfall?" Lucas asked.

"Thereabouts. Where exactly you want me to set down?"

"Got a map?"

"You bet."

"Let's get strapped in and I'll show you. Sounds like we have time to hash it out on the trip."

"If you've got to use the bathroom, now's the time."

"Thanks. I'm good."

Five minutes later the plane was rolling down the runway, bouncing over potholes as it picked up speed. Near the middle of the runway, it lifted into the air and banked lazily over the buildings as it made a gentle turn south. Lucas watched the landscape blur by, and after they'd leveled off, told the pilot to wake him a half hour outside Houston so they could figure out the best place to put down, and shut his eyes, hand on his pistol as he drifted off.

Chapter 48

Houston, Texas

Incoming shells screamed overhead as Duke bellowed orders into his radio. Explosions erupted in the mall buildings where the army had taken shelter, and panicked men and horses raced to get away from the unexpected and deadly bombardment that had begun minutes before, in broad daylight, just as the troops had relaxed after moving the entire camp.

The artillery fire had begun like a summer storm, coming out of nowhere, with no warning, the guns so far off that their firing was a faint thunder from somewhere south of the city center. That the cartel must have had a spotter who'd established their new location was a given, but it was too late to do anything about it now, when each explosion threatened to kill dozens and destroy the army's precious stores of food, water, and ammo.

"Fall back! Put a mile between us and the mall. Now!"

The troops scrambled to get clear of the kill zone that the mall had become, and teams of men half-dragged terrified mules hitched to wagons away in an effort to clear the destruction and salvage the cargo. Duke spurred his horse north to where Elliot and Luis were supervising setting up a new camp off the highway, a ten-minute ride farther away from Houston.

"We have to take out their artillery or we're dead," Luis said.

"Right, but our spotters have located their guns, and they're too far for us to hit. Well out of mortar range."

"Damn," Elliot said. "But smart of them. This way they can pick us off at their leisure, and we can't do anything about it."

Duke nodded. "They're obviously getting our location from forward scouts. So first order of business has to be finding those and neutralizing them, or we're going to be facing this every few hours." He looked to Luis. "I want patrols searching for anyone who could be cartel. Allocate as many men as it takes to ensure we're safe. We can't afford a repeat of this."

Luis issued instructions to his subordinates and rode off. Elliot shook his head and frowned as he watched the mall disintegrate into rubble through his binoculars. When he lowered them, his expression was dour. "It's a viable strategy. They've destroyed a fair amount of our supplies this last round. We only have enough food to go another couple of days. If we don't take the city, we'll be fighting on empty stomachs."

"Whoever is commanding them is savvy. I'll give them that."

"Especially since they have fewer men. Our scouts confirmed that they're severely undermanned after the last infantry attack. But they have the advantage of artillery and can obviously transport as many shells as they need to their position with the fuel and their trucks."

"Which is why we need to take the refinery without destroying it. That fuel's the whole reason we're here."

"At this point, we'll be lucky if we can get out with our skin. These attacks are depleting our resources in a big way."

"You don't have to tell me."

The drone of an engine from the north greeted them, and they turned and shielded their faces from the last of the sun's rays. Duke pointed at the sky.

"You see that?"

Elliot followed Duke's finger. "He's coming in for a landing." His eyes widened. "That's Lucas! Has to be. Tyler said he'd be here before dark!"

They watched as the plane shed altitude and then hovered over the asphalt before its wheels smoked on the pavement and it slowed, engines roaring. It rolled to a stop, and they galloped over. Duke grinned from ear to ear when Lucas dropped from the cockpit, though his smile turned to a scowl when he saw Lucas's mangled face.

"What's going on?" Lucas called over the engines.

"Artillery. They're shelling the new camp."

"How bad is it?"

"Bad enough. We've got to do something. We were thinking a final assault at dawn."

"Hold that thought. There's another option. Do you know where their guns are?"

Elliot nodded. "We do. One of our scouts confirmed the location. Near the refinery in Deer Park, which is well out of mortar range. Which is also where a lot of their troops are hunkered down."

"Show me on a map. I may have a solution." Lucas withdrew the map from his vest and unfolded it. "Where are they?"

Duke studied it and pointed to a spot in southern Houston. "There."

"Snake was planning to fly in," Lucas explained. "Apparently the Crew had been working on getting a missile system working at the air force base before they were overthrown. If we have men who are familiar with those systems, I can fly in with them, and we can see if we can get them functional and targeted on the cartel's artillery."

Duke and Elliot looked at each other. "I'll put out the word. With as many vets as we have, there has to be someone."

"Tell them it's the MGM-140 system."

"It might take a while."

"That's fine. I'll need some NV gear for the pilot and myself. I'd prefer to fly in after dark. Hate to have someone shoot us down, and we're an easy target while it's still light out. Let's try for an hour from now?"

"I'll alert the officers. We've obviously got our hands full, so it might take longer."

"I figured. Any idea where Ruby is?"

"I'll check."

"Please. I'm going to stay with the plane. When you get a chance, I'll need some men to unload it. We've got a bunch of grenades and mortar tubes. Oh, and some gold."

"Gold?" Duke exclaimed. "How is it that every time you go off, you come back with treasure, and all I ever get is saddle sore?"

"My positive disposition."

"Must be." He eyed Lucas. "What happened to your face?"

"Little complication. But I'll live."

Lucas returned to Clinton and gave him the two coins he owed him. He indicated the army. "You got enough fuel to do a short run?"

Clinton checked the fuel gauges. "We did better than I expected. What did you have in mind?"

Lucas told him, and the pilot made a face. "You're frigging nuts."

"Couple more ounces in it for you. You a businessman or not?"

Clinton thought about it. "Three and we're talking."

"Done. I'll get this unloaded and we can get out of here. If it's safe to shut down the engines, do so. Save gas."

Clinton killed the motors. The shelling had slowed, and ten minutes later the area was quiet, other than men screaming instructions and the groans of the wounded.

It was dark when Duke returned with Ruby and three men. He introduced them to Lucas after Ruby had hugged him and confirmed that the children were safe, if terrified from the shelling.

"What do you have planned that you need an old woman for?"

"You're a whiz at computers, if I recall."

"I wouldn't say that. Better than some, perhaps."

"Modesty doesn't suit you." Lucas looked over at Duke. "Can you unload while I talk to Ruby?"

"Yes, kemosabe."

Lucas walked with Ruby to the far edge of the highway and explained about the missile system. She rolled her eyes. "That's not some ordinary computer, Lucas. You're talking about trying to hack a military system that I know nothing about."

"That's about the size of it."

"I have no idea if I can do it."

"Only one way to find out." Lucas paused. "Those three have experience with the launchers. They can brief you on what to expect on the flight in."

"Behind enemy lines? In the hopes I can figure it out? That's crazy, Lucas."

"We don't have much choice. We're launching a final all-or-nothing attack first thing tomorrow. If we can't disable the big guns, we're toast, and this was all for nothing."

Her brow creased. "No pressure, then."

"None at all. As usual."

She sighed. "All I can do is try."

"That's all I'm asking."

They walked back to the plane, where the cases from the hold were now on the pavement. Lucas briefed the men on what he was planning and turned toward the plane. "The sooner we get there, the sooner we'll know if this can work. Duke? Rustle up some men to stow this stuff somewhere safe, and put that small bag in the command tent under guard. Understand?"

"Will do."

"Give me your radio. You have another handset?"

"In the tent. That's about half charged."

"Let's hope that's enough."

Duke shrugged and looked away. "I'll add it to my wish list."

Chapter 49

Lucas sat in the cargo area of the plane with Ruby and the men as it bounced along at 3500 feet, the higher altitude to make it harder for any enemy fire to hit it, assuming they could even locate it in the night sky. It was running without lights, everyone equipped with night vision goggles, the engines purring at halfway to redline.

"Explain about the guidance system," Lucas ordered a man named Kelly.

"It's a combination of a computer, a GPS, and a gyro. Not sure what generation we're talking, so the complexity is a question mark until we see what we're dealing with. We'll also need some way to power them. After this many years, they're guaranteed to be dead."

"Could that have neutralized the security system?" Ruby asked.

"Doubtful. I mean, anything's possible, but I wouldn't count on it."

Lucas thought for a moment. "Assuming we can get them working, what's the range? Payload?"

"Easily over a hundred kilometers, even if it's the oldest generation, so range won't be an issue. Payload will depend on the model, but at least a hundred bomblets."

"So these are cluster bombs?" Lucas asked.

"That's right."

"And you can program them accurately?"

"Should be able to," Kelly said. "But there are a lot of moving parts. The launcher. The solid fuel. The guidance system. Whether or not the GPS system is working. None of these are givens." He paused. "We'll know more once we see what condition they're in. Although you said the Crew was working on getting them operational, which implies they didn't. If that's the case, they may be nonstarters, because they had to have had some veterans with experience on them trying."

Lucas shook his head. "Maybe. Maybe not. They were also trying to get the refinery working, but it didn't take the cartel long to do what the Crew couldn't. They lost their best men when Magnus attacked Shangri-La, so the ones who were left were the least competent."

The plane began dropping, and Lucas called out over his shoulder to Clinton, "We there?"

"I'm going to do a pass to confirm the runway's clear."

Clinton shed altitude as they neared the field, and did a run over it before executing a gentle curve. "Looks fine. Grab something in case it's a bumpy landing."

He set the plane down gently, and it glided to the far end of the runway. Lucas studied the buildings and turned to the men. "What are we looking for?"

"Probably M270s."

"What's that?" Ruby asked.

"Mobile rocket launcher. It'll look like a big, boxy tank without the turret. We called them the finger of god. One launcher could carry enough missiles or rockets to blanket a square kilometer and destroy everything in it."

"Sounds like just what the doctor ordered."

Clinton rolled to a stop, and Lucas leaned forward. "Kill the engines so we don't attract attention."

"Customer's always right."

They disembarked and surveyed the area. Nothing jumped out, and Lucas instructed the men to split up and maintain radio contact. Ruby accompanied him, and they strode over to one of the long hangars, looking like two horror film aliens with their NV goggles covering their eyes and noses.

"It would have been helpful if they'd given you a better description of what we're looking for," she complained.

"I'm constantly disappointed by my enemies' unwillingness to open up to me."

She chuckled. "Why, Lucas, I do believe you just made a joke."

"Put a pin in it."

She slowed. "You take care of the Sierra situation?"

"They paid."

"I never doubted you. But it's been rough for the kids."

"I expect."

"Be good if you stuck around for a while."

"One thing at a time. I've got to figure out a way to defeat the cartel in the next eight hours before I try for father of the year."

"You know what I mean, and you know I'm right."

"Don't rub it in."

Lucas's radio crackled, and Kelly's voice sounded from it.

"I'm by the tower. There's an M270 here."

"On our way."

They ran to the tower, where the rest were waiting. Kelly was in the cab of the launcher, and when he saw Lucas, he hopped down. "No key."

"Can you hotwire it?" Lucas asked.

"I'll give it a shot."

Two minutes later, he emerged again. "It's dead. Not even a spark. So that's the first problem. You can't operate the launcher without power."

"Maybe we can use the plane's alternator to jump it, or bridge power from it to the launcher?"

"Possible. But do we have any cabling?"

"We can cut some from the buildings."

"Okay. Let me see if I can figure out a way to check the missiles."

Kelly climbed up onto the top of the massive launcher and fiddled with a panel. Ruby edged closer to Lucas and leaned into him.

"You realize what a long shot this is?"

"We have to try. Snake felt like he could get them working. So no reason we can't."

"Maybe he had information we didn't? Or maybe he got it wrong."

"Anything's possible."

Kelly lowered himself down the ladder at the back of the launcher and approached Lucas. "Let's see if we can power it. There's no way I can do anything with the missiles with the launcher closed up like this. Can't get to them."

Kelly and Ruby walked to the nearest building while Lucas retraced his steps to the plane and explained what he needed Clinton to do. The pilot eyed him skeptically, but agreed. "OK, buddy, it's your dime."

He started the engines and rolled the plane close to the launcher, and Kelly and Ruby returned with a coil of electrical cabling filched from the building installation. Clinton killed the engines, and Kelly connected one end to the starboard engine's alternator while Ruby held the other by the launcher. He joined her and twisted the ends to the positive and negative poles of one of the batteries, and gave Clinton the thumbs-up signal to restart the engine.

Twenty minutes later, it was obvious that even though the gambit had worked, the missiles were a different story.

"They're dead. No way to get power to the gyro computer. Assuming the GPS system is even functional," Kelly said.

"I don't think it is or we'd have used it on the plane," Lucas said.

"Then we're dead in the water," Ruby said. "I can't try to access the computers if they don't power up."

"How the hell did Snake plan to do it?" Lucas fumed.

"At this point we'll never know, but there's no way we're going to get anything accomplished here," Kelly said.

"There's absolutely no way to jury-rig something?"

Kelly shook his head. "Sorry. These are relatively sophisticated systems." He looked to the other two specialists. "Anything I missed?"

The men had a terse discussion amongst themselves and turned back to Lucas. "There's nothing we can do. Maybe if we had a few days and a generator and a backup battery source. But not here and now."

Lucas trudged back to the plane with Ruby and the men and told Clinton to return to the camp. The plane was silent as it lifted off, the men lost in their thoughts, the mood glum at their attempt having failed more miserably then they could have imagined. They were dropping again as they neared the highway when Lucas turned to Kelly.

"What do you know about mortars?"

"Fair bit. That's pretty primitive tech. Why?"

"Do the shells explode on impact from the force of gravity, or is there something that firing them activates?"

Kelly looked at Lucas with a confused expression. "No, they're basically falling at the speed of gravity when they drop. So it's impact that detonates them."

Lucas nodded. "Then we're not dead yet."

The plane touched down and rolled toward the new camp location, and Lucas leaned forward between the seats to speak to Clinton. When they stopped twenty yards from the camp, Clinton turned to Lucas.

"Not sure I have enough fuel to make it there and back, then to Oklahoma. So unless you can buy this plane and make it worth my while, the answer's no."

"Name a price."

Clinton thought for several beats. "Fifteen ounces. In advance. No offense, but I need to know you have it."

Lucas offered a hand. "Done. And I do." He looked to Kelly. "You up for another run?"

"What did you have in mind?"

Lucas explained his thinking, and Kelly's face lit up. "I'll have the men bring the cases."

Lucas checked his watch. "On the double. We're burning time we don't have."

Chapter 50

Lucas sat beside Clinton in the cockpit as the men finished loading the cases containing the mortar shells with the mustard gas into the plane. Elliot leaned against the fuselage and watched as he spoke in a soft voice with Lucas.

"This is brilliant, assuming they don't shoot you out of the sky," Elliot said.

Lucas glanced over at Clinton. "Slim chance of that. We'll be running dark, plus staying high enough that it would be almost impossible."

"I'll confess I have some ethical misgivings about it, though. I mean, it's chemical warfare. I know what mustard gas does to humans. It's as ugly as anything you can imagine, Lucas."

"Way I see it, it's us or them. We didn't invade Houston. They did. So they're the ones asking for this fight. And they've killed how many of our men? Couple of thousand by now?" Lucas sighed. "Look, I know it doesn't sit right with you. It's not my first choice either. But we have no chance of victory unless we take out their artillery and the majority of their men. And let's not forget – these are cartel killers we're talking about. The worst of the worst in Mexico, who kill over a few dollars. Slaughter whole families for amusement. If I'm supposed to get all weepy over sending a passel of them to meet their maker rather than our troops getting butchered, I'm afraid I'm out of tears."

"I'm not saying we shouldn't do it or that we have any choice. I'm just saying it's a horrible way to go."

"No question. But I'd go walk through our wounded and watch some of them die over the next few hours if you're that conflicted, and understand if we're unsuccessful, that's going to be just about everyone in the army by tomorrow." Lucas paused. "It's us or them. And I'm damn sure going to do everything in my power to make sure it doesn't wind up being us."

Duke approached, and Lucas twisted to address him. "Be ready to fall back to Dallas if something goes wrong," Lucas said. "If we can't neutralize the big guns, a dawn attack's suicide."

"Roger that. Although we're going to be eating the horses if we do. We'll be out of food soon."

Lucas turned to Elliot. "How long will it take for the gas to disperse so it's safe to push into the city?"

"In the area you bomb? Weeks. The surroundings? Depends on the wind. It can linger, so we'd be best to avoid it for as long as possible. I wouldn't want to go anywhere near it without a gas mask and protective gear for at least a few days, if not longer."

"Then half rations today and tomorrow. Depending on how it goes, we'll march halfway to downtown at dawn, but give the area around the refinery a wide berth…assuming we're successful."

"I have no doubt you will be."

Kelly climbed into the cargo hold with his two companions, and Lucas joined Clinton in the cockpit. "All right. Showtime. You think you can find their stronghold?"

"If it's by the Deer Park refinery, it shouldn't be too hard. That's a big piece of real estate. Pretty distinctive. I used to fly here all the time, so I know the area."

"Good. Let's get going."

Clinton guided the plane to six thousand feet, the engines straining under the weight of the load of mortar projectiles, and Lucas scanned the city below as they set a course south. Clinton spoke into his headset mic over the drone of the props to Lucas, who'd donned the copilot's phones.

"We should be over them in about five minutes or so. Spotting their artillery in the dark may be the hardest part."

"Could be," Lucas conceded. "But maybe not."

"What are you thinking?"

"If we can draw fire from wherever they're dug in, we can pinpoint them and drop our payload."

Clinton swallowed hard. "So your plan is to get us shot down?"

"Hopefully not. But if we can't make the guns out, that's plan B."

"You're nuts."

"Could be. Let's hope it doesn't come to that." Lucas managed a small grin. "Don't suppose you have any parachutes in this thing?"

"Very funny."

Clinton nudged Lucas with his elbow when they were on approach. "Looks like there are some fires down there, west of the refinery."

Lucas nodded. "Definitely a camp. Question is how far from the big guns they are."

"We're never going to be able to make them out from this far up."

"Don't be so sure."

Lucas flipped the NV goggles out of his field of vision and raised his night vision rifle scope from his M4 to his good eye. He peered through it and swept the buildings ahead and, when he lowered it, called out to the men in the rear.

"Get ready to start dropping them," he yelled, and then keyed his mic to speak to Clinton.

"Over to the right. There's a line of trucks and tanks. And it looks like at least ten howitzers. If we blanket this entire area, that should do the trick. Then we'll finish the run by hitting the refinery far enough from the main buildings to avoid destroying them, but close enough so the gas covers it, and we should be good to go."

"Sounds like a plan. Call out when we're a few seconds from being over them, and I'll cut the engines back to near stall speed."

Lucas did as instructed, and yelled to Clinton to start the bombardment run. Kelly pushed the fuselage door up, and the wind buffeted the interior of the cabin. He sat on the floor and braced his legs on either side of the opening as Clinton decreased the airspeed, and motioned to the men for a mortar shell. One of them handed him the first of the finned projectiles, and he leaned forward and dropped it into the darkness, followed closely by another and another.

The first explosion erupted in an orange blossom on the ground, and then an entire line of fiery detonations lit the area as the rest hit. Lucas screamed for him to continue dropping the projectiles, and Kelly complied, dumping another dozen into the night before Lucas motioned for him to stop.

Clinton banked hard and goosed the throttles forward, and the plane turned and lost a thousand feet as it set up for another run. Lucas indicated for Kelly to start bombing again, and he complied, pitching the shells out the door as fast as his men could hand them to him.

More explosions burst bright below them, and then Clinton twisted the yoke and pitched the plane hard left as he spoke into the mic.

"They're shooting at us," he warned.

"Let's do another pass. Climb until we're high enough so they can't see us."

"Bad idea."

"We can't stop until we've covered the entire area. Just do it."

"I didn't sign up to get shot out of the sky."

Lucas drew his Kimber. "You took the gold. Now do the job."

Clinton swore under his breath and executed another gradual turn while pulling back on the yoke, gaining altitude. Small-arms fire wasn't a real threat at more than two thousand feet, but heavy machine guns could pose a serious danger at twice that range to a slow-flying plane with no armor. Still, given the darkness, it was long odds they'd be hit, so he leveled off and eased off the throttle again, and Kelly got twenty shells through the door before they were past the target area.

"All right. Let's hit the refinery and call it a night," Lucas said. "Can you fly a circle around it? I want to choke them out, not blow up the tanks or the equipment."

"I'll do my best," Clinton said.

He pointed the nose of the plane towards the refinery. As he was completing the maneuver, the fuselage shook as a row of bullet holes appeared on the starboard wing. Clinton cursed and struggled with the controls.

"We're hit. Feels sluggish. They must have dinged something serious. We need to get back to the highway."

"No. We need to get the refinery."

"We might not make it home."

Lucas motioned with the pistol. "That's a chance we'll have to take."

Clinton's jaw clenched, and he manhandled the plane back to level flight and cut back on the power. "You'll only have one try. The fuel gauge is dropping. They must have nicked a fuel line along with the hydraulics for the flaps."

"Do your best."

The plane chugged over the refinery, and Lucas bellowed at the men to ready the shells. He keyed his mic and glanced at Clinton. "Take us down closer. We need as much accuracy as we can get."

"Bad idea."

"It wasn't a suggestion. Do it."

Clinton coaxed the plane down, and the airspeed indicator increased by twenty knots. When they were at the far edge of the grounds, Lucas instructed him to begin his bombing run turn, and gave Kelly the signal to start dropping the last of his payload. Kelly complied while the plane slowly circled the refinery, and then he called out to Lucas as he pulled the fuselage door closed, "That was all of 'em!"

Lucas nodded and turned to Clinton. "Okay. Get us back in one piece."

"Easier said than done. That engine could flare out at any moment. The gauge is showing it's nearly dry."

"Then pray."

The mall was on the horizon when the motor coughed and stopped, and the color drained from Clinton's face.

"I need to set down here. I can glide, but it's going to be touch and go."

Lucas twisted to Kelly. "Brace yourselves. We're going down."

Clinton fought with the yoke as the highway appeared out of the darkness below. The plane bucked as it descended, and after a bone-jarring bounce, it yawed in slow motion before tipping and flipping. The port wing shredded against the pavement and snapped off like it was made out of balsa, and then they were skidding upside down, leaving a trail of sparks and fuel in their wake.

The plane lurched to a stop. Lucas and Clinton were hanging upside down, supported by their harnesses, and Lucas fumbled with his releases. He unclasped them and lowered himself with his arms and then worked to free Clinton, ignoring the blood streaming down his face. He got him clear, and the pilot dropped to what had been the ceiling, and Lucas kicked his door open and dragged him out of the plane. He laid him on the ground nearby and then went back for Kelly and his men.

He stopped in the cockpit at the sight of Kelly, his head twisted at an impossible angle, wedged against the back of the plane. The other two were crumpled, motionless, and Lucas crawled past the seats to them and checked their pulses. The first man was dead, but the second was breathing, so Lucas dragged him forward and out the door and put him to rest beside Clinton, who was regaining consciousness.

The pilot blinked blood from his eyes and wiped it away and then took in the mangled plane, ethanol dripping from the remaining wing tip. The engine was still running, albeit roughly.

"Can you walk?" Lucas asked.

"Probably. We need to get away. She could blow at any time."

Lucas helped Clinton to his feet and then bent and heaved the injured gunner over his shoulder and began jogging toward the camp. They'd made it a hundred yards when the plane exploded in a fireball behind them, sending chunks of debris through the air in smoking arcs and a blast of heat against their backs.

Duke and Luis rode toward them on horseback, with at least fifty troops following with weapons at the ready. When they reached Lucas, Duke took in the bloody pilot and the unconscious missile tech before his eyes settled on Lucas.

"Looks like you've been busy. Do I dare ask how it went?"

"I could use a hand here."

Duke snapped his fingers, and two men dropped from the saddle and took the tech from Lucas, who looked up at Duke, his face expressionless.

"Mission accomplished. But we'll know for sure when we move out at dawn."

"How so?"

"If we're cut to pieces by their big guns, it didn't go as well as I think."

Duke snorted. "That's one way to tell, I guess."

Lucas checked his watch and then held it to his ear before shaking his head. "So much for that. I want to be inside the city before the enemy's been able to organize."

"Probably wouldn't hurt to get cleaned up and maybe snatch a few hours of sleep."

Lucas grunted. "I'll rest when I'm dead," he said with a tight smile. "Although a nap doesn't sound terrible."

Duke shook his head in wonder and lowered himself to the ground. "You go ahead and ride. My fat ass could use the walk back." He sighed. "You're really something, you know that?"

Lucas looked off at the camp and spit. "So I've heard."

Chapter 51

Julio lay on a bed in an abandoned hotel, a wet rag wrapped around his face. He'd been near the refinery when the bombing started, and before he'd realized what was happening, his eyes and nose had started burning like fire. That had been seven hours earlier, and what had initially seemed like the equivalent of a bad pepper spraying had escalated until he'd been unable to see and his throat felt like he'd gargled battery acid.

The reinforcements from Mexico had arrived the night before – fifteen hundred men, tired after a long journey from the border. They'd been asleep all of five hours when the shells had begun raining down on the artillery positions, jarring them awake. Julio had been caught unawares as he'd been inspecting the refinery, and had watched in horror as the big guns had been enveloped in a malodorous fog, followed shortly by the buildings filled with the new arrivals.

That something besides a bombardment was taking place quickly became obvious as men ran outside with their weapons, only to fall to the ground clutching their throats and coughing. By the time he'd radioed his lieutenants a warning that the enemy was gassing them, it was too late, and an entire ten-block-square area had been inundated with the agent, along with the majority of the men.

Julio's guards had rushed him away to the safety of the hotel, out of the hot zone, but they'd begun suffering from chemical blistering by the time they'd gotten him settled. He'd ordered them to summon a medic to attend to him, and was still waiting. That had been hours ago, and nobody had arrived, leaving Julio and two guards in the depths of the hotel. Chaotic transmissions from his radio advised him of the destruction of his empire in real time, as he sat powerless to do anything to stop it.

Julio gingerly removed the rag from his face and blinked. His eyes were on fire, and the skin around his mouth and nose was blistered beyond recognition, making it difficult to breathe. He tried to focus on anything in the room, but his vision was so blurred it was impossible to make out anything but shapes, and even those seemed distorted to the point they seemed alien to him.

He shifted on the bed and became aware that his hands and throat were also burning like he'd been cooked, in spite of having rinsed himself off and flushing his face with water prior to arriving at the hotel. He forced himself to look at his hands, and sour bile rose in his throat at the fuzzy sight: fingers ulcerated and broiled by the gas, the skin gone, and his tendons and veins exposed atop the bones.

He wanted to scream in horror, but his breath caught in his fried throat and all he could manage was a choked moan. Whatever they'd dropped on him was worse than anything he could have imagined, turning every moment into a waking nightmare. He had little hope that his condition would miraculously improve even as his flesh dissolved. As he degraded, he steeled himself for the only thing that would end his suffering.

Julio felt for his pistol, each tortured movement producing a thousand pinpoints of agony from every nerve in his body, and when his fingers found it, it was all he could do to grip the handle. His last thought as he pressed the barrel to the suppurating mess that was his chin was to damn the enemy army to the fires of hell; and then he squeezed the trigger and a hollow-point .40-caliber round mushroomed through his brain, and everything exploded in a starburst before going black.

Lucas stood at the base of one of the towering downtown skyscrapers, near what had once been a Creole restaurant, as Duke and Luis reported to him. They'd marched on the city at first light and hadn't encountered any resistance until they'd covered miles of deserted residential district and entered the metropolitan area.

"We've got a few firefights going, but nothing much to speak of. It's mainly mopping up, which I'm sure we'll be doing for the next week," Luis said.

Duke nodded. "Anticlimactic, after the last battles. I'd expected this to be our Waterloo, and it's turning out to be barely a scuffle."

"Obviously because you single-handedly routed the cartel," Luis said to Lucas.

"Two good men died helping me, and another's touch and go, so hardly single-handed. But I'm glad it saved so many of our troops' lives. We've lost too many already."

"True," Duke agreed.

Elliot rode up, followed by Ruby, with Eve and Tim seated together on Jax's back. Elliot lowered himself to the ground, handed Ruby the reins, and approached Lucas.

"Congratulations, my friend. It looks like the hard part's behind us."

"Maybe. But we still need to feed thousands of hungry mouths."

"True, but there are fish in the sea, and I'm sure the locals can help us source food once we've run the last of the scum out of town." Elliot sighed. "Speaking of which, Wink has requested a meeting as soon as it's convenient."

Lucas looked away. "I'll just bet."

Ruby dismounted with the kids, who ran to Lucas and hugged him. Tears rolled down Eve's cheeks as he knelt and hugged them back, and when he released them, they were both crying.

"Is it over?" Tim asked, his voice tight.

"For now." Lucas looked at Ruby. "We're going to make this area our base of operations. I want you all close to me from now on, so when we find a place to lay our bedrolls, I'll send someone for you.

Stay with Elliot for now. There's a lot of logistical BS I need to handle before the day's over."

"Of course, Lucas," Ruby agreed. "I'll stay out of your way. They just wanted to see you in the worst way."

"What happened to your face?" Eve asked.

"I had a…disagreement. Nothing that bad."

She nodded as though the explanation made perfect sense. "Are you going to stay with us from now on?"

"That's the plan, sweetheart. Although we're not going to be here forever. We still have a long way to go before we're done."

"As long as we're with you," she said.

Ruby took their hands and walked them back to the animals. Elliot smiled and looked Lucas over before shaking his head. "You do look like the losingest boxer in Texas."

"I feel like him, too."

"Well, let's set up shop in one of these buildings, because it seems like aside from organizing patrols to root out the stragglers, the fighting's done for now."

Duke frowned. "You really think the cartel's going to just write Houston off?"

Lucas explained his thinking. "If the refinery's still putting out diesel, we can get as many tanks as we need working. Between those and the big guns, they'd be facing a losing proposition. Besides, if Wink's right, we can probably do a deal where we sell them fuel in exchange for whatever we need from Mexico, so it may make more sense for them to coexist with us as trading partners rather than as slave labor."

Luis looked away. "I wouldn't bet on it."

"Neither would I," Lucas said. "But one thing I've learned is that there's always a surprise waiting around the corner. That wouldn't be the worst move they could make."

"Let's hope you're right," Duke said.

Lucas nodded again. "Hope for the best and prepare for the worst, isn't that the deal?" He gazed up at the building in front of him. "Let's find someplace we can hold court and get out of the sun."

"Lead the way, boss. I'd say you've more than earned it."

About the Author

Featured in *The Wall Street Journal*, *The Times*, and *The Chicago Tribune*, Russell Blake is *The NY Times* and *USA Today* bestselling author of over fifty novels.

Blake is co-author of *The Eye of Heaven* and *The Solomon Curse*, with legendary author Clive Cussler. Blake's novel *King of Swords* has been translated into German, *The Voynich Cypher* into Bulgarian, and his JET novels into Spanish, German, and Czech.

Blake writes under the moniker R.E. Blake in the NA/YA/Contemporary Romance genres. Novels include *Less Than Nothing*, *More Than Anything*, and *Best Of Everything*.

Having resided in Mexico for a dozen years, Blake enjoys his dogs, fishing, boating, tequila and writing, while battling world domination by clowns. His thoughts, such as they are, can be found at his blog:

RussellBlake.com

Visit RussellBlake.com for updates

or subscribe to: RussellBlake.com/contact/mailing-list

Books by Russell Blake

Thrillers
FATAL EXCHANGE
FATAL DECEPTION
THE GERONIMO BREACH
ZERO SUM
THE DELPHI CHRONICLE TRILOGY
THE VOYNICH CYPHER
SILVER JUSTICE
UPON A PALE HORSE
DEADLY CALM
RAMSEY'S GOLD
EMERALD BUDDHA
THE GODDESS LEGACY
A GIRL APART
A GIRL BETRAYED
QUANTUM SYNAPSE

The Assassin Series
KING OF SWORDS
NIGHT OF THE ASSASSIN
RETURN OF THE ASSASSIN
REVENGE OF THE ASSASSIN
BLOOD OF THE ASSASSIN
REQUIEM FOR THE ASSASSIN
RAGE OF THE ASSASSIN

The Day After Never Series
THE DAY AFTER NEVER – BLOOD HONOR
THE DAY AFTER NEVER – PURGATORY ROAD
THE DAY AFTER NEVER – COVENANT
THE DAY AFTER NEVER – RETRIBUTION
THE DAY AFTER NEVER – INSURRECTION
THE DAY AFTER NEVER – PERDITION
THE DAY AFTER NEVER – HAVOC
THE DAY AFTER NEVER – LEGION
THE DAY AFTER NEVER – NEMESIS
THE DAY AFTER NEVER – RUBICON

Books by Russell Blake

Co-authored with Clive Cussler
THE EYE OF HEAVEN
THE SOLOMON CURSE

The JET Series
JET
JET II – BETRAYAL
JET III – VENGEANCE
JET IV – RECKONING
JET V – LEGACY
JET VI – JUSTICE
JET VII – SANCTUARY
JET VIII – SURVIVAL
JET IX – ESCAPE
JET X – INCARCERATION
JET XI – FORSAKEN
JET XII – ROGUE STATE
JET XIII – RENEGADE
JET XIV – DARK WEB
JET XV – SAHARA
JET – OPS FILES (prequel)
JET – OPS FILES; TERROR ALERT

The BLACK Series
BLACK
BLACK IS BACK
BLACK IS THE NEW BLACK
BLACK TO REALITY
BLACK IN THE BOX

Non Fiction
AN ANGEL WITH FUR
HOW TO SELL A GAZILLION EBOOKS
(while drunk, high or incarcerated)

Printed in Dunstable, United Kingdom